Chasing the Devil's Breath

A Suspense / Thriller / Mystery

GEORGE R. HOPKINS

Copyright ©2017 by George R. Hopkins

All rights reserved.
ISBN: 1543033180
ISBN: 9781543033182
Library of Congress Control Number: 2017902356
CreateSpace Independent Publishing Platform
North Charleston, South Carolina

Other Suspense / Thriller / Mysteries
in the Priest and the Detective Series
by George R. Hopkins

Blood Brothers

Collateral Consequences

Letters from the Dead

Random Acts of Malice

Unholy Retribution

All of these suspense/thriller/mysteries can be ordered from your local
bookstore and are available at Amazon.com and in Kindle editions.

TO MY CHILDREN AND GRANDCHILDREN

(I am confident you have to be a big part of the reason I was born.)

Thank you.

May our grandchildren and their parents continue to grow in grace and wisdom.

Stephen

John

Max

Jack

Emily

Madelyn

Ella

Will

Tyler

Brayden

1

Staten Island, New York

When Tom Cavanaugh walked out of his house and saw the dead black-bird on top of his Jeep it could have been an omen. But he didn't believe in omens - at least not yet.

His immediate reaction was to toss the bird into the bushes, but he knew if his wife saw it, she would freak out. Fran would question where the bird came from, what caused it to die, was it diseased, was there a message in its death? She would look for meaning where there was none. So he looked around for something to pick up the bird. Now was a time he could have used a tissue, but Cavanaugh didn't believe in tissues. They were messy and a nuisance. He preferred using handkerchiefs. Carefully, he took out his handkerchief, lifted the bird, and tossed it in the backseat.

Driving away, he recalled the nursery rhyme his mother had sung to him as a child:

> *Sing a song of sixpence, a pocket full of rye.*
> *Four and twenty blackbirds, baked in a pie.*
> *When the pie was opened, the birds began to sing;*
> *Wasn't that a dainty dish, to set before the king?*

He wondered if the dead bird was a blackbird, a raven, or a crow. There was a difference. He used to know it. One was a scavenger looking for road kill. Another typically gathered in flocks.

Some kind of plight had killed a lot of blackbirds a few years before. They could, he knew, spread disease and be dangerous.

> *The maid was in the garden, hanging out the clothes,*
> *When down came a blackbird and pecked off her nose.*

Why, he thought, were so many of the nursery rhymes and fairy tales so violent? Humpty Dumpty had a great fall and all the king's horses and all the king's men couldn't put poor Humpty back together again. Jack and Jill went up the hill and Jack ended up breaking his skull. When the bough broke, both the cradle and the baby fell. The three blind mice ran after the farmer's wife who cut off their tails with a carving knife.

Hansel and Gretel were kidnapped by a cannibalistic witch. The prince leaps from the tower where his beloved Rapunzel once was held captive and is blinded by the thorns below. The Queen orders Snow White to be killed and as proof demands the hunter bring back Snow White's lungs and liver.

He shook his head. Mother Goose and the Grimm brothers were sick puppies. He wanted to protect his young son from the violence he had witnessed all around him as a cop. It was on the news, in the papers, on the Internet, on television, in the movies, and even in nursery rhymes. That was part of the reason he put his papers in and retired from the New York City Police Department.

He put the dead bird out of his mind. It was like changing a channel. He learned to do that on the job. It was a survival mechanism. He could compartmentalize. He turned on the radio. Today was a new day. The sun was shining. There wasn't a cloud in the blue sky. It was the first day of his new career. For the first time in his life, he would be his own boss. He had done his homework, his preparation, and now was on his way to meet his first client. Being a private investigator would give him more time with his family and less aggravation. At least, that was what former Detective Tom Cavanaugh initially thought.

■ ■ ■

When Cavanaugh arrived at what he called his "office," two women were outside waiting. His "office" had once been a "mom and pop" donut and coffee shop, but when Dunkin' Donuts moved in two doors down and Starbucks built a store on the next corner, Angelo Antonucci saw the handwriting on the wall and decided it was time to leave. He could have sold the property for a lot of money, but decided to rent it instead. Let his children and grandchildren divide the profit from the sale of the place in the future. It would be their inheritance. Now he and his wife Nina would get a little place in Florida where, he believed, old people in America go to die. With the rent from the store and social security, they would be happy enough. A few people looked at the store, but most wanted Angelo to make repairs to the roof, the pumping, and the electrical system. Angelo thought that was the buyer's responsibility. The only one who agreed to rent the store "as is" was Cavanaugh who learned about the store from one of Angelo's six sons. Marco Antonucci and Cavanaugh had gone to the Police Academy together and worked for a short time as patrolmen in Brooklyn.

Cavanaugh planned to make necessary repairs himself. He left most of Angelo's facilities in place including the countertop, the cash register, and the now empty display cabinets. On the walls around the store, the price list for donuts that were no longer available continued to linger as well as the tantalizing ghost-like aroma of the missing donuts. He bought a table from Costco, some folding chairs, a box of folders, and a few yellow legal writing pads. As much as Cavanaugh resisted modern technology, he consented to getting a phone, but not one of the latest smart phones. He insisted on an old flip-style wireless phone.

Cavanaugh checked his watch. He was fifteen minutes early for his appointment. He looked at the women waiting at his door. They looked like mother and daughter. The mother wore a black cotton mini-pleated dress designed to make her look thinner. It didn't work, however. She had caked-on makeup, too much lipstick, a twitch in her left eye, bedroom slippers, and unnaturally black hair. Her hands were shaking.

The daughter was a different story. A blue denim jean jacket covered a sexy low cut cleavage blouse. Above her 4.5 inch knee-high boots decorated with crisscross leather buckled straps, she wore a light blue and white embroidered short-short skirt with zippered leather sides she could have been poured into. She brushed her long blonde hair which cascaded across her left eye and looked at him. He saw smudged mascara beneath her blue eyes. "Are you Mister Cavanaugh?" she asked.

He nodded and opened the door.

"What kind of place is this?" the older woman asked.

"We're redecorating," he said motioning for the women to sit down. The older woman looked at the chairs as if they were a pile of dog dung. "Or you can stand, if you prefer." Eventually, they both sat.

"What can I do for you?" he asked.

"It's my son," the blonde said.

"My grandson," the older woman said.

"What about him?"

"He's missing," they said in unison.

"Did you report it to the police?"

"They don't do nothing," the older woman said.

"They think he ran away," the blonde explained. "In college he got into some trouble hanging around with the wrong crowd. I'm afraid something has happened to him."

"What kind of trouble?"

"My grandson is a good boy." Cavanaugh caught the glint of a gold lateral incisor.

"What kind of trouble?"

"Marijuana . . . alcohol . . .," the blonde murmured. "That kind of thing. . . ."

Cavanaugh looked at the women and listened. This was his first case – a missing or runaway addict. He thought of his own son. This was the world he would be growing up in. Would he and Fran be good enough parents to get their son through the tough times that lie ahead?

He glanced at the yellow pad on his table. It was blank.

"You're my first client," he said. "How did you get my name?"

"Mary suggested we contact you," the blonde answered.

"Mary?"

"Your sister-in-law Mary. Francesca's sister."

Mary Muscatelli was Cavanaugh's wife's sister. Mary was doing his marketing. She made up a website for him, put him on FACEBOOK, LINKEDIN, INSTAGRAM, and even set up a TWITTER account for him – none of which Cavanaugh knew how to use or had ever looked at.

"How do you know Mary?" he asked.

"She's my cousin," the blonde answered. "Her father was my mother's brother."

A cold chill rang up Cavanaugh's chest. Ralph Muscatelli, Fran's father, was once the notorious mob *capo di tutti capi* of Brooklyn. He was involved in gambling, prostitution, money laundering, drugs, loan sharking, and murder. He was what Cavanaugh and others would call "a bad ass." The police, the FBI, and all sorts of government agencies were unable to stop him and his organization. He was the original "Teflon Don." Nothing would stick to him, nothing until a lone assassin took him out for good with one shot as he was leaving a restaurant in Brooklyn. It made all the papers. After an intense investigation and a number of murders, Howard Stevens, a rogue former CIA agent, was killed in a gun battle with Cavanaugh and his partner, Morty Goldberg. It was believed Howard Stevens was Ralph Muscatelli's assassin and the case was closed.

Cavanaugh, however, knew differently. He knew that Ralph Muscatelli's actual killer was Cavanaugh's own brother, Father Jack Bennis. His brother decided to take matters into his own hands and mete out the "justice" police and government agencies were unable or unwilling to do. Although his brother never fully admitted it, Cavanaugh knew his brother had assassinated Ralph Muscatelli.

As he looked up from his blank pad, Cavanaugh studied the hopeful, soft blue eyes of Fran's cousin and the cold, hard dark eyes of the sister of the man his brother murdered.

■ ■ ■

Mompox, Colombia

Approximately 2,150 miles away, a tall, well-built man dressed in black walked into a quiet bar in the small town of Mompox in Colombia and ordered an American coffee - black, no sugar - in perfect Spanish. The bartender's dark weasel-like eyes darted from the stranger to the rear of the room where four people sat. One was a man dressed in a beige three-piece herringbone suit and a red bowtie sitting in the shadows against the wall sipping a French 75, the drink Rick Blaine's ex-girlfriend's Nazi officer ordered in *Casablanca*. Two burly men at the table with the man tensed and directed the AK-47s in their laps toward the tall stranger. The fourth person was a dark-skinned brunette who shifted her seat closer to the man with the red bowtie.

The stranger placed both hands on the weathered wooden bar and spoke to the bartender. "I'm looking for a man," he said.

"Please, señor. We want no trouble."

"I was told I might be able to find him here."

Beads of sweat began to form on the bartender's forehead. He glanced in the back of the room and whispered, "Please, señor, go back now. It is not safe to be here now."

The stranger heard a chair in the back of the room scrap along the floor. He turned and looked into the shadows. The thin man in the light suit rose from his seat. The two men at his sides leveled their rifles at the stranger. The woman crouched in her seat. The bartender ducked behind the bar.

The man with the red bowtie stepped into the light. "Who are you and what do you want?" he said in perfect English.

The stranger turned. "My name is Jack Bennis. I am a Jesuit priest newly assigned to St. Peter Claver Church in Cartagena."

"You are a long way from home, Padre," the man said.

Bennis saw the glint of the rifles aimed at him. "And to whom do I have the pleasure of speaking?" he asked.

"What's in a name? That which we call a rose by any other name would smell the same."

"The one I am seeking, I have been told, often quotes Shakespeare. Some call him El Apredido – the Learned One."

The man in the suit scratched his clean shaven chin and then folded his arms. "What do you want?"

The priest stepped forward. "I am looking for the man who develops and distributes a unique version of the Devil's Breath. Apparently, it's has been genetically altered and mixed with other drugs." He stared straight ahead at the man in the beige suit. "I want the man who is producing this to stop."

The men with the guns advanced from the darkness. The man in the suit held up his hands to stop the other men. He smiled and then laughed. It was a shrill laugh, almost like a little girl's laugh. He straightened his bowtie. "Go home, Padre. You are out of your depth here. Your boldness is acknowledged. Now leave. Go back wherever it is you came from or you will get hurt."

Fr. Bennis continued, "The man I am looking for knows the dangers in this chemically altered drug. I've heard it called the scariest drug in the world because it puts its victims into zombie-like states where they lose their memory and, more importantly, their free will."

"I see you are a brave and virtuous man, Padre, but I must warn you, as Shakespeare once said, some rise by sin, and some by virtue fall. Tread lightly or bear the cruelty that awaits the foolish."

The priest smiled. "There is another quote from *Measure for Measure* you should remember," he said turning toward the door. "'Virtue is bold and goodness never fearful.'"

The man in the beige three-piece suit and the red bowtie watched as Jack Bennis walked out of the bar into the hot midday sun. When the priest had left, the man turned to the bearded man on his left and said in perfect Spanish, "That man thinks too much. Such men are dangerous. Follow him. Find out what he knows. Then kill him."

The woman came up behind him and tugged at his arm. "No! You can't do that, El Apredido! He is a priest! It is bad luck to kill a priest!"

The man turned, looked down at her, bent over and kissed her gently on her forehead. Then he smacked her viciously in the face sending her sprawling across the table. His flute of ice, gin, and Champagne crashed to the floor. "No such man, as he, can be trusted. He is intelligent, brave, daring. Our plans go far beyond making and distributing the Devil's Breath." He reached down and yanked the brunette to her feet. "The hand that hath made you fair, hath made you good, maybe too good. 'Tis best to weigh the enemy, my dear, more mighty than he seems. "

He dragged the young woman over to the bar and ordered the bartender to make him another French 75. Then he flung the woman back into the arms of the other man with a rifle. "Take her out back. Do what you will with her. She is of no more use to me. Then kill her."

■ ■ ■

Jack Bennis walked slowly back along Mompox's narrow streets toward the hotel he was staying at for the night. The midday sun beat down on him. The streets were almost deserted except for the occasional sound of a motorcycle in the distance or the mooing of a meandering cow. He looked around at the white and gold colored stone buildings. His black clothes held the heat and clung to him like Velcro. From time to time he felt a slight breeze from the Magdalena River, but he knew by the time he reached the hotel he would be dripping wet and tired.

Mompox was once an important island-like town used by the Spaniards in sixteenth century South America as a port and holding place for the gold and silver they plundered. It thrived as a wealthy haven and storehouse for precious metals and jewels both because of its strategic location in the middle of the Magdalena River where it joins the Cauca River and because it served as a passageway from the ocean to the Andes Mountains for goods to be delivered upriver into the interior. But when the river began silting up, large boats were forced to seek other routes and its prosperity faded. Mompox became a dangerous place for visitors because of volatile politics and the warring violence of narcotic terrorists and paramilitary groups in the Magdalena Valley of Colombia. When the waters of the Magdalena River shifted again in the early twentieth century, however, the once prosperous Mompox began to revive, but this time as a remote tourist attraction because of the preserved, largely unaltered Spanish colonial architecture of its buildings, its colorful churches, its filigree gold artisans, and its celebrated religious ceremonies.

Father Bennis walked along whitewashed, tree-lined waterfront streets. He passed elaborate wrought-iron decorated doors, railings and windows. It was as if he had stepped back in time to colonial times. He passed a number of colorfully embellished churches and palatial homes. He stopped to wipe his brow in front of the municipal cemetery where statues of angels decorated white tombs surrounded by artificial flowers. A black cat ran across the road in front of him and one of the stone angels seemed to speak to him holding its finger up to its mouth as if to caution him.

But Jack Bennis already knew he was being followed. He expected it. One of the burly men with an AK-47 had been following him since he left the bar. Bennis recognized him as the one with the dark beard. He wasn't worried about him right now.

Walking slowly down the road, he was aware how alone he was. It seemed he was alone even when he was in a crowd. He missed his brother Tom, his sister-in-law Fran, his nephew Stephen, and his cockapoo Bella.

His thoughts kept questioning why he made the long trip from Cartagena to Mompox. For almost eight hours he endured a bumpy ride over rough roads in a noxious bus and then another two-hour ferry ride to get to Mompox. But why? To ask a notorious drug manufacturer to stop making drugs? It didn't make any sense. Had he totally lost his mind? Why would "El Apredido" listen to him? Hadn't he learned anything from the past? Back in Brooklyn, when he took matters into his own hands, it only resulted in the loss of many lives. Both the innocent and the guilty suffered. Why did he make this stupid, frustrating effort now?

But he knew. It was the letter. He had read it so often, he knew it by heart. It was long and rambling, but he remembered every word.

My dearest Jack,

I am truly sorry things turned out as they did. I will always hold you in my heart. You will always be the love of my life. I meant you no anguish. Please believe me. I miss you more than words can say.

Please forgive me. I am writing to you today to ask your help once again.

When I arrived here in Colombia, I accidently met my brother Santiago in Bogotá. I never spoke to you about him. He left Cuba when we were teenagers and I lost contact with him. His nickname was Chago. He is a shell of the brother I once knew. He looks terrible.

He told me he has been working for a drug cartel in Medellin. He said he wants desperately to get out, but he can't.

He was angry and nervous when I met him. He said life was hopeless for him and he was a failure. He told me there was a man known only as "El Apredido" in the town of Mompox who must be stopped. He is manufacturing a dangerous drug called the "Devil's Breath."

He said he heard terrible rumors about this drug and the power it has over people. He said this man is planning to do something Chago wants no part of. He wouldn't tell me what it was, but only that it was bad, very bad. He was afraid of this man and pleaded with me not to tell anyone. He said they will kill him if they find he has talked to me.

He wants help, but is afraid to ask for it. The police and government officials are all in the pockets of the cartels. He has no one to trust.

I don't know what you can do, but hoped maybe you could at least pray for him. He is really a good kid who just got mixed up with the wrong people.

Thank you for listening to my problems. I truly miss you.

With all my love — always and forever,

María

Some things Jack Bennis could not forget. Some things, try as he would, he knew he would never forget. He stopped and looked around as a boat sped down the Magdalena River past two fishermen in a dugout canoe. The bearded man with the automatic rifle following him ducked into an archway.

There was another time when he would have terminated the man in the beige suit and the red bowtie. It had been part of his assignment as a Special Operational Officer to assassinate people like him. And he was good at it – very good. But times had changed. He had felt a "calling" and became a priest. Once he had reverted to the special skills the government had taught him. He murdered two top crime bosses, but it didn't change anything. Good people died and new bad ones took the place of the ones he eliminated.

The street became ominously quiet. The only transportation he had seen since he got to Mompox was an old rickshaw, a few motorcycles, and some bicycles. It made sense that "El Apredido" would choose this place. Situated on the banks of a river and surrounded by swampy marshes and wetlands, Mompox was like an island without bridges making it difficult, almost inaccessible, to reach. Only one road ran out of Mompox. Despite its beauty and charm, few visitors would come to Mompox. It had taken Bennis almost ten hours to travel by bus and ferry to Mompox.

He had tried to help. He would stay the night and head back to Cartagena in the morning. It was up to God now. Santiago "Chago" Rodriguez would be in his prayers as his sister, María Isabelle, would always be. As a priest and a man, he felt his role in life was to walk in the footsteps of Jesus and to help. He was human, but his strength was in the hands of God. He had made promises to Him and he had promises to keep.

On the walk back to his hotel, loneliness overwhelmed him. He missed the woman whose letter drove him to come to Mompox to seek out El Apredido. He closed his eyes and shook his head. He tried to put her out of his mind.

Another slight breeze blew off the river. It stirred the hot air. Against his sweat drenched clothes it felt almost refreshing. He saw a small restaurant on the corner ahead of him. A few colorful umbrellas shielded patrons from the sun, but there seemed to be only one person outside. A cold drink would be great. He hesitated and then pushed on. There were drinks at his hotel, and the fan in his room would suffice.

As he passed the restaurant, another black cat darted across his path. Then a voice called out to him. He turned. Under a large yellow umbrella, a dark-haired woman in a loose blue dress sat on a white wrought-iron chair. He jumped. His heart skipped a beat. It was María Isabelle Rodriguez, the woman he had deliberately left in New York, the woman he was trying to avoid, the woman he had made this trip to help, the woman he was in love with.

■ ■ ■

Father Bennis stared at María. He shook his head. "What are you doing here, María? I thought you were in Bogotá?"

María sipped a glass of red sangria. Her hands were shaking. "And I might ask you the same question, Jack. I thought you were in Cartagena."

He looked at the half-empty pitcher of sangria on the table. "I got your letter. I came here to talk to El Apredido. I thought I might be able to change his mind."

"That was stupid!" she shouted. Her bright blue eyes sparkled. "I never asked you to come here! I only asked you to pray for my brother."

"And I will." He moved closer to her. "But why are you here?"

She finished her glass and poured herself another.

In the distance, he heard a motorcycle speeding toward them. Bennis stepped forward and sat down. He watched as the motorcycle passed by and asked again, "Why are you here, María?"

She avoided his eyes and raised her glass to her mouth. He grabbed her hand. "Why, María?"

She lowered the glass and leveled her eyes at him. "That man is evil. He is hurting people. He must be stopped."

He continued to hold her hand. She didn't pull away. "And how are you planning on stopping him?"

She looked straight at him. Her voice was cold and her eyes grew dark. "I am going to kill El Apredido!"

Bennis reached over with his other hand and removed the glass from her hand. "No, María. That is not the answer. Believe me. I know."

"You didn't have to come here. Now you are in danger. He will think my brother told you and he will kill you both."

Bennis gripped her hands in his. Her hands were soft and cold. "And how exactly did you plan to kill him?"

"I have a gun."

"It's not that easy, María. He has bodyguards with automatic rifles. You wouldn't be able to get near him."

"I will, Jack. Trust me. I will!"

He shook his head. "And what kind of weapon do you have?

She took a deep breath. A tear eked out of her left eye. "It's a pistol – a .45. I bought it in Bogotá."

Bennis smiled. "A .45 is a good weapon, but it's difficult to master. Have you ever practiced shooting it?"

"You're trying to stop me, Jack, but it's not going to work. I will kill that man!"

He grabbed her hands firmly. "Please, María, listen to me. No good can come of this. We will go back to Bogotá together and find your brother. I will take him with me to Cartagena and make sure he gets the best treatment available." He turned at the sound of another motorcycle roaring down the street. He recognized the distinctive sound of a Harley-Davidson. It slowed approaching the restaurant and stopped. The driver was a thin, young blond male with a crew cut. He looked at Father Bennis and María Isabelle, studied them for a few seconds, and then drove away.

"We must leave here," Bennis said. "Did you come by car?"

"I wish. It took me almost fifteen hours to get here by smelly bus and then another three hours in a hired Jeep...."

"Then we must take the first ferry out of Mompox in the morning. We will go to Cartagena first and then I will go with you to Bogotá to find your brother." He looked at the receding cloud of dust from the motorcycle. "But we must leave tomorrow."

"Will you come with me?"

"Yes. But first I want you to give me the gun you brought. Do you have it with you?"

"No. I left it at the hostel behind Santa Barbara Church."

"We will go to your hostel, get it and then you will come to my hotel and stay with me for the night. One of El Apredido's men has been following me. He will know you have spoken to me and you will be in danger."

María Isabelle pulled her hand away and wiped the tear from her eye. The edge of her lip began to curl into a smile. "Stay the night with you, Padre? This is an offer I can't refuse."

"Not like that, María. I told you I have promises to keep."

"Promises are made to be broken."

The guttural, thunderous retort of the Harley was coming back. Father Bennis tensed. He recognized the driver as the same one who had stopped and then roared away. As it came closer Bennis saw the gun in the driver's hand. He lunged for María, falling on top of her and pulling the table down as bullets flew about them and ricocheted off the table. The seconds that followed seemed like hours. They lay behind the table motionless until the shooting stopped and the motorcycle sped away crackling like a deafening heartbeat.

The priest rolled off María. She was shaking. He held her tightly and whispered, "Let's get out of here before he comes back and get that gun of yours! I think we're going to need it."

■ ■ ■

2

Staten Island, New York

Tom Cavanaugh studied the two women in front of him. He wanted nothing to do with them. "I have to tell you upfront. I'm not a licensed private investigator. I'm still waiting for my official license."

"Mary said you were the best," the younger woman said.

"Mary's prejudiced. Maybe it would be better for you to get a licensed P.I."

The older woman stood. She opened her large black rhinestone covered handbag that could have doubled as a horse's feedbag. "How much do you want?"

"That's not it. I think you would do better with someone else."

"My husband made a lot of money in the stock market and real estate. He was not like my brother. He was honest. I know my brother was a crook. He got what he deserved. I want you to find my grandson and bring him home. He is a good boy. He is my only grandson."

The mother took out a picture of her son and handed it to Cavanaugh. "Please, Mr. Cavanaugh, help us find my son."

Cavanaugh felt a twisting in his stomach. He studied the photo carefully. The boy was in blue graduation robes with his arms around his mother and grandmother. They were all smiling. Cavanaugh didn't want anything to do with this. But he identified with someone protecting their family. He listened.

Salvatore Anthony Russo was twenty-four years old. He was the product of a high school Senior Prom visit to the Jersey Shore that went awry. He never knew his father and was raised by his mother and grandparents in Chatham, New Jersey. According to his mother and grandmother, Salvatore was brilliant. He went to Yale, was graduated with Masters Degrees in both Environmental Engineering and Psychology, and moved to New York where he enrolled in a Ph.D. program at NYU. They thought he shared an apartment in Manhattan with a college roommate and may have had a steady girlfriend, but they never met either of them. They thought he worked somewhere on Long Island, but neither his mother nor his grandmother knew where. They both noticed a change in Sal's behavior over the last year. Sometimes he was his old self at family gatherings on Sundays. He would laugh and tell stories about the friends he had and some of the girls he dated. But other times, he was quiet, almost trance-like. He would nibble at his favorite foods, sit for a while in silence and then leave. No matter what, however, he would call his mother every Monday, Wednesday, and Friday and his grandmother every Tuesday, Thursday, and Saturday at precisely 1:00 p.m. They had not seen or heard from him in two months. His mother had tried calling his cellphone but it was out of service.

Cavanaugh scratched his head. "I hate to say this, ladies, but he's not a little kid anymore. He might have simply gone on a trip somewhere."

"It's unlike Sal not to tell us," his mother said.

"We are afraid something may have happened to him."

Cavanaugh tapped his pencil on the table. "What did the police say?"

"Bah!" the old woman spit on the floor. "They are scum! They said he was a big boy and he was probably just shacking up with some *gumare* somewhere."

Cavanaugh looked at the photo again.

"Please," they both said.

He had a bad feeling. He looked down at his yellow pad and saw he had written Salvatore Anthony Russo, his birthdate, social security number, cellphone number, and last known address. It wasn't much to go on, but it was a start.

Then he heard his own voice say, "Two months is a long time. I can't make any promises, but I'll see what I can do."

■ ■ ■

Staten Island – Brooklyn, New York

When the women left, Cavanaugh sat and stared at the faded price list of bagels and donuts on the wall. He really had to fix this place up. Maybe after this case, he would have some capital to invest in making this into a real office. Finding a missing person was not an easy task. The first twelve to twenty-four hours were the most critical. Salvatore was "missing" for over two months. Unless there was a reason to consider kidnapping or foul play, the police would not commit their resources to searching for a mentally fit young adult. If Sal was a child or a person with diminished mental abilities, the police would open a missing file on him and detectives in the Missing Persons Unit would investigate. But Sal was a twenty-four year old, intelligent male with no history of mental illness and no obvious reason to consider foul play.

Cavanagh knew that over 90,000 people go missing in the United States each year. The longer the person is missing, the less likely it is to locate him or her. Two months is a long time to be missing. If Sal didn't want to be found, chances were he wouldn't be found. Still, this was his first case and, as of now, his only case.

He flipped open his phone. The battery needed charging. *How is this possible?* he thought. *I hardly ever use the thing and now it tells me it needs to be recharged. I hate modern technology!*

He called his sister-in-law Mary, told her his phone was dying and asked her to find out whatever she could about Salvatore Anthony Russo. After telling her he planned to go to the last known address he had on Salvatore, he ended the call abruptly to save the battery.

Where do I start? Go with what you have. He looked at the yellow sheet. Salvatore's last known address was a start. Maybe the landlord or roommate could give him a lead. It would have been good if he could check phone records and employment records. They were there somewhere in what they called "cyberspace" or the mysterious "cloud." But even the police couldn't access them without a warrant and without probable cause no judge would grant permission. He was on his own on this one.

Salvatore's last known address turned out to be in Brooklyn across from the Old Stone House on 5th Street between 4th and 5th Avenues. The Old Stone House was the scene of the largest battle of the Revolutionary War on August 27, 1776. The playground in front of the Old Stone House was once a baseball field for the Brooklyn Baseball Club which later became the Brooklyn Dodgers.

Cavanaugh drove up and down adjacent streets searching for a parking space. Cars lined both sides of the street. Finding a spot to park in New York could be an agonizing, frustrating experience. The Park Slope area around the Old Stone House was being "gentrified" – whatever that meant. Rents had risen. For the young upwardly mobile, Park Slope was a stepping stone to the suburbs. The subway to Manhattan was a block away.

Cavanaugh had to park a few blocks away in a neighborhood that may have been changing, but the litter on the street and the homeless sleeping in doorways indicated this part of the city still needed some work. A few blocks away a softball game was going on in the park and the sounds of little kids playing in the playground and basketballs rattling off metal backboards could be heard. A new apartment complex gave signs of revitalization, but the street Cavanaugh found a parking spot on had not yet been "revitalized."

The closer he walked toward Salvatore's last known address, the louder the sounds of activity and life could be heard. In front of a three story stone building, he saw two bicycles chained to the railing by the steps. The outside door to the apartment house was open. Cavanaugh shook his head. *Leave it open, and they will come. Why don't people take care of their property? Just because you wouldn't do something, doesn't mean someone else is ready, willing, and able to steal everything you have from your money in the bank to the gold teeth in your mouth.* His wife Fran always told him he was too cynical, but he had been a detective for too long not to witness depravity in all sorts of forms. *It pays to be careful*, he thought.

According to his mother, Salvatore lived on the second floor with a former college roommate. Sharing apartments in New York was the only way some could afford the rent. Cavanaugh paused in front of apartment 2B. The door was scratched and secured with both the common key-in-knob lock and a dead-bolt lock. He took a deep breath. The odor of kimchi, popcorn, and marijuana hung like a cloud in front of apartment 2B.

He knocked on the door. No answer. Loud, cacophonous noises which Cavanaugh imagined some might call music come from within. He knocked again – a little louder this time. The music lowered and he heard footsteps. "What do you want now? I lowered the music. Okay? Now go away!"

Cavanaugh knocked again. "I'm not here about the music. I'd like to ask you a few questions about Salvatore Russo. I'm trying to locate him.... He won a lottery."

The music stopped altogether. There was a moment of silence and then the chain on the door was released and the double locks opened. A glassy-eyed man with red hair and acne peeked out the door. "Yeah?" he said. "I'm Sal Russo. How much did I win?"

Cavanaugh smiled and kicked the door open sending the glassy-eyed man back into the room. He was wearing checked boxer shorts, a wifebeater t-shirt and sandals. Through a cloud of marijuana, Cavanaugh saw two computers, three empty beer bottles, the remnants of three lines of cocaine on the coffee table and a naked woman asleep on the sofa.

Stepping into the apartment, Cavanaugh said, "You're not Sal. That's for sure. Who the hell are you?"

The skinny redhead's hands were shaking. He scratched his undershirt and looked somewhere beyond Cavanaugh. Then he heard the swish like the sound of a golf swing. The three bottles of beer and three lines of coke clicked and Cavanaugh started to turn. The blow from behind the door glanced off his shoulder and into his head. Then all went dark.

■ ■ ■

Cavanaugh awoke tied to a chair. The side of his head felt like it had been hit with a crowbar. His shoulder hurt almost as much as his loss of pride. How did he let himself walk into this? He lifted his head and looked around. The girl on the sofa was gone. Two men looked down at him. They stood in front of a white brick fireplace with a large painting of some sort over it. The skinny one with the acne picked at his face. His hands were shaking. The other one looked to be about 5' 8". Cavanaugh estimated his weight at around 125 lbs. He had long black hair to his shoulders, a fledgling Fu Manchu mustache, and wired-rimmed glasses. Both men were glassy-eyed. The one with the Fu Manchu held a softball bat in his hands. They were shaking.

"What do you want?" Fu asked. "Who are you?"

"I told you what I wanted. I'm trying to find Salvatore Russo. He won a lottery."

"You're lying. You're a cop."

"Let me loose and I'll explain everything."

"No! What do you want Sal for?"

"Listen, guys, I admit I was a cop once, but I'm not a cop anymore. I retired. I'm trying to find Sal for his mother and grandmother. They're worried about him."

"You're lying again."

"No, I'm not. You don't want to go down this road, guys. I'm just trying to find Sal for his mom. You guys know how mothers are. She's worried. She hasn't heard from him in over two months. Let me loose and we can discuss this as rational people. I figure you guys went to school with Sal."

"We don't believe you," the redhead said.

"Does Pimple Face speak for you, too, Fu Manchu?"

The two men looked at each other and the one with the bat shrugged. "What do we do with him?"

Cavanaugh planted his feet firmly on the ground. *This had gone far enough.* "I'll tell you what. Let me go and I won't bother you again."

"We can't do that," the redhead said.

"Then kill me. You didn't get the gun I keep in my ankle holster. There'll be a lot of blood and some cleaning up to do, but it could work."

"We can take him down to the cellar and dump his body in the incinerator."

"You'll need my gun to do that."

The redhead reached down to get Cavanaugh's gun. As he did, Cavanaugh brought both feet up into the redhead's jaw and then stood and swung his body into Fu Manchu smashing the back of the chair into him. The wooden chair broke. Cavanaugh grabbed the bat and hit both men with it. They went down. Redhead started sobbing. Fu Manchu's glasses flew into the fireplace and he started pleading, "Please don't kill us. Please...."

The two men crawled together and huddled on the floor in front of the fireplace.

"Where's the girl?" Cavanaugh asked.

They looked at each other and then answered in unison, "She left."

"Good. I don't need any witnesses." He removed his gun from his ankle holster. "I told you we didn't have to go this way. But you insisted. He aimed his gun at the two shivering young men. "Okay. Who wants it first?"

"No! No! Please don't do this! Please! We don't know anything!"

"That's not the answer I was looking for." He looked at the skinny redhead. His boxer shorts were wet. "Where did you guys first meet this Sal character?"

Redhead stammered, "We went to Yale together."

Fu Manchu added, "I was in a class with him at NYU."

"What can you tell me about him? Tell the truth and all of it and you might live to see another day." Cavanaugh shuddered about how he sounded like a character from a 1940s grade B movie.

But it worked. *Fear can sometimes be a great motivator.* The two men, Jacob "Redhead" Roberts and Dick "Fu Manchu" Cranberry, suddenly developed a severe case of verborrhea. They didn't know where Sal had gone, but they did give him information his mother and grandmother either left out or didn't know.

Sal, like Jacob and Dick, was into drugs. He participated in the Occupy Wall Street movement and had been a strong supporter of Bernie Sanders.

Jacob and Sal roomed together at Yale. According to Jacob, Sal was brilliant and multi-talented. He could sell anyone anything from drugs and term papers to the Brooklyn Bridge.

"Where did he get his supply?" Cavanaugh asked.

"I don't know," Jacob said. "There was a rumor around campus about a mysterious Hispanic exchange student, but I never saw him."

"Or her," Dick added. "He was pretty close with Cathy DeGaetano and Peggy Wall. They could have been his suppliers."

Dick was a biochemical major at NYU and met Sal there. He said Sal was quiet, moody, sensitive, and a genius. He told a story about how Sal railed against the Big Banks and Wall Street greed. He told him Sal didn't understand how his grandfather could work for Wall Street profits while poor people starved and went homeless. He added Sal had been seeing the naked girl Cavanaugh had seen on the sofa. They admitted they drugged her to take advantage of her. She was Sal's girl, but since he wasn't around, Jacob and Dick lured her back to the apartment hopefully for a *ménage à trois*. When she refused, they drugged her and were about to do what a famous comedian allegedly did. But then Cavanaugh arrived.

"From the looks of her, she was in no condition to leave on her own. What did you do with her?"

The two looked at each other again. Then Fu Manchu lowered his head and said, "She was unconscious. I carried her down to the basement after we tied you up."

"We didn't mean to hurt her," Redhead exclaimed. "She must have had a bad reaction…."

Cavanaugh stared at the two educated, immature morons sitting in pools of their own urine. *Einstein was right*, he thought. *The world is well on its way to creating a generation of idiots*. He looked at the huge oil painting hanging above them. It was an abstract painting of a figure with the head of a chicken, the torso of a man, and two serpents for legs. In one hand the creature held a shield and a whip in the other. He recognized it as the controversial symbol associated with both the Egyptian Sun god and a terrifying demon from Hell. Some of the Knights Templar in the 13th century adopted it and used it in their seals. "Where did you get that painting?" he asked.

"Sal painted it," Redhead said. "I told you he was talented."

"It's Abraxas," Fu Manchu added.

Cavanaugh nodded. The two pathetic creatures cowering before him were making him sick. When Cavanaugh extracted all he could about Salvatore Russo, he told them to turn around on their knees, close their eyes, and prepare to die. Both men were crying and pleading. "Shut up," he ordered. Quietly he backed slowly out of the apartment. He slammed the door as hard as he could when he left. The walls in the apartment shook. The picture over the fireplace fell. Glass shattered over the men, and. Jacob and Dick fainted.

■ ■ ■

Mompox, Colombia

Father Bennis grabbed María's hand and pulled her around the corner. The hostel María was staying at was back in the other direction. They moved quickly. People began appearing on the streets. They followed a zigzag pattern trying to shake the man following him with the AK-47. Bennis looked back and this time the man with the gun made no attempt to hide. In fact, he was gaining on them.

Holding María's hand, Father Bennis led her into the central municipal cemetery. Concrete white sepulchers lay on top of each other surrounded by monuments of stone angels, the Virgin Mary, and crosses and busts of long forgotten people. A few mourners looked with curiosity at the hurrying couple holding hands, but when they saw the man with the gun following them, the people scattered.

Bennis pulled María around the main building and stopped. It was time to act. A few moments later, the man with the beard and the AK-47 rounded the corner. He was met with a crushing right to his throat. He dropped the weapon and Bennis grabbed him around the neck and applied a chokehold. Within seconds, blood and oxygen were cut off to the man's brain and he passed out.

"Quick," Bennis said, "give me a hairpin or a tweezer from your pocketbook."

María looked surprised. "I don't have it! I must have dropped it at the café."

Bennis grabbed a bouquet of artificial flowers from a grave. He opened the AK-47 magazine clip, took the wire from the flowers, and pried open a bullet.

"What are you doing? We have to get out of here!"

"Patience, María." Bennis worked quickly like a surgeon. He took the gunpowder from a 7.62 caliber bullet and poured it into the magazine clip and the barrel. As the man with the beard began to regain consciousness, Bennis smacked his head with the butt of the rifle. "Now let's get the hell out of here and get that gun you left at the hostel."

Before retrieving María's .45 from the hostel, they found an empty bench in the Santa Barbara Plaza. The plaza was now busy with venders and shoppers. Bennis and María talked while the local people went about their daily chores around them. Bennis looked up and asked, "Where were all these people hiding?"

"They avoid the midday heat," María explained, "But the place comes alive at night."

Fr. Bennis leaned over and folded his hands as if in prayer. "We need to have a plan," he said. "The motorcyclist and the man in the cemetery.... They will know where I am staying and they will know you when they find your pocketbook."

"Maybe we should go back and look for it."

"No. That would be asking for more trouble."

María smiled. "By the way, Jack, we don't call it a pocketbook anymore."

He shook his head. "Well, you know what I meant."

"Why didn't you just take that man's rifle?"

"Don't you think we might look a bit conspicuous walking around with an AK-47? It's best this way. They'll still think we're unarmed. The ferry out of here in the morning will be crowded with people going to work on the mainland. I don't think they'll try anything there in front of a lot of people. The problem is tonight. You won't be able to go back to the hostel and I won't be able to go back to my hotel."

They sat in silence amid the passing pedestrians, vendors, motorcycles, and donkeys. After a few moments, Bennis took María's hand again and said, "'Diseases desperate grown, by desperate alliances are relieved, or not at all.'"

María frowned and looked at him. "And what does that mean, Jack? Is this another of your Kung Fu-Charlie Chan sayings?"

"No, María. It's from Shakespeare's *Hamlet*. It means desperate times demand desperate measures." He stood and pulled María to her feet. "It means we are going back to see El Apredido."

■ ■ ■

3

Brooklyn, New York

Anger swelled up in Cavanaugh like a rumbling volcano. *They were going to kill me. Educated idiots.* He shook his head. *And they vote!* He took a deep breath on the stoop of the apartment building. Why did he agree to look for this Salvatore Anthony Russo? He didn't really know him, and already he didn't like him. The first stop he makes, and he almost gets killed.

He rubbed his eyes. He wanted to go back to the apartment and beat the living shit out of both of them. There was a time when he would have. *How stupid could they be?* But then he thought about the girl. *What did they do with her? Was she alive? Could they really have dumped her body in the basement?*

There was only one way to find out. He went back into the building and found the stairs to the basement. It was dark and damp. There was a washing machine and a dryer in an anteroom. Farther down a corridor was the garbage room. The smell of garbage wrapped in black plastic bags hung like an invisible, nauseating vapor in the air.

"Hello?" he called as he groped for a light. "Anybody here?"

He heard scratching sounds in the far corner. A single light cord brushed across his face and he pulled the cord. Three large rats scampered over the garbage. Then he heard a groan from the corner behind him. He turned. In the dim light he saw a body under a few bags of garbage.

He bent over and moved the bags. There she was – naked, semi-conscious, but alive. He took his phone out and called his old police partner, Morty Goldberg. "Morty, no time to explain. I need a bus. Possible induced overdose from an attempted rape." He gave the address and added, "I'm in the basement with her now. I'll wait until I hear the ambulance. Then I'm gone. The perpetrators are in apartment 2B." He gave their names and then his phone died completely.

Cavanaugh went back to the laundry room and took some sheets from the dryer and covered the girl. He found her clothes under some more garbage and checked her wallet for her name and address. He put everything back and held the girl until he heard the police and emergency vehicles approaching. Then he quietly and quickly slipped out into the alley.

It started to rain as he walked back to his car. He recalled his mother watching the rain from their apartment window and singing with him, "It's raining, it's pouring. The old man is snoring. He went to bed, with a bump on his head, and didn't get up in the morning." *Another sick, morbid nursery rhyme.* He rubbed his shoulder and head. *Why did I agree to look into this? I almost got myself killed. I'm too old for this shit. The kid could be anywhere.* He realized as he approached the block where he parked his car, however, that some good had resulted from this experience. He had prevented a rape, possibly saved a life, and hopefully the two over-educated morons would pay for their selfish, callous criminal actions.

When he reached his car, however, his thoughts changed. *No good deed goes unpunished.* The side window of his car was smashed and his radio and E-Z pass were gone. When he got into his car, he smelled a foul odor and remembered the dead bird in the backseat. *Maybe there was such a thing as a bad omen.*

■ ■ ■

Mompox, Colombia

María Isabelle left the hostel carrying a lavender rainbow knapsack. When they were a block away, she opened the knapsack and handed Bennis a box wrapped in a colorful blouse and a pair of pink lace panties. He slowly removed the blouse and the panties to discover a large box of Kotex overnight maxi-pads.

"What's this?" he asked.

"It's what you asked for. I figured no one would look in the box."

Bennis froze when he opened the box and stepped back.

"What's the matter? You said you wanted it."

He recognized the gun immediately. His hands shook as he reached for it. This was a path he did not want to travel again. He felt the cold barrel. He balanced the gun in his hand.

"You look like you've seen a ghost," María said. "What's the matter?"

"It's *déjà vu* all over again."

"What are you talking about?"

He opened the clip. It was full – seven rounds. It looked very much like the standard Colt M1911 model. But it wasn't. It was a Mexican designed semi-automatic Obregón .45. It was a duplicate of the weapon he used to kill Ralph Muscatelli and another mob boss.

He closed his eyes. Images of the assassinations flashed across his brain. *Lead us not into temptation, Lord, but deliver us from evil.*

The gun seemed to jump in his hand as if it were alive. *I don't want to go down this path again. But something needs to be done to stop the spread of his new mysterious drug.* Was he being called to stop it?

He closed the magazine clip. *You can't be asking me to do this. Is it You or the devil?"*

"What's the matter, Jack?" María asked.

The gun seemed to burn into his hand. He shoved it into his belt and took a deep breath. The words of Shakespeare's Macbeth echoed in his mind. *If it were done when 'tis done, then 'twere well it were done quickly.*

He felt sick. He turned to María and said, "Let's go, María, and get this thing over with."

■ ■ ■

María Isabelle and Jack Bennis wove their way through the shoppers to the bar where Bennis had confronted El Apredido. "You'd better stay here, María. This could get messy."

"I'm going with you, Jack."

He argued. She persisted. He wished he knew how to handle a woman, but he didn't and realized few men, if any, ever really did. Finally, they entered the bar. It took a few seconds for his eyes to adjust from the sunshine outside to the darkness within. He looked around. Aside from the bartender, the room was empty.

"Can I help you, señor?" the bartender asked without looking up. He was a short man with jet-black hair, a large belly, and a moustache like a bird in flight. He reminded Bennis of Pancho, the Cisco Kid's companion. When the man looked up, he recognized Bennis. "Please, señor. I want no trouble. I warned you."

"Where is El Apredido?

The man's hands were shaking. "I am sorry, señor. I do not know of whom you speak. Please, señor, I want no trouble."

Bennis moved toward the man. The man reached for something under the bar. But Bennis was bigger, stronger, and quicker. He grabbed the man by his shirt and pulled him across the bar.

"Jack," María said. "I hear something in the back."

Bennis stopped and listened. Someone was crying beyond the back door of the bar. "Who is that?" he asked.

"I do not know, señor."

"You're lying, Pancho," Bennis said pulling the man over the bar and throwing him across the room. Before the man could get up, Bennis pushed him against the back door. The sounds were louder now. It was a man and a woman. The woman was crying and pleading. Bennis opened the door and flung the bartender through it.

In front of them a man straddled a woman on top of an overturned canoe. The woman's clothes were ripped and bloody. Her fishnet stockings were torn and scrunched around her ankles. Her right eye was swollen shut and she was bleeding from the nose and mouth. Bennis recognized the man. He was one of the burly men guarding El Apredido that afternoon. The man's AK-47 lay on the side of the canoe.

At the sound of the bartender crashing through the door, the man turned, lost his balance and fell off the canoe. The bartender crawled toward the stone wall in the enclosed courtyard. Bennis walked toward the man. María Isabelle started to go toward the woman. The woman rolled off the canoe and grabbed the rifle. Before anyone could stop her, the woman fired at her assailant. The sound of gunfire and bullets whizzing through the air enveloped the small courtyard. Within seconds, bullets ricocheted off the wall, pierced the canoe, and ripped through the man like a chainsaw.

Bennis stared at the man. His stomach looked more like piece of Swiss cheese oozing bloody spaghetti. He knelt and made a blessing over the man and then turned to the woman. María was holding her and trying to comfort her. He turned to the bartender, but he was gone.

"Come, María. We've got to get out of here," he said.

"But what about the woman and the man?"

"The man is dead. There is nothing we can do for him. Take the woman with us."

They went back into the bar where he took a checkered tablecloth from one of the tables and draped it around the woman. They left by a side door and walked in the shadow of a narrow alley for a few blocks. When they stopped, María reached into her knapsack and gave the woman one of her blouses to wear.

The woman's hands were cold and she was shivering. "I'm sorry, Padre. Please forgive me. I'm sorry. He was so bad. I'm sorry, Padre. Please forgive me."

Bennis reached out and held her hands. "God understands. He is all-merciful. The problem is man sometimes does not understand. We need to get you to safety."

As they crouched in the alley, they talked in whispers. The woman's name was Margarete. She was born in Medellin and was raped by her father, a member of the Calli Cartel, at the age of seven. She ran away from home when she was eleven and eventually made her way to Mompox. She thought things would be different here, but there were no jobs and she was desperate. Margarete resorted to doing what she had run away from. She made her living on the streets where occasional tourists, obnoxious drunks, and cheating husbands paid for her services. She was often abused and beaten. It was part of the job. She learned to trust no one. It was, she admitted to Bennis and María, a lonely, difficult life she was not proud of.

Tears poured from her eyes as she described some of the struggles she endured. She thought El Apredido would be different. He was a powerful man in the town. Police and public officials answered to him. But she soon discovered he was like the rest of them, only more brutal. She saw him kill and torture people and send his men off to kill others. He was a man without a conscience. She told how he sent someone to follow Fr. Bennis and kill him. When she tried to stop him, he hit her and turned her over to Manuel, the man who raped her on the canoe with orders to kill her after he finished with her.

"He is a bad man, Padre," she said.

"Where does he live?"

"I do not know. He has a place somewhere around here where he makes the 'Devil's Breath' you spoke about. But I do not know where." She looked down the darkening alleyway and sobbed, "He will kill me if he finds me."

Bennis wiped a tear from her cheek. "I think he will kill all of us, Margarete, if he finds us."

As the sun gradually went down, the sounds of music and laughter began to filter through the night. Bennis looked at María.

"It's like I told you, Jack, Mompox wakes up at night."

"We need to get out of here. I have more money and my passport back at the hotel, but they will be looking for me there. If I had it maybe we could bribe someone to get us out of Mompox. I don't think that would be a problem."

"I can go and get it for you, Jack."

"No, María. They saw you with me. That would be too dangerous."

"Then let me go," Margarete said. "They would not expect me. I can get what you need."

"No, Margarete. It is too dangerous. You said they would kill you."

"But they don't know I am alive and that I know you. They would not be expecting me. Even if they recognized me, they would think I was there for the reputation I have."

"I could give her some clothes from my knapsack, Jack, and they would not recognize her."

"I don't know. I don't like it. I don't want to put her life in danger."

It was dark now and the sounds of music and laughter were louder.

"Please, Padre. I want to do something good. You helped me. I need to help you. Please, Padre…."

"She's right, Jack. Margarete can do this. Trust her."

He sighed. It was two against one. "Never argue with a woman," his mother used to say. He told Margarete his room number and where his money and passport were and they waited in the alley until it was very late and the music and laughter dwindled into the silence of the night. They worked their way slowly back towards his hotel. Along the circuitous route they took, Bennis could not shake the feeling they were being followed. Frequently, he checked, but saw no one. He wondered if he was being overly cautious and a bit paranoid.

They stopped a block from the hotel behind a tamarind tree. He gave Margarete his key, thanked her, cautioned her to be careful, and blessed her.

Before she left, Margarete turned to Fr. Bennis and María. She kissed both of them on their cheeks. Her eyes were moist, but there was a smile on her face. She said, "My life has been a lonely road. Thank you for coming along…." Then, dressed in some of María's extra clothes, Margarete walked along the cobblestone roadway by the Magdalena River. They saw no one watching the hotel. Maybe he was wrong, but Bennis' gut told him to worry. She walked into the hotel, and they waited. Seconds turned into minutes – long agonizing minutes.

"It should not have taken her this long," María said.

Then suddenly, the night lit up and the sound of an explosion filled the night air. Glass and flames flew out of the window that once had been Jack Bennis' hotel room.

■ ■ ■

4

Brooklyn, New York

Cavanaugh wanted to call his sister-in-law Mary to find out what she was able to dig up on the missing Salvatore Anthony Russo. But his phone was dead. He got in his car and started driving. He wondered, *What would Superman do in the twenty-first century? Where have all the phone booths gone? And where did Clark Kent put his clothes when he changed into his Superman outfit? Wouldn't some homeless person have picked them up? If they were still there when Superman returned, wouldn't they be crumpled and dirty? And how would he go back to his job at the Daily Planet in a wrinkled suit possibly smelling of dried urine and cigarette smoke?* He wondered how many times Kent's editor Perry White had to talk to him about personal hygiene. *And wouldn't Lois Lane and Jimmy Olsen have complained about his unprofessional appearance and avoided going near him?*

He spotted a Starbucks and recalled they had Wi-Fi connections in their stores. But as he pulled to the curb, he realized he didn't have a charger with him. There was a Verizon store on the next block. He could charge his phone there and buy an adapter for the car. But there was a group of men and women wearing red jackets and holding signs and umbrellas in front of the store. They were waving and shouting at passing cars. Cavanaugh pounded the steering wheel. Pain shot up his shoulder to his head. He grimaced. *They're on strike again! And I'm not in the mood to be called a scab!* He had no idea what this strike was about. Maybe it was salary, maybe medical coverage, maybe job security, maybe retirement benefits. He didn't know, and he didn't care. He just wanted to find Salvatore Anthony Russo. After learning the little he did from Sal's friends, he really didn't like him and didn't care if he found him dead or alive.

. He planned to visit Sal's girlfriend. He had a lot of questions to ask her. But she would be in the hospital now probably getting her stomach pumped and giving reports to the police. He had her address.

With a dead phone, no radio, a missing E-Z pass, and rain pouring in from his broken window, Cavanaugh decided to take a trip to NYU to see what more he could find about the missing Salvatore Anthony Russo. As he turned onto Smith Street and headed toward the Brooklyn Bridge, the car started to bounce and veer to the right. The rain was heavier now. He pounded the dashboard. Pain shot through his shoulder and head again. "Shit!" he shouted. He had a flat tire!

■ ■ ■

Mompox, Colombia

El Apredido peered out his window into the dark night at the sleeping town of Mompox. He sipped another French 75 and savored the mixture of gin, sugar, lemon juice, and champagne. It had been an eventful day. The visit from the tall priest was somewhat unexpected. He expected someone would come, but not a priest. He smiled. The priest was a unique approach he had to admit. He nodded, "There's no art to find the mind's construction in the face." He would have killed the priest there and then if he had received the message before his arrival. But the letter did not come until after the priest left.

He turned from the window to his antique Spanish colonial desk and read the letter again.

> *This is your last chance. I cannot and will not*
> *tolerate your insubordination. Either you stop and*
> *decide to work with me, or I promise there will be serious*
> *repercussions. I will guarantee my way is best for all.*

It will save a lot of needless bloodshed. You may think
you are secure in Mompox, but trust me, you are not.
My people are on their way.
I trust you understand the urgency of this letter.

S.R.

It's not about selling drugs and accumulating profits. It never was. It's much bigger than that. I will not be deterred from my mission. "Our doubts are traitors and make us lose the good we oft might win by fearing to attempt." He studied the letter, then crumpled it up and threw it across the room into an abstract painting hanging over a 17th century credenza.

Trust him? What does he take me for? A fool? I have no tolerance for fools. The priest and the woman he met at the restaurant must have been sent by S.R. Had I gotten the letter first, they would be dead by now. But somehow they escaped, and one of my guards is killed and another ends up with a concussion. The bold priest is harder to kill than expected. But I will find both of them. Nothing happens in Mompox that I do not know. When they return to the priest's hotel room, they will meet their rewards for meddling in El Apredido's affairs. I do not make empty threats.

He turned abruptly back to the window at the sound of the explosion. He smiled as he saw flames leaping into the night sky from the hotel where the priest was staying.

That is my message to you, S.R.! No one will stop my plans. No cartel, no priest, no woman, no God, no one!

■ ■ ■

Brooklyn, New York

Cavanaugh sat for a while in his car and stared at the rain coming in his side window. His closest clue to finding Salvatore Russo might come from his girlfriend, Carolyn Hendershot, not NYU. Bureaucrats hid behind confidentiality and privacy rules. If reporters couldn't obtain copies of the President's college transcripts, how would he manage to pry information from a behemoth like New York University? No, the girl was a better choice. The ambulance would probably take her to the nearest hospital which would be New York Methodist Hospital. Depending on how bad her condition was, they might put her on a ventilator to assist in her breathing or they might pump her stomach, do toxicology tests, administer charcoal by mouth to absorb the drug, and give her a full psychiatric evaluation. Plus, there would be police reports to complete when she regained consciousness. He imagined they would keep her overnight to be on the safe side. Date drugs when combined with alcohol, he knew, could lead to a coma and even death.

If this were the case, he could call it a day and go home to get his phone charged.

Or, he could strike while the iron was lukewarm, at best, and go to the girl's apartment and see what he could find. It was a long shot. He knew how to pick locks, but what if she had a roommate? He didn't have a badge or anything to prove he wasn't a burglar. But then again, he had talked his way out of situations before. There was the time he took a woman he met at a bar back to her place and had just started to undress when her husband arrived. And then there was the time he held a suspected child molester by his feet from the roof of a precinct in Greenwich Village to get a confession and the Commanding Officer caught him in the act. He didn't quite remember what he said, but whatever it was, it worked.

He reached for the car radio to find out if the local news had reported on the attempted rape, but pounded the dashboard when it dawned on him that the creep who broke his window and took his E-Z pass had also stolen his radio.

He started the car and headed to Salvatore's girlfriend's apartment. He wanted this case over with more than he had wanted that set of Lionel trains with the Santa Fe engine for Christmas when he was a seven-year-old. He would take his chances on a roommate.

As he approached the Grand Army Plaza, however, he heard and felt the familiar sound of another flat tire. He took a deep breath and pulled to the side of the road. He turned and looked in the backseat. The dead blackbird seemed to peer back at him from his handkerchief. "If you know what's good for you, you'd better not be laughing at me," he shouted. Then he smiled and shook his head. "I'm talking to a freaking dead bird! I hate this case! I just hope I get my hands on this Salvatore before I totally lose my mind!"

■ ■ ■

After his car wobbled into a garage and he bought another tire, Cavanaugh looked like he stepped out of the shower fully clothed. His feet squished as he walked up to Carolyn Hendershot's apartment on Carroll Street. There wasn't any lock on the outside building door. He checked the names on the mailboxes and buzzed Carolyn's number. No answer. He buzzed again. No answer again.

He walked up three flights of stairs until he came to apartment 3B. He knocked. No answer again. He knocked again. Still no answer.

Working quickly, he picked the lock and let himself into Carolyn's apartment leaving a puddle on the carpet outside the door.

The apartment was a studio. He worked quickly scouring the room for a clue to Salvatore's whereabouts. By a sofa bed in the corner, there was a picture in a gold frame of Sal and Carolyn at an airport with palm trees in the background. He opened her drawers and rummaged through her clothes. All he found were some Mexican coins, a blank postcard from the Hotel Cozumel, a box of prophylaxes, a playbill from the *Book of Mormon*, a gothic faux gem lace necklace, a rhinestone hollowed out ring- bracelet, a retro-style octopus shaped alloy pendant, and a trendy moon-shaped pendant necklace. The jewelry was cheap and garish, but under the jewelry he found a stack of letters carefully tied in a pink ribbon.

He put the letters in his pocket just as he heard someone at the front door. He looked around. There was nowhere to hide. The door opened and a pale, thin, blonde looked at him. Her mouth opened in surprise. He recognized her immediately. Before she had a chance to scream or ask for an explanation, Cavanaugh began, "I'm the one who found you in the garbage room. I thought you'd still be in the hospital. You looked pretty bad back there when I last saw you. I figured I'd come here to see if we could gather some more clues about your assailants, Mr. Roberts and Mr.

Cranberry. I think we can put them away for some time. They won't be bothering you anymore."

She continued to stare at Cavanaugh as if she were in a catatonic state.

"Are you all right, Ms. Hendershot?"

She blinked and looked at the small puddle at her feet and then at Cavanaugh. "You're wet," she said. "You look wetter than a possum swimmin' in a dirty sewer."

"It was raining pretty heavy when I got here."

"You need to change your clothes. You're likely to get sick as a dog passin' peach pits."

"I'm fine, Ms. Hendershot. I thought you'd be in the hospital."

"I signed myself out. Hospitals give me the green-apple nasties."

"Did you give your report to the police about what Roberts and Cranberry tried to do to you?"

"I don't know what you're yappin' about. Jake and Dick didn't do nothin' to me. They're Sal's good friends."

"They drugged you and tried to rape you!"

"Mister, I don't know what you're talkin' about. I think you're as confused as a goat on Astroturf. I passed out. That's all. You're talkin' out of your ass. Jacob and Dick didn't do nothin' to me."

"They drugged you!"

"Mister, I sure think the wetness has gotten to your brain. You need to get out of them wet clothes. I have some of Sal's old clothes here if you'd like to change."

Cavanaugh shook his head and pointed to an etching on the wall. "Did Sal draw that?"

"Yep. He called it Abracadaver or somethin' like that."

"Abraxas."

"Yep. That's it. Supposed to be a devil of some sort."

"It's very unique. I like it. I wonder if I could get this Sal of yours to do a drawing like this one for me. Where could I find him?"

Carolyn Hendershot walked over to the computer on her desk. She looked out a window that faced a brick wall. "I don't know, Mister. Sal's a pretty busy guy. Sometimes I think he's busier than a funeral home fan in July. Besides, he ain't around here now anyway, Mister."

"Would you know where I could find him?"

She turned and studied him for a few seconds. "You're wet, Mister. Let me get you some dry clothes."

"No, I'm all right. Where can I find Sal?"

She sat on the edge of her desk. She looked weak and tired. "I'm from Lubbock, Texas, Mister. We do things a mite different down my way. I ain't got all the book learnin' Sal has, but I weren't behind the door when brains was passed out neither. My momma taught me the bigger the mouth, the better it looks when shut." She paused and folded her arms. "What are you really in my room for, Mister?"

Cavanaugh's feet made a squishy sound as he moved toward the door. "I'll level with you, Ms. Hendershot. My mother always told me honesty is the best policy especially with pretty women. I was hired by Sal's mother and grandmother to find him. They are worried because they haven't heard from him in months. Do you have any idea where he might be?"

"All I can tell you is he's okay. He's workin' on some kind of special project. That's all I know."

"What can you tell me about him?"

She rubbed her arms and Cavanaugh saw part of a tattoo on her left arm. The tattoo looked like some kind of mythical creature with the legs of a snake. "He's sharper than a pocketful of toothpicks," she said, "and he's so persuasive he could tell you to go to hell in such a way that you'd look forward to the trip. I don't know where he is now, but you can tell his momma she can bet the farm that he'll be back. If he says somethin', it's so. It's a calcified fact."

Cavanaugh stopped at the door and felt the letters in his back pocket. "Thanks for your help, Ms. Hendershot. Do you mind if I ask you one more question? You're from Lubbock, Texas. That's a long way from New York City. How did you meet Sal?"

A small smile cracked her tired face. "When I came to New York I didn't have a pot to piss in nor a window to throw it out of. I got a job as a waitress in a bar on 12th Street in Manhattan. That's where I met Sal. He would come in there with a group of guys from Con Ed or Wall Street or wherever. We hit it off faster than a prairie fire with a tailwind. He put me up here and I'll be here when he comes back."

Cavanaugh thanked her again, smiled and backed out the door closing it behind him. On the way downstairs, he knew what his next step would be. The Mexican coins, the Hotel Cozumel, the bundle of letters, and the apartment for his girlfriend. The pain in his head and shoulder slightly eased as he thought about how he would *follow the money.*

■ ■ ■

5

Mompox, Colombia

The heat from the fire swept over them like a torrid tidal wave. In moments the entire hotel was ablaze. María clung to Bennis' arm like a mother holding a sobbing child. But she was the one crying, not Bennis. His mind was calculating alternative plans. El Apredido was vicious and dangerous. Killing innocent people sleeping in a hotel meant nothing to him. His objective was to kill Bennis and María.

Jack Bennis knew they would have to leave Mompox. He didn't like running away, but he was with María and right now they were in no position to confront El Apredido. He needed a plan. Getting María to safety would not be an easy job. His old platoon sergeant's words echoed in his brain. "Remember the Seven Ps – Prior Proper Planning Prevents Piss Poor Performance."

Jack Bennis had dealt with catastrophes in life and death situations before. On a military mission, many years before, he and two of his men were wounded and abandoned in hostile South American jungles.

Despite his own wounds, Bennis endeavored to nurse the three of them back to health, removing bullets and shrapnel, stitching up wounds, foraging for food and water, and evading the real and potential dangers of the jungles. Surviving in the wild was not a problem for him. It was as if he wrote the U.S. Army Survival Manual. He knew nature can provide food to enable a person to survive. With few exceptions, everything that grows from the soil or that walks, crawls, or swims is a potential food source. The trick was knowing how to get the food and how to prepare it.

Initially, wounded and with hostile forces pursuing them, they used plants and insects as their main source of nutrition. These could be obtained more easily and more quietly than meat. The young Lieutenant Bennis fought through his own pain and scavenged for wild fruit and edible plants. Peanuts were an important source of protein. He dug out peanut pegs penetrating the ground. He picked berries off plants. From a leguminous tree he found fleshy, juicy, pod-like fruit. Later, he would find wild mangos and bananas, catch fish and trap animals.

Their primary source of protein in the beginning, however, was insects. Ants, grasshoppers, and termites were plentiful and a high source of protein. Woodgrubs, the larvae of wood-boring beetles, were found in rotten logs, in the ground, and under the bark of dead trees. Some of these white, slimy, worm-like creatures could be almost three inches in length. They ate them raw or boiled or roasted them.

Finding water in a jungle was probably the easiest part of survival. One can live many days without food if you have water. The leaves on the rainforest ground are large and are useful in collecting dew and rainwater. Bennis and his men followed animal tracks to streams and rivers, but the problem was purifying the water without attracting the attention of their pursuers. He solved the problem by digging pits and making rock-type ovens which he used to boil the water and food at night.

No, surviving in the wild was not a problem for Jack Bennis. The problem was taking María Isabelle with him.

He looked at her clinging to his arm and wondered how she would react to eating snakes or cleaning and eating fresh-killed squirrels. He recalled splitting the hide of an agouti from tail to throat, being careful not to pierce its stomach, cutting away and removing the bladder, trying to save as much blood as possible as a good source of food and salt. He had been trained to use everything possible, including scraping the meat from the head, boiling the eyes and brain, cracking the bones and scrapping out the marrow, and using the bones to make weapons.

He put his right arm gently around María and reached into his left pocket with his other hand. He felt the pink Connemara marble Irish rosary beads his mother had given him to keep him safe and the dog tags of PFC Jimmy Ward. The men in his squad back then called Ward "Happy" because he was always smiling. He never complained and never had a bad word to say about anyone.

"Happy" was an orphan with no known family. He joined the Army when he was eighteen because he felt it was his duty. He was a tall, muscular teenager from the Midwest. "Happy" was one of the men wounded in that aborted mission a lifetime ago. "Happy," however, never made it out of the jungles. He died of septicemia probably resulting from the gunshot wound to his lung. Bennis did all he could to save "Happy." He acted as a shaman. He extracted capsaicin from wild hot chili peppers and applied it to "Happy" to relieve some of his pain. He used white willow bark as a remedy for inflammation and pain. He tried using the leaves from the birch tree which act like cortisone as an anti-spasmodic, antifungal, detoxifying diuretic.

But he and Sgt. Manny Rodriguez watched as PFC Ward's fever rose, his breathing rapidly increased, and his heart rate rose. "Happy" became confused. He thought he was on a merry-go-round and kept calling out for the mother he never knew. He stopped urinating and showed serious signs of edema as his fever increased. Bennis knew shamans used a wide variety of herbs, lianas, flowers, and leaves for medicinal purposes. Studies had shown the bark and wood of the pau d'arco tree boosts white blood cells and kills bacteria, and a woody vine called cat's claw fights pain. Bennis searched the woods frantically for anything that might help "Happy."

But on a damp day in August, PFC Ward looked up at Bennis and smiled, "Thanks, Lieutenant, for everything you've done. You're a real good guy. It's been a pleasure serving with you." Then "Happy" closed his blue eyes and slipped into a coma. He died a day later and they buried PFC Ward beneath a giant sandbox tree. Bennis kept Ward's dog tags both as a remembrance of him and as a reminder that man will never understand God's plans.

Father Bennis looked up into the night sky and prayed silently as embers from the hotel fire floated aimlessly upward. He didn't want to let María down as he felt he had PFC Jimmy Ward. Maybe it was the smoke that caused him to choke when he prayed, "Not my will, but Thine be done."

■ ■ ■

Staten Island, New York

Follow the money. It worked with terrorists. It should work here. Miss Carolyn Hendershot was a bar waitress. Granted they made good tips, but not good enough to have traveled to Mexico and stayed at Cozumel. The picture at the airport of Sal and Carolyn meant they went together. Where did the money for the trip come from?

When he returned home, Cavanaugh charged his cellphone and called his sister-in-law, Mary Muscatelli. "Did you find anything on this Salvatore Russo?" he asked.

"I'm fine, Tom. Thank you for asking."

"I'm sorry, Mary. It's been a rough day and I have a splitting headache. How are you and what did you find on this Salvatore Russo?"

"Thanks for asking, Tom. Your mother-in-law soiled herself three times, the washing machine broke, and I was unable to get much about Russo. Maybe that's the most significant part. The colleges wouldn't release any information about him. Privacy laws and all that crapola. I tried to work my way around the IRS, but apparently he never filed any tax reports. He doesn't have a driver's license and as far as I could discover he has no credit cards."

Cavanaugh sat in silence for a few moments and then said, "Does Fran know about her mother?"

"I called her. She's here helping me."

Cavanaugh bit his knuckle, looked at his yellow note pad and asked, "What do you and Fran know about your Aunt Vincenza Russo, and your cousin Deborah Catherine."

"I'm putting you on speaker, Tom, so Fran can hear, too."

He heard Fran's voice in the background. "We didn't really know much about them, Tom. Aunt Vincenza was my father's sister, but we never associated much with them. I think they live someplace up in northern New Jersey in a rich area. The only time we saw them was at funerals and weddings."

"What can you tell me about them?" he asked.

Mary commented first, "Aunt Vincenza scared me. She was tough. I remember she had a gold tooth and I couldn't stop staring at it when I was young. She told me to stop looking at her or she would pluck my eyes out. I think she was kidding, but she scared the heck out of me."

Fran added, "I think there was some kind of scandal back when we were younger. They tried to hush it up, but our cousin Deborah apparently got knocked up in high school and had a baby. Deborah was beautiful but pretty free with her body the way I heard it. I think the father of the baby was the valedictorian of the school. No one ever really knew for sure, however. The whole thing was hush-hush. My uncle was a big time Wall Street broker. He didn't want any scandals."

Cavanaugh thanked Mary and Fran and asked them to keep digging. After hanging up he went to the refrigerator and pulled a Beck's beer from behind the orange juice. He went back into his den and closed his eyes. His head ached where that educated fool with the Fu Manchu beard had clocked him with the softball bat. How was he going to find this Salvatore Russo if there was no paper trail? His gut told him Sal's two classmates knew more than they said and, he felt sure, Sal's girlfriend Carolyn was holding out on him. In fact, the more he thought about it, the more he felt Sal's mother and grandmother knew more than they told him, too. What were they holding out on him? And why?

He sat back and took a long swig of his beer. It felt good. Real good. Almost too good. He took another long drink and emptied the bottle. He looked at the green bottle and thought he had the ability to be an alcoholic. He rose to get another beer and felt something in his pocket. Of course! The letters! Maybe they would give him a clue as to where this Russo guy was hiding out or had disappeared to.

He untied the pink ribbon and opened the first letter. He frowned and asked aloud, "What the hell is this?" The letter read:

> DeaR carolyn,
>   yoUr Girlfriend Was cOrrect. the RocK formationS are Wonderful, wILd, Lofty, and beauTiful. Regret You not wITH me. gOiNg tO the norTH sEction eaRly Saturday or Sunday at nOOn. wish me luck.
>   love, sal

I thought this guy was supposed to be brilliant, Cavanaugh thought. *I guess no one ever taught him to write. I think they did away with teaching grammar and penmanship in school years ago. I heard they don't even teach cursive writing anymore. How are today's kids ever going to be able to sign their checks? Even I can write better than this.*

He opened the next letter.

> dear carolyn,
>   ITS BEautiful hEre. Nothing but Azure skies, MOuNTans, Heavy wiNds, EvEnings Dull. TomorrOw will try to Swim in thE ocEan. I FantasIze Tumbling SofTly wIth siLLy Wild dOlphins RocKing in the waveS. After Supper i Keep REadDing FOReign papers for More wOrld NEws. Yesterday Wondered wHEN a Hungry pErson will REFUSE being puShed Around. Someday i would liKe to ask HIM, "HAVE YOU EVER BEEN TO COZUMEL?"
>   love, sal

The writing was in the same style. It was irregular, almost slipshod. There was no consistency. Was he too arrogant to follow a formal style of writing? Cavanaugh knew when he wrote he printed everything in capital letters, but Sal Russo went back and forth like an erratic ping pong player. He flipped through the other letters. Maybe his mind travelled faster than his hand. The letters were all written in this same apparent haphazard way.

There was no uniformity in any of the letters. And, what was even more shocking, some of the letters made no sense. "Fantasize tumbling softly with silly wild dolphins rocking in the waves." *What kind of a nut is this Salvatore Russo?*

He looked at the letters again. They didn't make sense. Sal Russo, from all he had learned, was smart, articulate, and meticulous. The painting of Abraxas over the fireplace in Redhead and Fu Manchu's apartment was carefully and methodically created. According to his mother and grandmother, he had earned a couple of post-graduate degrees. He would have had to write term papers. Why would he now throw capital letters around like a 300 pound man with high blood pressure pouring salt on a McDonald's cheeseburger?

He went to the refrigerator again and pulled another bottle of beer from under a head of lettuce in the vegetable bin. He held the cold green bottle against his head. His head seemed to ache more when he thought about the letters. They meant something. But what?

"Yesterday I wondered when a hungry person will refuse being pushed around." It wasn't worded very smoothly, but it fit with what Redhead and Fu Manchu told him about Sal's participating in the Occupy Wall Street movement and his being a strong supporter of Bernie Sanders. The missing Sal Russo was concerned with social inequity, but why would he ask a hungry person if he had ever been to Cozumel?

Cavanaugh placed the top two letters next to each other and studied them. The first one read, "DeaR carolyn." The second letter's greeting was, "dear carolyn." Why the capital D and R in the first letter and not in the second letter? Did the capital letters mean something? Or was he just careless?

He grimaced as he took the beer bottle from his head and took a long gulp. He remembered Roxanne Fraum. She was a beautiful blonde who loved her beer and could chug a bottle of beer faster than anyone he knew. They were in the same English class in high school, and Mrs. Hensley constantly reprimanded Roxanne for writing about herself with a lower case letter "i." Roxanne would dot the lower case "i" with a small heart. He always thought it was cute, but it drove Mrs. Hensley wild. This gave him an idea and he picked up a pencil and underlined only the capital letters in the first letter.

> <u>DeaR</u> carolyn,
>   yo<u>U</u>r <u>G</u>irlfriend <u>W</u>as c<u>O</u>rrect. the <u>R</u>oc<u>K</u> formation<u>S</u> are <u>W</u>onderful, w<u>IL</u>d, <u>L</u>ofty, and beau<u>T</u>iful. <u>R</u>egret <u>Y</u>ou not w<u>ITH</u> me. g<u>O</u>i<u>N</u>g t<u>O</u> the nor<u>TH</u> s<u>E</u>ction ea<u>R</u>ly <u>S</u>aturday or <u>S</u>unday at n<u>OO</u>N. wish me luck.
>   love, sal

He wrote only the capital letters down on his yellow pad: "DRUG-WORKSWILLTRYITONOTHERSSOON." Gradually, the letters formed words and made sense! "Drug works. Will try it on others soon." It was a simple code. Salvatore Russo was cautious. But why? And what drug? And why try it on others?

He turned to the second letter and underlined only the capital letters.

> dear carolyn,
>   <u>ITS</u> <u>BE</u>autiful h<u>E</u>re. <u>N</u>othing but <u>A</u>zure skies, <u>MO</u>u<u>NT</u>ans, <u>H</u>eavy wi<u>N</u>ds, <u>E</u>v<u>E</u>nings <u>D</u>ull. <u>T</u>omorr<u>O</u>w will try to <u>S</u>wim in th<u>E</u> oc<u>E</u>an. <u>I</u> <u>F</u>antas<u>I</u>ze <u>T</u>umbling <u>S</u>of<u>T</u>ly w<u>I</u>th si<u>LL</u>y <u>W</u>ild d<u>O</u>lphins <u>R</u>oc<u>K</u>ing in the wave<u>S</u>. <u>A</u>fter <u>S</u>upper i <u>K</u>eep <u>RE</u>ad<u>D</u>ing <u>FOR</u>eign papers for <u>M</u>ore w<u>O</u>rld <u>NE</u>ws. <u>Y</u>esterday <u>W</u>ondered w<u>HEN</u> a <u>H</u>ungry p<u>E</u>rson will <u>REFUSE</u> being pu<u>S</u>hed <u>A</u>round. <u>S</u>omeday i would li<u>K</u>e to ask <u>HIM, "HAVE YOU EVER BEEN TO COZUMEL</u>?"
>   love, sal

The capital letters again spelled out a message. ITS BEEN A MONTH. NEED TO SEE IF IT STILL WORKS. ASK RED FOR MONEY. WHEN HE REFUSES ASK HIM, "HAVE YOU EVER BEEN TO COZUMEL?"

Cavanaugh went through the others letters. Beneath the rambling, sometimes incoherent sentences, there was an encrypted message in each letter.

I TOLD YOU IT WORKS. NOW GO BACK AND OFFER TO GIVE THE MONEY BACK TO RED.

IT REALLY WORKS. EVEN AFTER THREE MONTHS HE DID NOT KNOW WHAT YOU WERE TALKING ABOUT.

IF YOU NEED MORE MONEY WHILE I AM AWAY TRY THIS WITH YOUR BOSS BIG LOUIE.

ENTERING FINAL PHASE NOW. THEY WILL BE SORRY.

Cavanaugh studied the messages. What was Salvatore Russo up to? What was this drug he was talking about? He seemed to be experimenting with it on others. But why? Where was he now? Who were Red and Vic? Why did the missing Sal send these coded messages buried in his letters to his girlfriend? What was the final phase? Who were the "they" and why would they be sorry? This case had more questions than answers.

Cavanaugh finished his beer and stood up. It was time for a little experimenting of his own.

■ ■ ■

Manhattan, New York

Cavanaugh thought he knew the place where Carolyn met Sal. He remembered it from his days assigned as a patrolman in Manhattan. It was a couple of blocks away from the Con Edison electrical substation on 14th Street. He had been there many times. The bar itself was sleazy; the food tasted like cardboard, and the beer was routinely stale and lukewarm. But it had half-naked waitresses and an active backroom where gambling of all sorts took place. You could bet on anything from horses to dogs, from the attendance at a Met game to the time to sing the Star Spangled Banner at a Knick game. They would play Ferret Bingo and wager on the next person to play James Bond and the size of Donald Trump's "Johnson" as well as high stakes poker. The local cops looked away and were richly rewarded for their myopia or nearsightedness. Cavanaugh was young and single then. He knew the score, but never accepted a dime. He went there for the half-naked waitresses and the hopes of making a different kind of score.

That was a long time ago. He wondered if things had changed. He heard the place was raided during Rudy Giuliani's time as mayor, but under Mayor Bill deBlasio things had pretty much reversed themselves. He didn't have to wait long to discover things were back to the past, but with new additions. Looking through the front door he saw the bar was crowded with men in suits, workers in overalls, and waitresses in G-strings. But there were a lot more women there and male waiters who also wore G-strings!

The music and laughter were loud and the place smelled of alcohol, perfume, and hormones. On the wall a large chart entitled "Ghoul Pool" hung over a long list of names. He recognized some of the names of elderly actors, politicians, athletes, scientists and world leaders. The chart indicated the pot was now $2,000.

A strong hand swung out in front of him blocking his access. "You planning on entering the Grim Reaper Lottery, Detective?"

Cavanaugh reacted immediately. He pushed the arm back with one hand and swung his other hand toward the voice. A huge hand grabbed his hand in mid-air. "Easy, Detective. It's me."

The voice was familiar. It was deep and had a trace of a Spanish accent. He looked up into the smiling face of Francisco Thomas, the ex-fiancé of María Isabelle.

"What are you doing here?" Cavanaugh asked.

"I could ask you the same thing, Detective, but I won't."

"I thought you were pitching with the Yankee farm team."

"I was and things were going good, but my arm went out again. I'm working as a bouncer here now. What about you?"

Cavanaugh backed out of the bar so he could hear better. "How do you stand the noise, Francisco?"

Thomas pointed to his ears. "I put cotton in my ears. It helps."

Cavanaugh felt his head pounding to the music. "I'm looking for a missing guy named Sal Russo. Have you ever heard of him?"

"No, sir. I've only been working here about a month. I can ask around for you if you like."

"No. That won't be necessary, Francisco. Can you tell me if a thin blonde named Carolyn works here? "

"Oh, sure! I like her a lot. She's the girl from Texas. *Muy bonita.* She reminds me of María Isabelle. Have you heard anything from her? Last I heard after she broke our engagement, she went off to South America to work in the missions or something."

Cavanaugh's head felt like it was about to crack. He didn't want to get into a discussion of María Isabelle. That would lead to a discussion of his brother. He knew something had been going on between María and his brother. He didn't want to know what. He just knew. His brother was a priest, but he saw the look in his eyes when he was with María. Now they both were in Colombia. What his brother did, he reasoned, was none of his business. Jack Bennis was an adult and whether he was a priest or not he was capable of taking care of his own business.

"No, I haven't heard a thing since they, I mean, she left."

"They?"

"Sorry. That was a slip of the tongue. I heard she left with a group of nurses for someplace in Colombia. If I hear anything, I'll let you know." His speech became more rapid. He wanted to change the topic quickly. "Can you do me a favor? Do you happen to know someone named Louie who works here? I need to talk to him."

"Do you mean Big Louie? He's the manager of this place."

"Yeah. That's the guy. Is he here now?"

Thomas looked around. "I didn't see him, but things are pretty busy now. He usually comes in around 11:30 to check the receipts. Just between the two of us, he's pretty cheap and is afraid someone might be skimming off the top. But he's probably right about that. Do you want me to have him call you?"

"No. I'll come back and talk to him. It's really no big thing."

Cavanaugh turned and walked slowly back to his car. It's always hard finding a parking place in Manhattan. He had been lucky and found a spot a block away close to a McDonald's and across the street from a liquor store and a bodega. The odor of hamburgers and French fries hit him like the bouquet of roses and he suddenly felt hungry. He couldn't remember the last time he ate. As he approached his car, however, he lost his appetite. His left front headlight has been smashed. He looked around. A woman strolled by with a baby carriage. A homeless man with a sign reading, "Help the needy" lay next to the doorway of a nail salon. Two well-dressed men walked side by side talking into their cellphones. No one looked at Cavanaugh. This was New York.

He opened the car and looked into the back seat. The dead blackbird's head peered out from his handkerchief. "I guess you didn't see anything either," he said. As he turned and looked at the broken glass, he started to put random acts together like a jigsaw puzzle: the broken car window, the stolen E-Z pass and car radio, the flat tires, and now the broken headlight. Coincidences? Maybe. But he never really believed in coincidences or omens. Was someone sending him a warning message about trying to find the missing Salvatore Anthony Russo?

■ ■ ■

6

Mompox, Colombia

Sirens blared in the night and people ran toward the burning hotel. María Isabelle clung to Jack Bennis' arm. It was hard and strong like the tree they were hiding behind. She nestled her head into his shoulder. He could smell her lingering favorite perfume, the familiar shampoo she used, and her perspiration. He breathed deeply and savored everything about her. He wanted to pull her closer and kiss her. He wanted to taste her lips and inhale her breath.

"What are we going to do now?" she asked.

He looked into her eyes. He felt her fear. It was tangible. His eyes watered. He wanted to tell her not to worry, that it would all be all right. But that was a lie, and priests aren't supposed to lie. He took a deep breath and pulled her closer. He leaned down and kissed her with all the passion that had been building up in him since he first realized he was in love with her. Then he closed his eyes and whispered softly in her ear, "It'll be all right, María. Don't worry. We'll find a way."

■ ■ ■

Manhattan, New York

Cavanaugh bought a large black coffee and a roast beef hero with cheese, lettuce, tomato, onion, and plenty of mayonnaise at the bodega and waited in his car. At 11:45 p.m., he got out of his car and headed back to the bar. It was still noisy, but the crowd had thinned out. The Ghoul Pool was up to $2,500 and he noticed Rosie O'Donnell's name had been added to the list. Francisco was still at the door.

"Is Big Louie here yet?" Cavanaugh asked.

"Not yet, Detective. I expect he will be arriving soon."

"What's he look like?"

"Oh, you can't miss him. He's big. Well, large might be a better word. He's about half my size and twice my weight. He usually wears loose clothes. He's got a cheap black toupee that looks like he bought it at a Halloween party store. You can't miss him."

Cavanaugh thanked Francisco and walked a few stores down and waited outside a closed Verizon store. As he waited he thought about why anyone would want to stop him from investigating the disappearance of Salvatore Russo. Little Miss Texas knew more than she said. From the letters he read, it was clear Sal told her about his plans. But what were they? Had Carolyn tipped someone off? Were the stolen E-Z pass and car radio part of the plan to stop him? Or were they separate? She was unconscious when he found her. She wouldn't have had the opportunity to get someone to break into his car. Or was it all just a coincidence?

He turned and looked down the street. A man in his early fifties waddled down the street. The man stood about 5' 2" and must have weighted over 300 pounds. He shuffled along with a large leather bag dangling from his left hand. He wore an extra-large black sweat suit and a blue Yankee cap pulled down over his face. Judging from the bulge under his sweat shirt, Cavanaugh figured he was probably carrying a weapon – and whatever it was, it was big – possibly a Smith & Wesson .44 Magnum. *A little fat man with a gun too big for him.* Cavanaugh shook his head. *Pathetic. A man with a Napoleonic complex who thought he was Dirty Harry.*

Cavanaugh took a deep breath and moved toward the man. He was going into unexplored territory. Men like Big Louie could be dangerous. Insecure men with big egos and large guns were unpredictable. As he grew closer to the man, he saw the man move his right hand toward the bulge on his side.

■ ■ ■

Mompox, Colombia

María Isabelle's right hand moved down to Jack's chest and unbuttoned his black shirt. Slowly yet deftly, she unbuttoned one button after another. Her head followed her hands and she kissed his torso. Her lips lingered over old wounds and scar tissue from the past. They lapped against his skin like the soft ripples on a lake. Her tongue rolled circles around his nipples. And her fingers methodically worked their way toward his belt buckle.

He focused on the moment and surrendered reason to passion. The crackling fire of the hotel, the sounds of curious onlookers and volunteer firefighters faded away like an FM radio going through a tunnel. He looked down at María and patted the top of her head.

Then he heard it. It sounded like a dislodged pebble or a footstep on the gravel path. It was very close. He turned and saw the man he had hit in the cemetery. He was less than twenty yards away. His head was bandaged. His eyes screamed hate and revenge. He raised his AK-47 and took careful aim. At this range a blind man could hit both Bennis and María, but the burly man with a beard wanted a head shot. He wanted to blow Bennis' head open like an exploding pumpkin. Bennis tried to push María's head away. But it was too late.

The bearded burly man pulled the trigger.

■ ■ ■

Manhattan, New York

"Excuse me, sir," Cavanaugh began. "You're Big Louie, aren't you? Can you spare a fellow a couple of dollars? My car ran out of gas and I ...."

"I don't know you, creep. Get out of my way before I blow a hole through you," Louie replied.

Cavanaugh saw Big Louie reaching under his sweatshirt for his gun. It was now or never. "Have you ever been to Cozumel?" he blurted out quickly.

Louie's hand stopped. His face lost all expression. His eyes stared straight ahead. It was like he was suddenly paralyzed. He stood motionless in front of Cavanaugh like a figure in Madame Tussaud's wax museum. A large UPS tractor trailer barreled across 12th Street and blasted its air horn at a couple making out next to a blue Toyota Camry. The woman screamed and the man pulled her away. Big Louie didn't flinch.

Cavanaugh didn't believe his eyes. Louie was in some kind of hypnotic trance. What had Salvatore Russo done to Big Louie? And how did he do it? Cavanaugh seized the moment. "Give me half the money in your wallet?" he said.

Big Louie dropped his leather money bag and reached into his pocket. Robotically, he handed Cavanaugh half the money in his wallet. Cavanaugh counted out two hundred dollars. *Now what do I do?* Cavanaugh thought. *I can't just leave him here like this.* "Now go ahead about your business," he told Big Louie.

The little, fat man picked up his bag and walked past Cavanaugh like he wasn't there and went into the bar. Cavanaugh watched Francisco nod at Louie as he brushed by him.

Cavanaugh looked at the money in his hand. He couldn't keep this. It was like he had just robbed the man. Then he remembered Russo's coded message to Carolyn, "Now go back and offer to give the money back." If Sal Russo was right, Big Louie would not know what he was talking about. And so he waited for Louie to collect the club's proceeds from the night. As he waited he thought about the drug Sal Russo had developed. But where was he? Why had he disappeared? And how was he going to find him?

An hour later, Big Louie exited his club. The empty leather bag he had taken in with him was now heavy, and he listed slightly to his left. In his right hand he gripped a large Smith & Wesson .44 Magnum at his side. Big Louie was ready for trouble. How do you approach a man carrying a lot of money with a gun in his hand? Cavanaugh decided on the direct approach.

He stepped forward with the money in his outstretched hand and said, "Mr. Louie, this is your money. I'm giving it back to you." Big Louie leveled the gun at Cavanaugh. "Beat it, creep!" he said. "I warned you before. Get out of my sight before I blow a hole through you!"

Cavanaugh stepped back and watched Louie wobble down the street. He looked at the two hundred dollars in his hand. He had never robbed anyone before. He thought he should have felt an adrenaline high of some sort, but instead he felt guilty and dirty. Then his headache roared back again. Trying to find the missing Salvatore Russo was proving to be more than he bargained for.

■ ■ ■

Mompox, Colombia
The sound of the rifle rippled through the cacophony of sounds in the night. Jack Bennis fell on top of María beside the tamarind tree. This was it, he thought. "You know neither the time nor the place," he had been warned. This wasn't the time nor the place he envisioned meeting his Maker. What would he say? How would he be judged?

He awaited the pain. But it didn't come. Bennis turned to look at his assassin. The bearded burly man's rifle dropped from his hands. The man's face looked like it had been sprayed with red paint. The man reached for what was left of his face and toppled backward like a dead tree. The gunpowder Bennis had placed in the barrel of the AK-47 in the cemetery had exploded and sent pieces of metal into his face. Bennis stared at a shard sticking out of the man's right eye as he crashed to the ground.

Blood poured out of the man's face and his beard smoldered from the explosion. Bennis pulled himself up and stared at his would-be assassin lying motionless on the gravel with a spring from the AK-47 protruding from his eye like a corkscrew. The man's rifle lay at his feet, a tangled mess of wood, metal, and plastic. His forehead had been ripped open and parts of his brain eked out like soft, thick, black, white and red fatty noodles.

Bennis turned to María and pulled her up. "We need to get out of here!" he said. She turned to look, but he blocked her view and pushed her forward. The bearded fat man's death would not stop El Apredido. Bennis knew there were only two ways out of Mompox – one by a long, bumpy, narrow, pot hole, often flooded, two lane road through desolate farmlands, swamps and marshlands; the other by boat. "I think our best bet is the ferry," he said. He checked his watch and touched the .45 in his belt. "Let's go now and wait for the early morning ferry."

As they walked away from the fire and the dead man, he thought about the parable of the watchful servants. How true it was that we don't know the time we will die. The gospel tells us to be prepared, to be watchful, but we forget. He had forgotten. The bearded man had forgotten. Would he be better prepared in the future?

He re-buttoned his shirt as they walked through the early morning darkness toward the ferry's pier. They stopped behind an abandoned shack overbooking the ferry's dock. They sat leaning against the weathered wood. He put his arm around María. She was quiet. She hadn't said anything since the shooting. He wished he could read her mind. Was she scared, anxious, embarrassed, ashamed, guilty, or pleased? He didn't know. Words did not come to him so he simply held her. She closed her eyes and he gently patted her head. In the silence they sat and waited for the ferry out of Mompox. While María slipped into a fitful sleep, Jack Bennis remained alert. He could not shake the feeling they were being followed.

■ ■ ■

Staten Island, New York

It was early morning when Cavanaugh drove over the Verrazano-Narrows Bridge. As he drove from Brooklyn to Staten Island, he had a habit of singing "Bali Hai" from *South Pacific*. He smiled as he thought how his wife Fran hated it when he would sing in his tone-deaf voice, "Bali Hai may call you, any night, any day. In your heart, you'll hear it call you: 'Come away …. Come away.'" He loved coming home to Staten Island. It had become his special place of peace and rest.

He was bellowing, "Here am I, your special island. Come to me…. Come to me," when he drove through the E-Z pass only toll booth. He pounded the steering wheel and shouted, "Shit!" when he realized, too late, he no longer had an E-Z pass! At one time the bridge was the longest suspension bridge in the world. It wasn't any more, but Cavanaugh thought the $16.00 toll must make it one of the most expensive bridges to cross. Normally, if he used his E-Z pass he would save more than $4.00, but someone had stolen his pass.

He looked at the $200 on the seat next to him. To Cavanaugh it was dirty money. He thought it had a peculiar smell. But that might have come from the dead blackbird in the backseat. He thought he could smell the money on his hands. In all his years as a New York City policeman and detective, he had never taken a bribe. Now, on his first day on the job as a private detective, he robs a man of $200. This was not the way he envisioned the start of his new career. He turned and glared at the dead blackbird in the backseat. He was starting to believe in omens.

■ ■ ■

Mompox, Colombia

As the early morning sun rose, Bennis glanced down at the ferry that would get them out of this beautiful cultural oasis frozen in time that had become a death trap for María and him. The ferry looked like a cheese box on a raft. It was three levels high. The top level was open except for the pilot's control cabin. The second level was open on both sides with a series of metal benches running from one side to the next. Trucks and motorcycles would lineup around the wooden box in the middle. It did not look particularly seaworthy, but as his mother had told him, "Beggars can't be choosey."

Scanning steadily around the shack he saw a growing line of passengers and vehicles waiting to board the ferry. The air was damp and he savored the smell of the freshwater Magdalena River. Bennis noticed a small, skinny boy with a large sombrero and no shirt squatting beside an assortment of fruit to sell to passengers off to work. A few yellow lulos, orange grandillas, and spiky yellow uchuva lay at his bare feet next to salted avocados. The boy locked eyes with Bennis and then turned toward an old barn on a hill across from them. The boy's eyes swung back toward Bennis. He was giving him a signal.

Bennis peered out from behind the shack and saw something move slightly behind a donkey and some cattle by the barn across the road. It looked like a motorcycle jutting out from the side of the barn. As the people started to board the ferry and the vehicles slowly parked on the sides of the elongated box in the middle, the motorcycle behind the cows remained motionless. As the sun rose more, however, Bennis saw the cyclist was the same thin, young blond with a crew cut who shot at them at the corner restaurant.

The ferry blasted its horn and men prepared to untie the ferry. "Come on, Jack," María said. "We're going to miss the ferry."

Father Bennis checked the man on the motorcycle. He was carrying an automatic rifle. "No, María. Wait here until I give you the go sign. The man who shot at us from the motorcycle is behind the building across the way. I'm going to sneak up behind him. Don't go until I give you the signal."

"I have to get on that ferry, Jack. My brother needs me."

"It's too dangerous, María. That guy across the way is checking everyone out."

"What's the matter with you? You've changed. You weren't afraid before."

Since the incident at the tamarind tree, he knew he had changed. The awkward silence between them was palpable. It had happened so quickly. He should have stopped her. But he hadn't.

"I'm not afraid, María. It's just not smart to walk in the open now. I'll circle back and come up behind him. Don't move until I tell you it's clear."

Bennis went back along the dirt road and then cut through the field behind the barn.

The ferry blasted its horn again and prepared to pull away from the shore.

Bennis was fifty feet from the cyclist when he looked up and saw María dashing with another man toward the ferry. The cyclist raised his rifle. Bennis reached for the .45 in his belt. "No!" he shouted. "Stop!"

Before Bennis could aim, the cyclist fired and the cattle scattered in different directions.

In the distance, Bennis saw María and the man running with her fall to the ground amidst a cloud of dirt and gravel. The cyclist swung around toward Bennis. But he was too late. Bennis fired María's .45. Then he leaped over the cyclist and tumbled down the hill toward María.

The man next to her was dead. He looked like a laborer on his way to work. Bullets had shattered his spine and blown off much of his head. María lay next to him. She had been shot. Her clothes were covered in blood. She was breathing heavily. Her eyes flickered. "Stay with me, María. Stay with me!" he said holding her in his arms.

She tried to say something. He leaned closer. "Stay with me, María!" he pleaded. Her voice was raspy. "You are a good man, Jack Bennis."

He felt her body shake and then she closed her eyes.

■ ■ ■

7

Staten Island, New York

Cavanaugh awoke to his brother's dog Bella licking his face. He looked at the clock. It was almost 10:00 a.m. He never slept this late. As he struggled to get up, his headache returned. He felt the bump on the side of his head and cursed under his breath. Fu Manchu could have killed him with that bat. When he moved his head, the pain returned like a sharp knife drilling into his head.

A note on the coffee machine told Cavanaugh his wife had taken their son and gone to her mother's. Fran's note told him to be safe and that she loved him. He smiled and was getting ready to take a hot shower when the phone rang. The caller ID indicated the call was from another country. *Probably someone calling from Africa to tell me I just won a lottery in England or inherited a huge amount of money from someone he never heard of.* All he would have to do was send a cashier's check for a few hundred dollars to pay for the bank transfer of funds. He let the phone ring and stepped into the shower.

The warm water felt good and he lingered in the shower wondering what his next step would be in trying to locate the elusive Salvatore Russo. The letters were the main thing he had to go by. He wrapped a towel around himself and went back to the letters. Russo and his girlfriend had been in Cozumel, Mexico. Perhaps, he was still there.

The phone started ringing again. He checked the number. It was the same number as before. He smiled. *The lottery winnings must be really pretty high now or the scam artists were pretty desperate.* He let it ring.

He went back to the letters. They lay sprawled out on his desk next to an empty bottle of Beck's and his yellow legal writing pad. He checked the envelopes expecting to see postmarks from Cozumel, Mexico, but the postmarks were instead from Bogotá, Colombia.

The phone rang again. This was getting to be annoying. The same international number. He picked the phone up and shouted, "No. I don't want any! Now take my name off your goddamn list!"

The voice on the other end of the line spoke in halted English. "Will you accept a person to person call from a Jack Bennis in Mompox, Colombia?"

It's my brother, Cavanaugh thought. *What's he calling me from Colombia for?*

"Yes," he said and waited as the line was connected.

"Thomas, is that you?" a voice said.

"Yes, Jack. What's up? Why are you calling me? Are you all right?"

"Yes and no. I'm fine, but María has been shot."

"Shot? What the hell happened?"

"It's a long story, Thomas. She's in a coma and in critical condition. If it weren't for Chico, a little twelve-year-old street urchin selling fruits by the ferry, we might have lost her. Somehow he had a cellphone and called for an ambulance immediately. It's still touch and go."

"What can I do, Jack?"

"María has a brother. His name is Santiago Rodriquez. His nickname used to be Chago. I am at the hospital here in Mompox. I have no way of reaching María's brother to let him know what happened. I was hoping you might be able to pull a few strings and get the message to him."

Cavanaugh scratched his head. First, he is looking for a person he has no idea where to find. Now his brother asks him to locate another person in another country to give him the bad news about his sister. "Where can I find this Santiago character?"

The line crackled with static and then Bennis replied, "I'm not quite sure, Thomas. I thought I would leave that to your detective skills. The only thing I know is María said she met him in Bogotá and that he was mixed up in some way with the Medellin drug trade. She said he had lost a lot of weight from when she last saw him which was many years ago and that he looked nervous and anxious. He didn't want her involving the police."

Cavanaugh's eyes darted to the Bogotá postmarks on Carolyn Hendershot's letters. "Bogotá?" he asked.

"Yes. She accidently bumped into him there. He told her about some-one here in Mompox who was manufacturing a drug called the Devil's Breath."

Cavanaugh frowned. "I'll see what I can do, Jack. How can I reach you if needed?"

"I'm staying at the hospital now with María. The situation is a bit dicey at the moment and I don't want to leave her alone."

"Are you ok?"

"I'm fine, Thomas. Don't worry about me. Try to get the message across to her brother. I think he should know."

"How can I reach you if I need to?"

"I don't have a phone. You could call the hospital and they could try to reach me, but that may cause additional problems. Probably the easiest way would be to call Chico, the kid who called the ambulance. He can get a message to me."

Cavanaugh wrote Chico's name and phone number on his yellow legal pad. He hesitated a moment and then asked, "What did you mean by 'additional problems'?"

There was silence on the line for a few seconds and then Jack said, "It's just that the hospital is pretty busy and not many people here speak English. Your message might get lost in transit. Besides, Chico is a street-wise kid who speaks English."

Cavanaugh sensed his brother was lying or at least leaving a lot out. Now wasn't the time to argue with him. He knew from experience Jack Bennis was an independent, stubborn, at times pig-headed, impetuous in-dividual. But so was he.

■ ■ ■

Mompox, Colombia

"What do you mean he's dead?" El Apredido shouted into his phone. "First, you tell me Manuel is killed. Now you tell me Carlos is dead. How did this happen?"

The voice on the other end of the line stuttered. "We … we are not sure, El Apredido. His face was burned. It looks like his rifle exploded."

"What about the priest? Was he killed in the fire?"

"Again, El Apredido, we are not sure. The only body found in his room thus far was that of a woman."

El Apredido stood and slammed his fist into his desk. "What do I pay you for? You are the goddamn police chief! Give me some good news. Alejandro was at the ferry. Did he see the priest get on the ferry?"

There was silence on the other end of the line.

"Speak to me, you rump-fed ronyon! What do you hear from Alejandro?"

The police chief's voice trembled. "We have heard nothing from him."

"What? This cannot be!"

"There was a shooting at the early morning ferry, El Apredido. There was a lot of confusion. One man was killed and a woman severely wounded. The man was Nelson Famdel Gomez, a laborer on his way to Santa Ana. The woman is not yet identified. She is in a coma in the hospital. We have not located the shooter."

"But where is Alejandro, you whoreson beetle-headed drudge? He was riding a Harley-Davidson bike for Christ's sake! You would have to be blind and deaf not to find him."

"My men are looking for him, but we have not found him or his motorcycle."

"Find him, or I will find your pretty little wife and your children. You know I mean what I say!" El Apredido pounded his empty fist into his desk again. He took a deep breath and looked out the window at the still smoldering hotel in the distance. Then he glanced across the room at the crumpled message lying on the antique credenza under an abstract painting of Abraxas. *More will be coming soon*, he thought. *I must be prepared*. He spoke slowly and deliberately into his phone. "El Capitán, one more thing. Let me know if any strangers come by boat or car to Mompox."

"I want no trouble, El Apredido."

"Have no fear, El Capitán." He looked at the smiling demoniac figure on the wall with its chicken-like head, shield, and serpent legs. "You need not trouble yourself about dirtying your hands any more than they are already. The gold I pay you for is for information. I will supply any actions that need be made. And you will look the other way like the flap-ear'd knave I pay you to be."

■ ■ ■

Staten Island, New York

Cavanaugh's brother's words sank in like a Mack truck in quicksand. *María Isabelle was shot. But how and why?* What had his brother gotten himself into this time? He rubbed the bump on his head. *Why does life get so complicated?* he wondered.

He looked at the telephone number he had scribbled on his yellow writing pad. Maybe this Chico kid could explain things to him. He dialed the number. Eventually, a young voice answered.

"This is Tom Cavanaugh," he said. "My brother is Father Jack Bennis. He told me to call you."

"Sí, señor. He is in the hospital with his lady friend."

Lady friend? That's one way of putting it, Cavanaugh thought. "Can you tell me what happened?"

"Sí, señor. A man on a motorcycle was hiding behind a barn by the ferry. I saw him and tried to warn your brother. I didn't know your brother was a priest."

"Yeah, well sometimes I forget, too. What happened?"

"Your brother, the padre, left the woman he was with. They were hiding behind a shack on the other side of the road. He went back around the barn. When the ferry started to pull away, the woman ran to it. Nelson Famdel Gomez ran with her. He was always late. He works in Santa Ana.

He has a wife and family here in Mompox. He is rarely early for the ferry, but if he is, he always buys a salted avocado from me."

"What happened next?"

"The man behind the barn, his name is Alejandro, started shooting at Nelson and the woman. Then your brother …. I couldn't see from where I was, but he shot Alejandro and jumped over his motorcycle and fell down the hill to the woman."

"How do you know my brother shot this Alejandro?"

"I heard a shot and when your brother ran to the woman he had a gun in his hand."

"Did the police arrest him?"

"No, señor. They are looking for the shooter of Nelson Famdel Gomez and the woman."

"But you said my brother shot him?"

"Sí, señor. It was a perfect shot. Right between his eyes."

Cavanaugh's years as a homicide detective told him something was missing. "Why are the police still looking for the shooter if you saw him and he is dead?"

"Sí, señor. I found the body and pulled it into the barn. I buried it under a lot of hay."

"What about the gun and the motorcycle?"

"The gun was an AK-47 and the motorcycle a Harley-Davidson. I took them both."

Jack Bennis had told Cavanaugh María Isabelle was in the hospital and in critical condition. There was nothing more this Chico kid could tell him about her. But young Chico was another story. Who was he? Why did he help Bennis? Why did he hide the body and take the gun and the motorcycle?

"How did you know the name of the man who shot this Nelson guy and the woman?"

"Sí, señor. His name is Alejandro López. I will always remember him. He killed my father and mother."

The young boy's voice was calm, factual, and emotionless.

"What?" Cavanaugh asked.

"Sí, señor. I remember him well. My father was editor of the local paper. He wrote a story about a man here in Mompox who is making a dangerous drug. My father wanted him stopped. One night, twelve weeks ago, it had been raining. I heard a motorcycle pull up to our home. I got up and looked out my window. The man had blond hair cut very short. My father and mother went to the door and Alejandro López shot them both. He came into our house and set fire to my father's office. He didn't see me or my sister who was sleeping."

"You have a sister?"

"Sí, señor. She is only seven. I carried her out. The house burned down. She cried a lot when she learned our parents were dead."

"Where is she now?"

"They took her to Magangué. I think she is in some kind of boarding school there. I haven't seen her since they took her."

"What about you? Why didn't they take you, too?"

"They tried, but I ran away, señor. I wanted to find the man who killed my parents. Your brother killed him for me. Now I must protect your brother. Someday, I hope to find the man who sent Alejandro to kill my parents."

Cavanaugh marveled at the simplicity of youth. Things were black and white to Chico. Tragedy and trauma had swept into his life, but Chico was a survivor. There were no complaints in his voice, no whining about his plight, no expressions of sorrow. He followed his own code. He didn't know if this were a good thing or a bad thing. Chico reminded Cavanaugh of a poem he had read many years before by William Ernest Henley called "Invictus." In the fell clutch of circumstances, Chico did not wince or cry aloud. Under the bludgeonings of life, his head may have been bloodied, but was unbowed. Chico was a survivor. This twelve-year-old street urchin was the "master of his fate," the "captain of his soul."

Or at least he thought he was.

■ ■ ■

Cavanaugh dialed his old police partner, Detective Morty Goldberg. "Hello, Morty. It's me, Cavanaugh." He heard the groan on the other end of the phone.

"I thought I got rid of you when you retired. What do you want now, *meshuggener*?"

"Did I ever tell you I love it when you speak Jewish?"

"And how many times have I told you, it's Yiddish, not Jewish? I'm a busy man, Cavanaugh. What do you want this time?"

"You hurt my feeling, Morty. Didn't I give you a solid on the Carolyn Hendershot woman?"

"Some solid. She wouldn't press charges and signed herself out of the hospital. You gave me nothing but *tsuris*! The Captain is threatening to write me up for wasting police time."

"Yeah. Sorry about that. I heard she wasn't very cooperative."

"You heard?"

"That's not important now. I'm calling you to do me another favor. You remember María Isabelle?"

"Of course. She is your brother's good friend. She's a good person."

"Right. Well, he just called me and told me María's been shot and is in critical condition in a hospital in Mompox, Colombia."

"*Gevalt*! What happened?"

"I'm not quite sure right now. But he asked me if I could locate her brother in Bogotá and tell him."

"How can I help?"

Cavanaugh looked at the yellow pad on his desk. "I don't have any more connections now, Morty. I was hoping you might be able to check somehow with the police down there. The brother's name is Santiago Rodriguez. He used to go by the nickname Chago."

"That's not much to go on, Tom. Rodriguez is a pretty common name."

"Yeah. I know. Apparently, he is mixed up somehow with the Medellin drug cartel. He didn't want María to contact the police. I thought he might have a record down there and I might be able to get an address to track him down. It's a long shot, Morty, I know, but you're the only one I can trust to find out."

"I'll check my files. I think I remember someone down there from a conference a few years ago. I'll reach out to her and see if she can help."

"She?"

"Yes, Tom. Wake up. It's the twenty-first century. A number of recent studies at Wall Street law firms found women received more positive comments than men. It's about time they were acknowledged as being able to do some jobs as well as or better than men. Lt. Marion Fraumeni is a top flight criminalist."

"Oh, Morty, don't tell me you've been drinking that liberal soup again! Is this Fraumeni person at least pretty?"

"She's gorgeous. Knockdown, drag out gorgeous. She could have been a model. No offense meant to Francesca, but you would eat your heart out if you had to work with her."

"I'm getting too old to argue, Morty. I'd appreciate it if she could give me some way to locate María's brother. He's probably a low-line pusher or he might even be locked up for all I know. I just want him to know about his sister."

"Will do, Tom. Please keep me informed about María. If there is anything else I can do, just give me a call."

Cavanaugh hung up and glanced at the letters on his desk. The postmarks were from Bogotá, Colombia. María's brother was in Bogotá. They both were involved some way with drugs. Could there be a connection? Probably not, but maybe Santiago Rodriguez had heard of the supposedly brilliant American Salvatore Russo. It was another very long shot.

He dug out an old edition of the Yellow Pages and started calling airlines. It would have been easier to use a computer, but Cavanaugh never learned how to use one and didn't intend to learn. Calling the various airlines proved frustrating and irritating until he found a cooperative representative named Carol Orazem at one of the airlines. She sounded like she was from the South, Georgia probably, and she went out of her way to help. She suggested he call a Sue Dietrich, a travel agent she knew and worked well with. Ms. Orazem assured him he could trust Ms. Dietrich to get him the best deal possible. Cavanaugh called and found Ms. Dietrich everything Carol Orazem said she was. She was helpful, efficient, and very knowledgeable. He was surprised to discover the prices for a flight from New York to Bogotá, varied in price from less than $200 to more than a thousand dollars and the flight time, depending on the number of stops, varied from a non-stop from Newark International of six hours to a two stop flight of over twenty hours. He promised to call Ms. Dietrich if he decided to make the trip to Bogotá.

He got up to make himself a cup of coffee when the phone rang again.

■ ■ ■

8

Mompox, Colombia

A small boy wearing a large sombrero walked into the main entrance of the Mompox's San Juan de Dios Hospital. He went up to a gray haired woman with bronzed, wrinkled skin and the smell of mothballs behind the reception desk. He asked if anyone had seen his mother. He said someone told him she had been shot down at the ferry. The woman looked up and attempted to touch his hand, but he pulled back. Her eyes were watery when she told him delicately she was in intensive care.

"Can I see her?" he whispered.

The woman frowned and told him he couldn't see her right now. She added, "Your father is with her."

The boy's sad eyes hid the smile he held inside at the irony. The old woman thought the padre was his father. "Then can I please see my father?' he asked.

The woman called the security guard over and mouthed something to him. The security guard was a big man with a large stomach, slouched shoulders, and a weathered face. He stared at the shirtless, skinny boy with the huge sombrero on his head. He didn't believe the boy.

The boy read the security guard's look like a neon sign on a starless night. The boy turned his distraught face up a notch or two. Finally, the guard shrugged, pulled his blue striped trousers up over his protruding stomach and ambled down the hall. As soon as he was gone and the woman behind the desk turned away to answer the phone, the boy slipped quietly into the stairwell and headed up to the intensive care unit on the second floor.

The boy waited in the stairwell and opened the door a fraction. The cold smell of Iodoform, antiseptics, and bleach greeted him immediately. He pulled back as he saw the security guard trundle out of the elevator and down the hall. He stopped at a room across from the nurses' station. The guard went into the room and came out a minute later – alone, muttering curses under his breath.

The boy waited until the security guard disappeared into the elevator and then he crawled past the vacant nurses' station. He slipped into room. A tall man dressed in black sat in a chair by the bed. In his hands he held what looked like pink rosary beads. On the bed, a woman lay with tubes and all sorts of machines monitoring her vital signs.

"Psst, Padre, it's me, Chico," the boy whispered.

Fr. Bennis turned. "How? How did you get in here?" he asked.

"Magic, Padre," the boy replied. "I spoke to your brother. He seems like a nice guy. I told him I was watching over you."

Jack Bennis folded his rosary beads and put them back in his pocket. "You're incorrigible, Chico."

"I don't know what that means, Padre. I hope it's not bad."

"It's not, Chico. But why are you here?"

"I wanted to tell you, I hid the body under a haystack in the barn. It should buy us some time."

"Buy *us* some time?"

"Sí, Padre. I also took the motorcycle and the gun. We may need them later."

"What's this *we* business?"

The boy placed his index finger over his mouth. "Quiet, Padre. We don't want to be disturbed." He looked at the woman in the bed. "How is she doing?"

"She was hit a few times. The bullets narrowly missed her heart. She lost a lot of blood. If you hadn't called for an ambulance she might have bled out at the ferry. I have to thank you for that. "

"No *problema*, Padre. You killed the man who murdered my parents. Great shot, by the way!"

Bennis frowned at the boy. "She's in a coma, Chico, in very critical condition and the doctors honestly don't give her much of a chance."

The boy looked back at María Isabelle again in the bed. "Do they know who she is?"

The priest's eyes flashed from María to the monitors and then back to Chico. "No. She had no identification on her."

"Who do they think you are?" the boy asked.

"I didn't say. I just came with her and nobody asked."

"They will soon, Padre. You can bet your ass on that!"

Bennis smiled.

"Oops! Sorry about that, Padre, but it's true!"

"You're right, Chico. But where did you learn your English if I may ask?"

"Movies, Padre. I used to watch a lot of American movies when I had a home. I love Clint Eastwood, Sean Connery, John Wayne, Humphrey Bogart, Eddie G. Robinson...." He stared at the priest and added, "Somebody's out to kill you, Padre. You need to get out of here before they start asking questions."

Bennis rubbed his chin. He hadn't shaved in a couple of days. "You're right again, Chico. But this isn't your problem. You've done enough already and I appreciate that."

"I'm not done, Padre. You killed the man who killed my parents. I owe you." He looked back at María lying ensnared in tubes and wires. "She's in good hands now. They'll take good care of her. There's nothing more you can do for her here."

"I can pray for her."

"You can pray for her somewhere else, too. As long as they don't know who she is, she's safe. You being here puts her in added danger." Chico looked out the window. "A police car just pulled into the parking lot. We've got to get you out of here. The Mompox police might be slow, but they're not *that* slow. Follow me. The police will be here soon asking questions you don't want to answer."

Jack Bennis knew the twelve-year-old was right. Yet he felt like he was abandoning María. There was nothing he could do for her here. She was unconscious and in the best care available. Plus, he had to get out of the hospital. Both their lives depended on it. He rose, gave María a blessing, and placed a kiss on her forehead. "I'll be back for you, María. I promise," he said.

■ ■ ■

Staten Island, New York

Cavanaugh didn't recognize the phone number. *Just what I need,* he thought, *another wonderful chance to lower my interest rate or to consider the wonders of a reverse mortgage.* "Hello," he half shouted into the phone.

"Mr. Cavanaugh, this is Vincenza Russo," a shrill voice on the other end of the line announced.

"Oh, Mrs. Russo, how are you doing?"

"That's not the point of this call, Mr. Cavanaugh. How are *you* doing? Have you located my grandson yet?"

Cavanaugh scratched the bump on his head. "With all due respect, Mrs. Russo, I only started looking for him yesterday and I really didn't have much to go on."

"I'm paying you to locate Salvatore. That's all I want. I don't want you prying into his private affairs. Just tell me where he is and I will talk to him. It's simple. You tell me where he is and I'll do the rest. Do you understand, Mr. Cavanaugh?"

Cavanaugh understood he had been hit over the head, tied to a chair, broken into a woman's apartment, stolen some of her letters, and shaken down the owner of a gambling bar in Manhattan. The only way he could possibly find Salvatore Anthony Russo was to pry into his private affairs. Maybe that was the problem. Good old Aunt Vincenza didn't want Salvatore's dirty linens exposed to the world.

"I have made some progress, Mrs. Russo. I still don't have a direct location for him, however, but I believe he may be in Mexico."

"Mexico? What the hell would he be doing in Mexico?"

"I don't know, Mrs. Russo. But I may need to take a trip down there to check things out. With your permission, of course."

"I don't want you prying into his affairs, Mr. Cavanaugh. If you locate him and just let me know where he is. I will personally follow up. Is that clear?"

"Abundantly, Mrs. Russo. Now do I have your permission to follow up? I promise not to confront him."

Mrs. Russo cleared her throat and made rasping sound. "I want no police involved! Is that clear?"

Cavanaugh knew Salvatore was involved with drugs. Whatever drugs they were, they were special. He had the two hundred dollars from Big Louie to prove it. Was Vincenza Russo behind his stolen E-Z pass, radio, flat tire, and broken headlight?

"Do you have someone following me, Mrs. Russo?"

"That's ridiculous! Why would I do something like that? I hired you to find my grandson. Don't be ridiculous, Mr. Cavanaugh!"

"Fine. Then I will follow up the leads I have and get back to you. Okay?"

She cleared her throat of phlegm and he pictured her spitting into a handkerchief. "Excellent. As long as we understand each other. And no police are involved."

He thanked her and hung up. He knew he may need to involve the police, but he had avoided the question. Looking at the phone, he felt like a politician on Meet the Press. Whatever the question was, they usually managed to avoid directly answering it. He shook his head. The headache returned with a sleazy feeling. What kind of a world had Salvatore Anthony Russo dragged him into?

■ ■ ■

Mompox, Colombia

Jack Bennis followed little Chico as he led him down the stairs and through the hospital's damp laundry room. As they raced through a labyrinth of dank tunnels, still halls and dusty storage rooms, he recalled the words of Isaiah, "…and the lion and the sheep shall abide together, and a little child shall lead them." He wondered if there ever were going to be a time when the wolf would dwell with the lamb and people would live in peace and harmony.

When they reached an emergency exit, Chico peered out, checked the parking lot and saw the vacant Mompox police car. Then he motioned for Bennis to follow him along a narrow cobblestone path beside the hospital. Gradually, the path dissipated into thicker and thicker vegetation. "Where are we going, Chico?"

"Have faith, Padre," the boy said as he disappeared behind a thick shrub of plumeria rubra. The large green leaves parted for the boy as some of the brittle branches broke oozing a white mucous-like substance. Bennis followed. His black shirt caught on the thick, thorny stem of a Crown of Thorns plant.

"Come on, Padre. It is not far now."

"Where are we going, Chico?" Bennis repeated.

The priest was following the child. Bennis wondered who was the lamb and who was the lion. Where was this twelve-year-old boy leading him? Just then he saw it. Hidden behind a spiny palm tree was the Harley-Davidson of the blond man who shot María.

"I hid it here, Padre, because they will be looking for it. We must use it now to get away."

Bennis ran his fingers through his hair. "Get away to where, Chico? The police will be looking for this. And this motorcycle makes a loud, distinctive sound. They can easily follow the sound."

"Sí, Padre, I know. But why does it make this sound?"

Bennis touched the black metal and eyed the tallboy seat. He estimated it was a late model Street 500. "The sound comes from the engine design. The Harley-Davidson engine has two pistons but its crankshaft has only one pin and both piston rods are connected to it."

"I do not understand what you are talking about," the boy confessed. "Hop on and I will drive you to my safe place."

"Hop on? Chico, you can't drive this thing!"

"There is no time to waste, Padre. I got it here and if we leave now and go through these woods we can get to my place. But we must leave now! Hop on! I know the way. You do not."

Bennis looked down at the skinny, bare-chested boy with the big sombrero. *This is crazy*, he thought. But he found himself getting on the bike behind the little boy and moving steadily through the woods to the unique sound of the pop-pop...pop-pop...pop-pop of the Harley-Davidson and the sounds of breaking branches and scattering birds.

■ ■ ■

Staten Island, New York

Salvatore Anthony Russo had become a pain in the ass and an enigma to Cavanaugh. Where was he? Why had he dropped out of sight? What was he planning? What was this "drug" he was apparently working on? How did it work? And why, as he fumbled around to try to find answers, did someone break into his car and smash his headlight? Were the break-in, the flat tire, and the shattered headlight merely coincidences or something else? Cavanaugh never believed in coincidences. He agreed with the adage about coincidences being like a rotten egg in that they leave unpleasant odors. But then again, he thought of the dead blackbird and realized he had never believed in omens before either.

Wherever Salvatore Russo was, right now he didn't give a shit. María Isabelle had been shot! His brother was in some kind of trouble. And to Cavanaugh, family comes before some smartass drug dealer. Grandma Vincenza with her gold tooth and her nasty attitude would have to wait.

He paced around the kitchen and made another pot of coffee. He hated not being able to investigate properly. As a first grade New York City detective, he had a host of ways to obtain information, but as an unlicensed private detective he felt like he was drowning in a rip current unable to reach the life preserver. The world had passed him by. He didn't know how to use the computer. He barely knew how to use his cellphone.

His headache returned. For the first time in his life, he realized he was dependent on others. He hated the feeling. His sister-in-law Mary did his computer work for him and now he had to call in favors to help his brother.

The phone rang. He spilt his coffee reaching for it.

"Hi, Tom," Morty Goldberg's voice began. "I contacted Lt. Fraumeni down in Colombia for you. It's only an hour difference in time down there."

"Did she give you an address?"

"Do you want to take a guess how many Rodríguezes there are in Bogotá, let along Colombia?"

Cavanaugh closed his eyes and grimaced.

"Santiago limited it to probably a couple of thousand. She couldn't be sure."

"What the hell am I going to do now?" Cavanaugh asked. "How do I find this guy?"

"You may be in luck on that one, but I'm not sure. The nickname Chago did get Marion's attention."

"Is he some kind of junkie or drug pusher?"

"Let's put it this way. The Chago she knows by reputation. He has no criminal record, but he is the alleged head of the Medellin drug cartel in Bogotá."

Cavanaugh's hand traced the bump on his head. "What? That can't be. María's brother, a drug lord? I don't believe it."

"Marion's checking it further. She has actually had him in for questioning once. She says he looks like you described him to me. He's swarthy, smart, and shrewd, but, she emphasized, he's extremely dangerous. He is not a native-born Colombian. She thinks he may have come from Cuba a number of years ago and worked his way up the drug trade ladder. His full name is Santiago Rodriguez. She thinks he's the man you are looking for."

"This is nuts!" Cavanaugh exclaimed.

"Do you want me to have her tell this guy about his sister? Marion said everyone in Bogotá knows him. But there may be a problem actually finding him. She said she knows someone who she thinks can get a message to him."

"No, Morty. Thanks for everything. This is something I have to handle myself."

"What do you mean, Tom?"

Cavanaugh hung up and started planning his trip to Colombia.

■ ■ ■

Mompox, Colombia

Chico drove the motorcycle through dense jungle and thick underbrush. Jack Bennis held on for dear life, ducking his head under low lying branches. The bike bounced and jerked almost throwing Bennis off. After what seemed like an eternity, the boy slowed and stopped behind a huge boulder covered with moss. "We must walk from here," he announced. "Be watchful, Padre. There are jaguar and poisonous snakes in this area."

At the word jaguar, Bennis stopped. A chill ran through his chest. As a Black Ops officer, he had seen the horrific, bloody remnants of jaguar attacks. That was a long time ago, but the images were as fresh as a recent color photo. He remembered the powerful jaguar bite which could crush the shell of an armadillo or a turtle and pierce the skull of a cow, a tapir, or a man. It was a stealthy, carnivorous animal that would silently stalk and ambush its prey. He looked around at the trees above and the underbrush ahead. He shuddered at the memory of the head torn from its body by a jaguar's fatal, violent bite to the brain of a six-month-old baby boy he witnessed along the Padomo River in Venezuela.

He recalled reading stories of Gonzalo Jimenez de Quesada and how in his search for the mythical "City of Gold," El Dorado, many of his conquistadors were butchered by jaguars as they slept in their hammocks at night.

"See those scape marks, Padre, the tracks, and that *meirda* over there. They are signs of a jaguar."

Bennis looked at the scrape marks, the tracks, and the tubular, tapered feces. He looked in wonder at the boy. "How do you know. . .?" he started to ask, but the Chico waved his sombrero forward and said, "I live here, Padre. It is not too far away now. Follow me, but be watchful where you step. There are also pit viper snakes around here. They are most poisonous."

As he followed the boy deeper into the jungle he smelled dampness and danger. His fear of snakes went back to the stories he learned as a child. It was a snake that tempted Adam and Even in the Garden of Eden. What had he gotten himself into? It might have been safer to hide in the streets and alleys of Mompox until he could come up with a plan to help María Isabelle and get them both of them safely off the island.

But what about El Apredido? He had sent people to kill him. He had blown up the hotel he was staying at and killed Margarete. He had most probably sent the blond crew-cut man on the Harley-Davison to kill both him and María. El Apredido needed to be stopped.

Hopefully, his brother Tom could reach María's brother and he could come to be with her. Bennis planned to talk with him and help him in any way he could to kick the drug habit he had. From what María said in her letter, it seemed Santiago had come to the realization he had a problem and understood his need to get help. Bennis would help him. He would work to help him believe in a higher power.

Then they would go to the police and stop El Apredido. There may be a few complications in the plan, but with Santiago and María's help together they would put an end to El Apredido's production of the Devil's Breath.

A branch whipped across his face, and he looked up. A large boa constrictor dangled from a limb above him. He watched it start to slither down the tree trunk towards him. He ducked and heard Chico whisper somewhere ahead, "We're here, Padre. Come quick."

Bennis looked around. Chico was nowhere in sight. He seemed to have been swallowed up in the dark shadows of the jungle.

"Over here, Padre." The voice came from low below a prickly sticker bush in front of him. Bennis crouched and peered behind the bush.

Chico's voice came from a small fissure behind the bush and in front of a huge boulder.

"Down here, Padre," Chico urged.

Bennis looked at the gap in the ground. The opening was concealed in such a way that it was barely noticeable. Chico was small. Bennis was big. He didn't know if he could even fit. He didn't know how deep the hole was. Then he heard the snake slithering through the brush toward him. He didn't hesitate. He jumped into the opening in the ground.

■ ■ ■

Jack Bennis landed with a thud. He rolled over. The ground was hard. It was dark and dank, but he realized he was in a narrow passageway of some kind. He heard Chico roll something in front of the entrance sealing them in and sealing the boa out. Then Chico lit a flashlight and asked if he was all right.

The walls lit up in a golden hue. The walls were decorated with red ochre primitive art designs and murals. The floor was paved with what looked like gold. The slabs were mortised and grooved to fit together in such a manner that they were almost slip-proof. Chico helped him up. "Be careful of your head, Padre, but follow me. In the next room the ceiling is higher."

Jack bent over and followed the young boy down a narrow, low path. Gradually, the passageway widened and they entered a large underground room. Buttresses held up the walls and supported a twenty foot high curved ceiling. In one corner of the room, which appeared to be the size of a football field, there was what looked like a garden in which the lumps of earth were pieces of gold. In the garden were cleverly fashioned stalks, leaves and ears of corn – all of which were pure gold.

"Where am I?" Bennis asked. His voice reverberated through the room and seemed to echo down tunnel entrances around the room. In front of him water cascaded into a deep chasm at the far end of the chamber. There were gold statues and artifacts all around. Statues of shepherds armed with slings and staves guarded immobile sheep by the garden. What looked like an altar of some sort stood in the center of the room. All were made of gold and silver. There were pots, vases and every kind of vessel around the room cast from gold.

As Chico shown his flashlight round the room, Bennis noticed a number of unlit sconces fixed to the walls of the cave. Chico motioned to a golden chair. "Sit, Padre, and I will tell you what I know." A cool breeze swept through the room as Chico set his flashlight down and sat at the priest's feet. "My father used to tell me stories of how the Spanish King Ferdinand back in 1511 ordered his colonists to get gold by whatever way they could. Hernando Cortes did this with the Aztecs in Mexico. But even after Montezuma gave him his empire's treasures it wasn't enough for the Spaniards, and they fought the Aztecs until they defeated them. Francisco Pizarro did this with the Incas in Peru who were known to mine gold and store it because they worshipped the Sun god, Inti. Pizarro declared war on the Incas and, after capturing their King Atahualpa, had him killed even after he paid a ransom of six tons of gold. The conquistadors were brutal and cold-blooded in their quest for gold, Padre. Stories of their slaughters and stealing spread quickly.

"Here in Colombia, my father told me, the Muisca civilization lived in this area. When a group of conquistadores led by Gonzalo Jimenez de Quesada started looking for the City of Gold, legend has it that the Muisca hid their gold in tunnels along the Magdalena River."

The priest leaned forward. "I heard many stories of mysterious tunnels running from Mexico through many other countries. Supposedly, the indigenous people hid their precious metals and artifacts in these tunnels and used them for religious sacrifices and as a sacred burial place."

The boy looked at the priest and said, "I don't know what 'indigenous' means, Padre."

"Sorry, Chico. You seem so knowledgeable sometimes I forget you are only twelve. Indigenous means the people who live in a particular area. Like the Inca were indigenous to Peru, and the Aztec to Mexico." Bennis stood and started walking around the room. He stopped in front of a nine foot gold statue of a fierce-looking warrior. Alongside of the statue was another of a smaller man with the tail of a jaguar.

"Do you know who this statue is supposed to be?"

"No, Padre."

"I believe it is supposed to represent the mythical Goranchacha said to be the prophet of the Muisca people your father told you about. The smaller statue is of his second-in-command, an Indian with a long tail. Goranchacha was a harsh, cruel ruler. The story goes that the Sun wanted to reincarnate in human form and performed this through a young maid who remained a virgin. The daughters of the leader of the village would leave their houses every day and climb a hill to see the Sun rising in the east. There they would lay down naked under the Sun waiting to become pregnant by the sunbeams. One of them supposedly did become pregnant and gave birth to a large emerald. She wrapped the emerald in cloth and in a few days the emerald turned into a boy, whom they named Goranchacha, son of the Sun."

The boy removed his sombrero and scratched his head. "I did not know of that legend, Padre, but it sounds very much like the stories the priests would tell of the birth of Jesus."

"Similar, Chico, but different. We believe Jesus was the son of God, but he preached peace and love, not war and hate." He wanted to explain why he believed Jesus was truly the son of God and Goranchacha, a legend. But he was tired, frustrated, and angry. He lacked the energy to discuss apologetics with the twelve-year-old. His mind was not on the spiritual. It was focused on the temporal and some very unchristian thoughts. The woman he loved had been shot and might die. He changed the topic by pointing to tunnel entrances around the chamber. "Where do they go?" he asked.

"I fell through the one on the right when I was digging after my parents were killed. That is how I found this place. One tunnel is blocked by a lot of stones. Another tunnel is lined with beds cut into the sides of the walls. There is a terrible smell in that tunnel. I have been afraid to go in the other tunnels."

"I saw you down at the ferry this morning. You were selling fruit. How do you get out of here if there is a dangerous jaguar outside?"

"Sí, Padre, Sergio wakes me up every morning. He is a spider monkey. He is hiding now, but you will see him later. His tail was bitten off by the jaguar. I helped him then. He helps me now. When I get up, I walk into Mompox. On the way, I steal a few fruits from the fields. The farmers don't miss what I take. I use the money to buy batteries for my flashlights and to save money for my sister."

"How do you get out of here if there is a jaguar lurking outside?"

"Sí, Padre. I go back to the hole I fell through. It is safer that way. I did not take you that way because we were in a hurry and I did not want anyone following us. Everyone in Mompox is afraid of the jaguar. But I knew you had a gun."

"Chico," Father Bennis said, touching the .45 in his trousers and looking about the room, "you are literally sitting on a goldmine here. The things in this room are worth more money than I can imagine. Why steal fruit when you could take some gold articles and sell them and move somewhere else? You would be a rich man."

"Sergio and I eat the leftover fruit. We do not need much. The things you see around us, Padre, are sacred. I will not let greedy people destroy them. Today, you killed the man who killed my parents. I was hoping someday I would find him. But he was following orders. I want the man responsible for my parents' death punished."

"Do you know who that person is?"

"Sí, Padre. Everyone in Mompox knows. He has an old shack in the wetlands where he tortures and kills his enemies. No one goes near there. If you are seen, you will die."

"Who is this man, Chico?"

"He is the man who tried to kill you yesterday and again today. People know him only as El Apredido."

■ ■ ■

9

Staten Island, New York

Cavanaugh dreaded making the call. He made the plane reservation. He packed a few clothes, a toothbrush, and shaving gear. He made another pot of coffee and sat by his desk staring at the phone. What would he say? How would he tell his wife, Francesca, he was leaving for Colombia? It was so much easier when he was single. He thought about just leaving her a note, but he couldn't do that. He had a wife and child to think about. Maybe he should have the Colombian cop relay the message. It would be easier. But it didn't feel right. María Isabelle had been shot. His brother was in some kind of trouble. He needed to go to him and find out what was going on.

He stared at the phone. He could hear Fran's voice telling him it was stupid to make the trip. Maybe it was, but he felt it was the right thing to do. He didn't want an argument. He just wanted to go and get whatever needed done over with.

He jumped at the sound of the phone ringing. He picked it up quickly. His hand was shaking. It was Fran.

"Hi Tom. I was wondering if you planned on coming over to Mary's tonight for dinner. Mom's doing much better and Stephen had a good nap this afternoon. What do you say?"

"I … I can't, Fran," he mumbled.

"What do you mean? Are you all right? You sound like something's wrong."

"I got a call from Jack. María's been shot and she's in a coma."

"Oh, my God! Where is she? How did it happen? Is Jack okay?"

Cavanaugh took a deep breath. "I don't know all the details. I didn't actually speak to Jack for that long. Some kid from down there gave me most of the details." He hesitated and then added, "I plan to catch a plane to go down there tomorrow morning."

"What? Are you out of your mind? You can't just up and go to Colombia like that!"

"Why not? Jack asked me to tell María's brother that she's been hurt."

"Can't you just call him like a normal person?"

"Fran, you don't understand. It may be difficult to find her brother. After I do, I plan to go to Jack and see if he needs any help."

"Your whole family needs help, Thomas Cavanaugh. What about your wife and son?"

"I shouldn't be gone for too long. It should only take a couple of days, a week at most."

"And what about my cousin Sal? Weren't you supposed to be trying to locate him?"

Cavanaugh rubbed his head. His ear was hot. "I am …. I will be. I think he may be somewhere in Mexico."

"Mexico is a big place, Tom, and be honest, you haven't got a clue where Sal is."

Cavanaugh took a sip of coffee. It was cold. "Fran, I'm going to Bogotá to tell María's brother the news. Then I'm going to find my brother and see if he needs help. Your cousin's been missing for almost three months. Another few weeks won't make a big difference. Besides, the more I learn about this cousin of yours, the more I don't like him!"

He sat back in his chair and breathed a sigh of relief. He felt like a weight was off his chest. But then he became aware of silence on the other end of the line. "Fran," he asked, "are you still there?"

A few long seconds later, she spoke. "I'm going with you," she said.

"What? Are you crazy? You have a child to take care of."

"My sister Mary will mind him while we're gone."

"No! It's too dangerous! You can't go!"

Her voice was calm and determined. "I am going, Thomas Cavanaugh! That's final!"

He sensed he was suddenly losing the battle and the weight was back, only heavier. "Fran, Mary can't take care of Stephen and your mother at the same time. Be reasonable."

"My other sister Susan is coming home from college. She can help."

Cavanaugh was grasping at straws. He knew Fran could be an immovable, inflexible person. "What about the dog? It's too much to ask!"

"If the dog is a problem, we can put her in a kennel."

"But, Fran, be reasonable. Someone shot María. She's in critical condition. It's dangerous down there."

"All the more reason you need help. If you forgot, you don't speak Spanish. I do. It can be like a honeymoon for us. As I recall we never really had a real honeymoon."

Cavanaugh got up and carried the phone into the kitchen. He opened the refrigerator and grabbed a bottle of Beck's. "Fran," he pleaded, "please. You will only get in the way. I don't want you hurt."

"We can act as a team. Consider me your translator, and you get to sleep with me, too."

"I don't like this, Fran. It's too dangerous."

"If you remember, we've been in dangerous situations before and survived. Besides, I'm a woman. You'll be safer with me beside you. The bad guys don't look to hurt women."

Cavanaugh closed his eyes and shook his head.

"I'll be home in about an hour unless I hit traffic on the Staten Island Expressway. I'll pack my bag tonight and we'll be ready to start on our 'delayed honeymoon' in Colombia tomorrow."

Cavanaugh hung up, opened the beer bottle, and drained it in one long gulp. Francesca could be impossible, inscrutable and incredibly ingenuous. "I'm a woman," she said, "you'll be safer with me beside you." How safe was María? Somebody shot her. She could be dying in a hospital somewhere in Colombia. Being a woman hadn't protected her. Cavanaugh sighed. This trip was bound to be difficult to begin with. Now it was going to be unbelievably challenging. He smiled, however, realizing how lucky he was to have a loving wife like Fran.

■ ■ ■

That night Cavanaugh and Fran sat at their kitchen table and talked. He told her all he knew. According to Lieutenant Marion Fraumeni, Morty Goldberg's contact in Bogotá, María's brother, Santiago Rodriguez, was a drug lord. He might be difficult to contact, but Lt. Fraumeni knew someone who might be able to arrange for a meeting. The boy who called Cavanaugh told him María had been shot and was in a coma. Bennis wanted Cavanaugh to notify her brother. That was all the information he had.

"Who is this Marion Fraumeni?" she asked.

"I don't know. Morty met her at a conference a few years ago. He says she's reliable."

"What does she look like?"

"You've got to be kidding. How do I know what she looks like? I never met her!"

"I've heard the police in Colombia are all involved with the drug cartels."

"Be serious, Fran. They all can't be crooked. Plus, I trust Morty's judgment."

Fran stood up and walked to the refrigerator. She reached in a poured herself a glass of sauvignon blanc. She sipped her drink and stared out the window. When she turned, she wiped a tear from her eye. "What happened to María and your brother?"

Cavanaugh shook his head. "I don't know, Fran. I don't even know where he is. He's in some town I never heard of. I tried calling the kid back, but the call didn't go through. Maybe he's out of range or in a blackout area. I'll call him again when we get to Colombia."

"Who would have shot her? I hope she'll be okay."

Cavanaugh remained silent.

"I really like María, Tom. I always have. Is she going to be all right?"

"I don't know, Fran. We'll see her when we get down there."

Fran poured another glass of wine. "What was she doing with your brother? I thought they were in different cities."

"I have no idea, Fran. We'll find out when we get down there." He looked at his watch. "I made reservations for you. If we are going to leave in the morning, you need to pack, and we need some sleep."

Fran nodded and headed upstairs to pack. Cavanaugh sat nursing his beer. His hands wrapped around the bottle. It was warm now. He didn't usually pray, but staring at the green bottle of beer in his hands, he did. He wondered where the path they were about to pursue would end. He remembered the dead blackbird in the back seat of his car. He exhaled deeply realizing he would not know until they reached the end of the road. And he was frightened - for Fran, María, and his brother. "God help us all," he whispered.

■ ■ ■

Bogotá, Colombia

The flight to Bogotá wasn't as bad as Cavanaugh expected. A late call to travel agent Sue Dietrich secured passage for Fran and him on a non-stop flight from Newark, New Jersey. Its departure time of 1:45 p.m. left them time to make last minute arrangements. The Jet Blue flight was scheduled to arrive in Bogotá at 4:37 p.m. From their house on Arthur Kill Road, it was less than a twenty minute cab ride to Newark International Airport. He worried about leaving his son with Fran's sister, but Fran's insistence on going with him left him no choice. There was no way he could bring little Stephen with them even if he wanted.

Cavanaugh's former partner, Morty Goldberg, made arrangements for Lt. Marian Franmeni to meet them at El Dorado International Airport. The steward on the flight helped make the six hour flight more palatable. He told jokes and challenged the young honeymoon couple from Matawan, New Jersey, across the aisle from them if they could name all the Presidents of the United States. He was originally from Cordoba, Argentina, what he called the "Heartland of Argentina." His name was Walter McKinley Cummings, and he was tall and thin with a strong chin, blond hair, and a bronze complexion. Despite his name, Cavanaugh guessed somewhere along the line he was of Germanic heritage. Walter knew the names of all but three of the U.S. Presidents. The young couple from Matawan could only name two. Cavanaugh knew them all.

When they landed in Bogotá, Cavanaugh gave the steward the names of the three missing Presidents and learned Walter's family immigrated to Argentina from Germany. The steward was proud of the fact he was named after the German poet Walther von der Vogelweide. Cavanaugh smiled knowingly and made a mental note to learn who this poet was. Then he gave the steward something to think about. "Now you know the names of all the U.S. Presidents, but do you know which President had the most children, which President had a pet alligator, and which was the only President who never married?"

Walter stood for a moment in the hatchway as passengers were hurrying to depart. People pushed and bumped into Cavanaugh. Fran gave the man behind her an elbow. A deep voice from somewhere behind them shouted, *"Fuera de mi camino!"*

The pilot tapped Walter on the shoulder and motioned toward the door. Cavanaugh took the hint. "Take care, Walter, and thanks. You made the trip better than I expected."

"But what's the answer?" Walter called after them.

Cavanaugh turned, waved, and said, "Look it up, Walter! You're a bright guy!"

As they waited for their luggage, Fran asked, "So?"

"So what?"

"So which President had the most children, a pet alligator, or was a bachelor?"

Cavanaugh shrugged his shoulders.

Fran punched him in his arm. He winced as the pain shot up to his injured shoulder. "Okay, okay. I give up. John Tyler fathered fifteen children,

John Quincy Adams had a pet alligator, and John Buchanan was the only unmarried President."

Fran asked, "How do you know so much worthless shit?"

"I don't know. I guess it goes back to those long stakeouts I made when a cop. I found it made the time go faster reading arcane, obscure facts."

Fran looked up at him and kissed him. "You're weird, Tom Cavanaugh."

"I've heard that before," he smiled and gave her a bear hug.

■ ■ ■

Leaving the airport terminal, they were hit with a blanket of hot air and a voice calling, "Mr. Cavanaugh, over here." He turned and saw a dark skinned woman in a green uniform and a baseball cap reading, "Policía." She looked about fifteen-years-old and stood a little over five feet tall. Her well-endowed bosom, however, told Cavanaugh she was older than fifteen. She stood, arms folded, next to a white Ferrari 348 convertible with green letters reading, "Policía."

"Looks like someone was expecting us," Cavanaugh said walking toward the woman and the car. As he got closer, he saw the two gold bars of the Colombian National Police lieutenant. "Lt. Marian Fraumeni?" he asked.

"Yes," she said and then motioned toward Fran. "Who's the woman? I was told you were coming alone."

"This is my wife, Francesca. She wanted to come along."

Fraumeni extended her hand. Her grip was deceptively strong. "I welcome you both to Bogotá, but you need to know this can be a dangerous place and the person you asked to meet is most dangerous. I hope you didn't plan on making this a holiday."

"We don't plan to be here that long, Lieutenant." He stared at the Ferrari convertible behind her. "Where did you get the wheels? I guess the Colombian Police are doing very well."

Lt. Fraumeni did not smile. "You might say it is a gift from your government. Your people arrested Hernando "Scratch" Gomez, a notorious drug trafficker. We confiscated his vehicles."

"And you got the Ferrari convertible? Nice work, Lieutenant."

"As you say in your country, 'Rank has its privileges.'"

Beads of perspiration formed on Cavanaugh's forehead. He was tired and didn't feel like playing games with the lieutenant. "So where can we find your mysterious, elusive, dangerous Santiago "Chago" Rodriguez? As soon as we find him, we will leave you and your fair city."

Fraumeni's face remained passive. "I don't know where he is. His location is a mystery to most of us."

"But according to Detective Goldberg, you interviewed him a while back."

"Yes, but I had to go through an intermediary."

Fran raised her hands and shook her head. "I don't believe this! You are the police for God's sake! Why can't you find this guy?"

Fraumeni stared with cold, steely eyes at Fran. "First, Mrs. Cavanaugh, this is Colombia. Things are different down here. Second, according to reliable sources, Chago runs the biggest drug cartel around here. If he doesn't want to be found, he won't be found."

Cavanaugh took a deep breath and relaxed his shoulders. "So how do we contact him?" he asked.

"There is a madam here in Bogotá. She runs a very lucrative house of prostitution," Marion Fraumeni stated.

"Prostitution?" Fran exclaimed.

"Yes, Mrs. Cavanaugh. Prostitution. I think you know what that means."

Fran's face flushed and she stepped toward the police officer. Cavanaugh pulled her back. "Go on, Lieutenant. We're listening."

"For a number of reasons, including poverty, prostitution is widespread here. Adult prostitution is actually legal in designated 'tolerance zones.' Enforcement and restriction, however, are difficult. Organized crime networks make this even more difficult. There is only one person I know in Colombia who bridges the gap between legal and illegal. She is the madam I spoke about. She can arrange a meeting for you with Chago – if she wants to. She determines if you see him or not."

"Who is this person and how do we reach her?"

"She is tall, attractive, meticulous, and very business oriented. She goes by the name Aunt Jo."

Cavanaugh and Fran exchanged glances. Then Cavanaugh said, "Okay, just tell us where we can find this Aunt Jo and we'll be out of your hair and your city."

Lieutenant Fraumeni smiled for the first time. "I think there is one more thing you should know. In addition to being smart and crafty, Aunt Jo is ninety-two-years-old."

Cavanaugh wiped his brow. Fran's mouth opened and she stared at Fraumeni.

"Aunt Jo," Fraumeni continued, "is very close to Chago. Rumor has it she supported him when he first came to Colombia. They are very close – like mother and son. Some say even closer. You give her your message, but she determines if the message gets through to Chago."

Fran exclaimed, "This is ridiculous! We came all the way down here to tell this drug dealer that his sister has been shot, and you're telling us he may not get the message?"

Fraumeni nodded. "It depends on whether Aunt Jo thinks the message is important enough."

Fran turned and kicked one of the tires on the Ferrari. "I have never heard such a cock and bull, stupid way of doing things!" she shouted. "The man's sister has been shot for God's sake!"

The Lieutenant shrugged. "I'm only telling you the way it is. Chago is a violent, dangerous man. A lot of people want him dead. Aunt Jo is his first line of defense."

"Okay, I get it," Cavanaugh said. "Where can we find this Aunt Jo?"

Lieutenant Fraumeni wrote an address on the back of her business card and handed it to Cavanaugh. "If you wish, I would try to deliver the message for you."

"No. That won't be necessary. My brother asked me to tell María's brother the news and I will. Thank you for your help."

The police lieutenant extended her hand to both Cavanaugh and Fran. "My number is on that card. If you need help of any kind, call me.

Where you are going, you may need backup." Then she turned, got into the Ferrari convertible and roared away out of El Dorado International Airport Terminal.

■ ■ ■

10

Mompox, Colombia

He stood before the full length mirror and draped his red bowtie under the collar of his white handmade silk shirt. Few men knew how to tie a bowtie. Perhaps that was one of the reasons he wore one. It was a symbol of his superiority. He was not like "most men."

He crossed the longer end of the tie over the shorter end. There was still no news of the priest and his hired assassin, Alejandro López. He looped the longer end over where the two ends crossed. He liked the symbolism of the red bowtie. Red was the color of blood. It symbolizes man's mortality and was meant to remind others of his ability to inflict pain and death. He smiled at the irony of the Earl of Kent's comment in *King Lear* about being a gentleman of blood and breeding. El Apredido considered himself a true gentleman, but he whispered to the image in the mirror, "Vengeance is in my heart, death in my hand, blood and revenge are hammering in my head."

He folded the dangling end of his red bowtie to make a loop over itself. The rest was like tying a shoelace. Where had the priest and his man disappeared to? The phone rang. In the distance he could still see the smoldering smoke from the hotel. The phone rang again. He tightened his bowtie pulling gently at the looped portions and admired himself in the mirror.

The phone rang again. He turned and picked up the phone.

"El Apredido?"

"Yes. Have you found my man or the priest?"

There was a moment of silence, and then the police chief said, "We have located Alejandro López."

"It is about time. What does he say about the priest and the woman he was with?"

Another hesitation. "He didn't say anything. He is dead. We found him buried under a haystack in the barn by the ferry."

"How did he die?"

"One shot to the head. Looks like a .45. Right between his eyes."

"What do the witnesses say? Who did it?"

"No one claims to have seen anything. They claim they were on the ferry and it was about to cast off."

"Balderdash! Someone must have seen something! What about his motorcycle?"

"We have been unable to locate it, El Apredido. The theory is some-one stole it."

"Brilliant! It is such fools as you that make the world full of ill-favored children! There aren't too many Harley-Davidsons in Mompox. Find it and you will find the person who stole the bike and probably killed Alejandro!"

El Capitán paused again. "A few people think a young boy may have taken the motorcycle. We can't be sure."

"You can't be sure? Find the boy or I swear I will kill your family a hundred and fifty ways! You know what I can do. You have seen what goes on in my private factory on the lagoon to my enemies."

El Apredido slammed the phone down toppling a gold statue on his desk of Cerberus, the three headed hound who guarded the entrance to Hades. As he bent to pick it up, he smiled. El Capitán would soon learn the fate of those who crossed El Apredido. He never gave a thought to what the police chief might have been thinking.

■ ■ ■

Muisca Tunnels of Mompox, Colombia

Jack Bennis did not sleep well in the tunnel. It was cold and damp. But he had slept in cold and damp places before. It was the dreams. He tossed and turned on the hard beds carved into one of the stone tunnels. He recognized the smell of death and had seen catacombs like this one before. He dreamed of killing the man whom he met in the bar. Why had El Apredido tried to kill him? Why did he target María? Old instincts kicked in. He had been trained in the Army to kill. And he was good at it.

But voices interrupted his dreams. "Forgive your enemies as I have forgiven you." *No! María was a good person. She meant no harm. Take me, not her!* "Vengeance is mine." *He can't get away with this. He had Chico's parents killed. He must pay.* "Not your will, but mine be done!" *The words are easier said than done. El Apredido must be stopped. Am I the one meant to stop him?*

He awoke with a start. Something jumped on his chest. He pushed it away. In the dark, he couldn't see what it was. It jumped back on him. Bennis screamed, "Get away! Get away!"

Chico's voice echoed down the tunnel. "Padre, it is only Sergio! He means you no harm." The light from Chico's flashlight darted across the walls until it rested on Sergio, the spider monkey with no tail, sitting on Bennis' chest. "It is time to get food," the boy said.

Bennis reached up and touched the monkey. It seemed to smile at him in the dancing light. "What about the jaguar?"

"We will leave through the tunnel I first fell through. I have built some stairs there from fallen rocks. It is close to the wetlands and I can show you where El Apredido has his house of death."

They walked down the tunnel for some time. The path began to slope downward and the ground became slippery. Bennis felt the walls. They were slimy and little rivulets of water eked slowly down them like a widow's tears. He felt the presence of bats hanging ominously overhead and heard the scurrying movements of rats as the flashlight guided them forward. Chico led the way with Sergio perched on his shoulder. Bennis felt he was walking in the valley of death. He had never felt claustrophobic before, but he did now. All he wanted was to breathe fresh air and gaze at the sky. This was no place for a twelve-year-old to live.

Gradually, he felt the ground begin to rise and they climbed a steep incline. In the distance, Bennis saw a thin stream of light. And then he heard them. He ducked his head as a cloud of bats swarmed over him returning from their evening feeding. When they reached the hole where Chico had fallen through, they climbed out and Chico carefully placed shrubbery and foliage across the entrance. Sergio stayed in the tunnel.

They walked a quarter of a mile through the forest until they came to what looked like a lake. "This is part of the wetlands that surround Mompox," the boy said. He pointed to a number of dilapidated faded wooden shacks huddled close together on stilts in and around the banks of the water. Small canoes and hollowed out boats were tied to the stakes holding up the buildings. Clotheslines hung between some of the buildings. Worn wooden planks formed shaky paths from the shore to the houses. They reminded Bennis of river homes he had seen in the Mekong Delta of Vietnam and Kampong Khleang, Cambodia.

"The poor live here," Chico explained. "On the other side of the wetland, the rich live in better homes." He gestured to one building in the middle of the wetland. It stood forebodingly alone. Planks of gray wood hung off its sides. Its windows were boarded up. But smoke emanated from its corrugated tin roof and a motorboat was moored at its deck. "That is where people say they hear people scream and plea for mercy as El Apredido cuts them up with chainsaws and then feeds them to the crocodiles in the water."

Chico handed Bennis his flashlight and a cellphone. "Hold this, Padre. I must go now to gather fruit for Sergio, you and me. Stay here. You are safe here. I will also try to learn how your woman friend is doing in the hospital. You can call me if you have any problem."

Bennis looked at the cellphone. "Where did you get this?"

"It was Alejandro's. He doesn't need it anymore. I also took his money. I will buy more lights for the tunnels with it."

"Let me go with you, Chico. It is too dangerous for you to go alone."

"I will be fine, Padre. You in your black clothes will stick out like a black bird in a flock of herons. Maybe I will buy you some new clothes, too. Alejandro will not mind."

Before Bennis could argue, Chico scampered away through the trees like a squirrel. The priest watched the boy quickly disappear in the dense foliage. Bennis knew the boy was right. El Apredido would be looking for him, but he had a bad feeling. The last two people he had left alone met tragedy – first Margarita, then María. Would Chico be the next? He turned his eyes toward the house in the middle of the wetland. Prayers stuck in his throat. All he thought about now was making El Apredido pay for his sins.

■ ■ ■

Bogotá, Colombia

Cavanaugh stood in the airport arrival entrance and looked around. He savored a momentary breeze from the Andean peaks in the distance. The air was clean and fresh. Bogotá was the heart of Colombia. It was its capital and largest city. Situated on a high plateau known as the Bogotá savanna, the city was approximately 8,660 ft. above sea level. Possibly up to ten million people lived here, and he was looking for one person - Santiago Rodriguez. Ten million to one. He smiled. Still, the odds were better than trying to locate Fran's cousin, Salvatore Russo. Here at least he had a possible contact, a ninety-two-year-old madam named Aunt Jo. He shook his head and a dull pain returned. The pain was less, but it reminded him of the danger that might lie ahead.

"Fran, why don't I drop you off at the hotel and you can get settled while I go try to find this Aunt Jo?"

She looked up at him. "No way, José. We are in this together. I go with you."

A taxi pulled up to them and Cavanaugh resigned himself to the fact that he wasn't going to win this battle with his wife. He gave the driver the address and they proceeded out of El Dorado International Airport along Avenida El Dorado. Traffic was heavy. The driver took them through the cobbled historic downtown and by preserved colonial buildings, luxury apartments, modern high-rise businesses, museums, trendy restaurants, parks, boutiques hotels, churches, and bars. As they drove south and then southeast, poorer neighborhoods appeared. The streets were dirtier and the buildings run down. Paper and litter lined the streets.

The driver slowed when he entered the red-light district or the "Tolerance Zone," as Lt. Fraumeni called it. Prostitutes stood on every corner and leaned on graffiti lined walls, sat in dirty doorways, and congregated in shadowy alcoves in between. They wore tight, colorful short-shorts with bare midriffs. They came in all colors, sizes, and nationalities. Some were very young, some older, some skinny, some overweight. A few walked up and down the streets twirling blue or yellow umbrellas. The streets were littered with discharged coffee cups, paper, empty food containers, and garbage. The air was heavier here and smelled of sadness and desperation.

This was not the neighborhood Cavanaugh wanted to bring Fran into. A sense of dread swept over him. Why had he allowed her to come along? Then he realized he hadn't "allowed" Fran anything. She made her own rules. He had no ability to control her. She was her own person and that was part of the reason he loved her. But still he worried about her as he looked out the cab window at the seamy, sleazy area around them.

The driver pointed out the famed brothel La Piscina (The Swimming Pool) and the El Castillo brothel which he said has been designated as having "architectural patrimony." He admitted he didn't know what that meant, but thought it was intended to attract more clients.

They drove slowly by a partially destroyed building. The driver explained that many years ago some radical university students were making a bomb in an apartment in the building when it accidently exploded, killing them, the neighbors, and a woman walking past. The government, he explained, has a policy to rebuild things destroyed by terrorism, but when it was discovered the building had been bought with drug money, they left it as it was and no one else had bothered to repair it.

On a corner, at a minimarket called Danny's, the driver made a sharp left and proceeded out of the red-light district.

As the neighborhood improved, Cavanaugh asked, "Where are you taking us?"

The driver turned and frowned, "I'm going to the address you gave me."

"But we are going to see a madam called Aunt Jo."

"Santa Fe is the red-light district, señor. It's a slum. It can be much dangerous at night. Aunt Jo's place is not around here. She is a class act."

"You know Aunt Joe?" Fran asked.

"Sí. Everyone in Bogotá knows Aunt Joe. She is a legend. She could run for President if she wanted."

As they drove, the environment changed. Traffic thinned. The streets became winding and tree-lined. Cavanaugh saw rippling creeks, nature paths, and parks. The road ascended up the mountainside into a dense forest. The air became clearer and cooler. Large iron gates appeared before them and opened as they approached. A half-mile up another twisting, narrower road, they saw a huge red brick building with stone turrets on both sides looming like a fortress ahead. Two people stood on either side of an intricately carved solid oak door. One was a tall, well-built man in a black tuxedo and a black top hat. The slight bulge under his jacket told Cavanaugh he was armed. The other was a tall, voluptuous, curvaceous woman in a V-neck full-length white lace evening gown. She wore an emerald and diamond tiara and her long reddish-brown hair cascaded off one shoulder and down her bare back. Her smile was warm and bright, but he wondered where she kept her weapon hidden.

Cavanaugh asked the taxi driver to wait, but he told him he could not. "I am not allowed to wait, señor. Aunt Jo arranges return transportation for visitors."

As the two elegant porters opened the door for them, Cavanaugh felt conspicuous and underdressed in his green and white Jets' jersey. But an even deeper sense of danger returned. The area was cleaner, classier, and more luxurious, but he knew it was still dangerous – perhaps even more dangerous.

■ ■ ■

Mompox, Colombia

Chico's first stop was a small farm where he picked three pineapples. He remembered his father telling him how some of the farmers in the region had experimented with growing a particular kind of pineapple called the Golden Pineapple. It didn't need much water or even rich soil. It needed full sun and there was plenty of that in Mompox. He put the three stolen pineapples in a burlap bag and headed for this next stop. One of the pineapples would be for him and the Padre, another would be for Sergio, his adopted spider monkey. The last pineapple was for Ronaldo Vernon, the owner of a supermarket in Mompox.

Ronaldo ran the local market. He was a big man who was pushing fifty years now. His hair was thin and he walked with a limp due to a knee injury when he played for the Union Magdalena in Santa Marta. Ronaldo had been a rising Colombian footballer. He and his good friend of Andrés Escobar Saldarriaga were defenders. They had both attended Colegio Calasanz and graduated from Instituto Conrado González. They both became professional footballers, but Andrés went on to be a member of the Colombian national team. Ronaldo often told Chico how he might have been a part of that team except for a severe concussion he suffered playing against Universitario Popayán at Ciro López Stadium in Popayán.

Ronaldo was a good talker and Chico could be a good listener. He told Chico how he was at the 1994 FIFA World Cup match against the United States. He saw his good friend stretch out to cut off a pass from an American midfielder. Ronaldo and thousands of others watched in dismay as Andrés' slide inadvertently deflected the ball into his own net. The score resulted in a United States victory of 2-1.

But that wasn't the end of the story. Ronaldo, Andrés, and some other friends went to a few bars that night in the El Poblado neighborhood in Medellin. After they split up for the night, some men approached Andrés in the parking lot of the El Indio nightclub. They argued with him about his scoring the winning goal for the other team. One of the men was a personal bodyguard of a major Colombian drug cartel boss who allegedly lost a lot of money on the outcome of the game. Andrés was shot six times and died a short time later.

Ronaldo blamed himself for leaving his friend alone. He was looking forward to his friend's wedding only five months away. Ronaldo never kicked a soccer ball again. He moved to the remote town Mompox and opened a food market. He told people he left football because of his concussion and knee injury. But everyone knew the real reason had something to do with guilt, frustration, and anger. The sport that he loved had been corrupted and he wanted no part of it.

Ronaldo never attended another soccer game. And, although fans and reporters encouraged him to attend, he never went to the unveiling of a statue in Andrés' honor in Medellin.

Still, when questioned about why he left football, he would often quote his late friend's famous line, "Life doesn't end here."

Chico liked Ronaldo. He was kind, he told good stories, and he was always willing to help if he could. But Chico knew Ronaldo was a business man. The third pineapple was barter.

"Good morning, Ronaldo," Chico said peeking through the open window of the supermarket.

The store owner turned stiffly on his bad leg. "Chico, what are you doing here? You should be in school."

"I am on my way. But I am late. I hoped you could give me a chocolate bar to give my teacher.'

"I run a business here, Chico. As much as I like you, I can't give my store away for you."

"But señor Ronaldo, surely one chocolate bar will not put you out of business."

Ronaldo laughed. "No, but it is the principle of the thing, Chico. If I give to you then I would have to give to other boys and girls who would come asking for candy."

"Sí, I understand, señor Ronaldo. How much do you charge for a pineapple - a ripe, juicy Golden pineapple?"

Ronaldo scratched his head. "Oh, Chico, a good pineapple costs much more than a chocolate bar."

Chico smiled and pulled a pineapple out of his bag. "Would you be willing to trade this beautiful Golden pineapple for a chocolate bar? I really want to give it to my teacher."

Ronaldo reached for the pineapple and squeezed it gently. "This is a good pineapple, Chico. Where did you get it?"

"I am late for school, Ronaldo. I found it on the way here. I thought you might be willing to take it in exchange for a chocolate bar."

Ronaldo reached behind the counter and handed Chico two Chocolate Santander bars. "You drive a hard bargain," he said. "Now be gone with you and get to school before I change my mind!"

Chico smiled, dropped the chocolate bars in his bag and disappeared down the street in the direction of the hospital. When he reached the hospital, he saw a security guard talking and smoking with two police officers by their car. He slipped around the parking lot and entered the hospital by a partially opened side door. He then proceeded carefully to the emergency station where an overweight nurse stared into a computer screen as her fingers tapped quickly on her keyboard. Chico snuck up behind her and gently put his hands over her eyes. "Guess who?" he whispered.

"Chico!" she said and swirled her chair around away from her computer.

He reached into his bag and pulled out the two Chocolate Santander bars. "I brought something for you, Nurse Nancy. Do you still like chocolate?"

"Where have you been, Chico? Is everything all right?"

"Sí, Nancy. My sister is doing well in school."

"What about you? Where are you staying? Have you been going to school?"

"Sí, Nancy. I am doing fine. My teacher gave us off today. I thought I would bring you a present. I hope you still like chocolate."

Chico knew Nancy when she was slim and attractive. His mother was Nancy's best friend and was supposed to be her matron of honor at her wedding. But the wedding never happened. Her fiancé, Miguel Colon, was a reporter for Chico's father's newspaper. Miguel had been working on an exposé of a new drug that was being produced in Mompox. The day before their wedding Miguel's mutilated body was found floating in the Magdalena River. Chico overheard his father tell his mother that he thought El Apredido was responsible for Miguel's murder.

After her fiancé's death, Nancy had started eating voraciously and she hadn't stopped. Chocolate was her nemesis and the chocolate wild blackberry bars he gave her was a bribe Chico felt would get him the information he needed. When she saw the bars he gave her, she tore the wrappers off them like a stripper on crack.

As he watched her devour the chocolate, he asked, "I was wondering, Nancy, how is that woman who was shot at the ferry doing. She looked pretty bad when I called for an ambulance."

She closed her eyes and slowly chewed the dark chocolate and cherishing the sweet acidic taste of the fresh, ripe berries. "This is good, Chico. So good!"

"The woman, Nancy. How is she doing?"

"I shouldn't be telling you this, but she seems to be doing better," she mumbled through a mouthful of chocolate. She swiveled back to her computer and touched a few keys. A chart appeared on the screen. "She had three bullets removed from her back. One was very close to her spine. She's still in a coma. The doctor doesn't know if she will walk again. Nobody knows who she is. She had no identification on her."

Chico heard the door at the end of the corridor open and the security guard and one of the police officers appeared. "Sorry, Nancy, but I have to go. Got to get back to school."

"I thought you said you had the day off?"

Chico turned and started running down the hall. "I lied, Nancy. Enjoy the chocolate!"

"Hey, you!" the security officer yelled. "Stop where you are!"

Chico ran around the corner and knocked over a tray of food. Both men started chasing him. "I think that may be the kid the chief told us to find," the police officer said drawing his pistol. "Stop kid!" he shouted. Chico ran like his life depended on it – and it did.

■ ■ ■

11

Mompox, Colombia

The phone rang in El Apredido's den. It was the police chief. "We stopped five Mexicans in a Mercedes SUV on Route 78. They are not talking, but they were armed with machine guns, automatic rifles, and enough ammunition and explosives to start a war. What do you want me to do with them?"

El Apredido tightened his red bowtie. Anticipation was more than half the battle. "Confiscate their weapons." He hesitated a moment before adding, "Then kill them."

El Capitán gasped. "But they have done nothing wrong. How can I do that?"

"They are terrorists. Make it look like a gunfight if you have to. Then dump their bodies in the wetlands. The crocodiles or caimans will get rid of the bodies. If you are too squeamish, I will send my men to do it!"

El Capitán grimaced, but El Apredido couldn't see it. He continued, "What about Alejandro's motorcycle and the boy reported to have been seen riding away with it?"

"I just received a report from my men at the hospital. They think they saw the boy and are in pursuit."

"Find him, El Capitán. Getting the Mexicans was a start, but ...." He looked up at the abstract painting of Abraxas. "But we have scorched the snake, not killed it. Find the boy and he will lead us to the priest." The figure in the painting seemed to nod its chicken-like head in agreement and move its serpent-like legs. "Yes," El Apredido said placing the phone down, "the priest must die."

■ ■ ■

Bogotá, Colombia

Cavanaugh and his wife walked into a huge, high ceilinged rectangular room. Aunt Jo's brothel was beyond Cavanaugh's imagination. Red velvet cushioned chairs were spaced evenly around the walls. Medieval and modern painting of nymphs, cherubs, and angels lined the walls in gold frames of various sizes. There were nymphs lying by streams and dancing with Bacchus. There were loving, playful, thoughtful cherubs interspersed with the nymphs and angels who descended golden stairways and played musical instruments. Soft, peaceful music played in the background. The smell of lilacs filled the air.

They were met by a tall redhead in a tight fitting full-length white gown. "Greetings to you," she said in perfect English. "My name is Judith. I believe you are Mr. and Mrs. Cavanaugh and you have come to see Aunt Jo. Please have a seat." She motioned to a red loveseat in the center of the room. "Aunt Jo will see you in a few minutes."

Fran poked Cavanaugh in the ribs. "How did she know who we are?"

Cavanaugh's eyes were scanning the room. He had never seen so many naked women before in his life. In one corner of the room was a statue of Bacchus holding grapes as a nymph and a child clung to him. In another corner stood a sculpture of two naked, faceless women embracing. Next to them was a bronze carving of two naked men engaged in sex. He turned to his left and saw a statue of Pan assaulting a goat. To his right was a reproduction from the Indian Khajuraho temple of an orgy involving three women and a man. He shook his head. This place had something for almost everyone. His eyes were drawn, however, to a modern painting in front of them of a naked nymph reclining in a red poppy field. The nymph's eyes seem to stare at him.

"How did she know who we are, Thomas?" Fran asked again.

"Ask Aunt Jo yourself," he said pointing to the naked nymph in the poppy field. Suddenly, the painting opened and a beautiful, tall, slender woman appeared. Her skin was smooth and seemed to glow. Her long, straight black hair hung over both shoulders with a bang covering most of her forehead. She smiled at them and said, "Greetings, Mr. and Mrs. Cavanaugh. I am Aunt Jo. I understand you wish to talk with me. What can I do for you?"

■ ■ ■

Cavanaugh and Fran stood. He stared at the statuesque woman. She was beautiful. Fran's mouth dropped. She shook her head. "You can't be Aunt Jo!"

"But I am, my dear," she said. "Please, have a seat and tell me why you wish to see Chago."

"But they told us you were ninety...."

Aunt Jo smiled. "Actually, Mrs. Cavanaugh, I will soon be ninety-three."

"But ...."

"Yes. I have been told I do not look that old. Perhaps it is because I take care of myself. It is something more people should do. I also do not frequently associate with old people. But enough about me. Why do you want to see Chago?"

Cavanaugh cleared his throat. "My brother is a Jesuit priest. He and Chago's sister have been very close. According to my brother, María Isabelle met Chago when she arrived in Bogotá. She hadn't seen him in a long time and she thought he looked skinny and worried. She contacted my brother and told him her brother was mixed up in some way with the Medellin drug trade and asked him to help. She said her brother didn't want her involving the police. He told her there was someone in Mompox making a drug call the Devil's Breath...."

Aunt Jo stiffened. Her smile evaporated. "Cut to the chase, Mr. Cavanaugh."

Fran said, "The bottom line is María has been shot. She is in a hospital in Mompox and in critical condition."

"Who shot her?"

"We don't know," Cavanaugh said. "After I deliver the message, I ... I mean we plan to go to Mompox to find out more and see if we can help."

Aunt Jo folded her arms. "This would not be wise." She clapped her hands twice and six people appeared behind them - three women and three men. Each was dressed in formal attire and each held a handgun. Cavanaugh recognized the rectangular end of the barrel. They each had a Russian made MP-443 Grach pistol. It was the standard sidearm of the Russian military.

"It is best that you go now. I assure you I will deliver your message to Chago. A car is waiting outside to take you back to Bogotá."

Fran started to protest, but Cavanaugh gently pulled her back. He motioned to the people who now surrounded them. "We're not going to win this battle, Fran. Let's not tempt them to kill the messengers." He bowed to Aunt Jo, thanked her, and followed their armed guards out of the mansion and into a new black limousine parked in front.

As they drove away, Fran asked, "Where are we going?"

"It's our belated honeymoon, remember?"

"The only thing I remember is we left our luggage in the taxi that took us here."

Cavanaugh noticed the driver was listening. "Then it's off to the airport. I read somewhere UNESCO declared Mompox a World Heritage Site in recognition of its outstanding colonial architecture. It's supposed to be beautiful. Because it is such a remote place, the pace is slower and its beauty hasn't been spoiled by greedy developers and crass, obnoxious tourists."

The driver turned slightly. He spoke in Spanish. "With your permission, señora, there are no flights to Mompox. The best way to get there is by bus and ferry."

"What did he say?" asked Cavanaugh.

"He said there are no flights to Mompox. We have to go there by bus and ferry."

Cavanaugh realized something strange was going on here. The driver understood English. Why did he address his comment to Fran in Spanish?

How did he know she spoke Spanish? Aunt Jo was everything Lt. Fraumeni had said about her. In addition to being tall and beautiful, she was thorough, well-prepared and well-organized. He didn't know why or exactly where she was leading them, but he decided to go along for the ride. With an eye on the driver, Cavanaugh said, "It is what it is. After all, we're on our honeymoon, aren't we? This should be a chance to see the country. Tell him to drop us off wherever the bus leaves for Mompox."

Cavanaugh noticed the driver lean back and smile.

■ ■ ■

Mompox, Colombia, Rain Forest

Father Jack Bennis looked up at the sky. It was darkening and the air had grown slightly cooler. He leaned carefully against a giant sandbox tree that stretched high above him. Its leaves were massive. He knew the sap of the tree was toxic and had been used in the past as poison for arrows. He tried to pray for María Isabelle and Chico. The boy had not returned and soon it would be dark.

He heard rustling sounds in the shrubbery around him and a series of dark shadows shot across the path ahead of him. He squinted into the fading sunlight. Whatever the shadows were, they were moving closer. He heard feet snapping twigs. He took out María's .45 pistol. Directly in front of him, a large reddish-brown barrel-shaped body appeared. It looked to be about four feet long and two feet tall. It stood on webbed feet and stared at him. It was bigger than a rat, or a squirrel, or a cat. He leveled the .45 at the creature. Suddenly, it started to bark like a dog and the area around Bennis was filled with similar cries. The bushes and underbrush stirred as the shadowy creatures on his right and left quickly scampered away. The one in front of him, however, stood motionless, locking its eye on him. He studied the creature as it studied him. It had a short head, blunt nostrils, and its eyes and ears were near the top of its head. He recognized it now. It was a capybara. Bennis raised his arms and gave his best interpretation of a jaguar's roar which sounded more like a chronic cough, but was close enough to scare the capybara. It turned and ran.

As the capybara disappeared into the underbrush, the silence of the night fell on him like a suffocating blanket and Jack Bennis was left to think about Chico and María, the real jaguar lurking somewhere in the growing darkness around him, and El Apredido.

It was then that Bennis remembered the cellphone Chico had left him. Chico said he had taken it from Alejandro López, the man who shot María. The priest laid the pistol on his lap and pulled out the cellphone. He checked recent calls. There were five recent calls in the last two days and one text. The text read, "KILL THE PRIEST!"

The calls and the text were all from the same number. Alejandro was kind enough and careless enough to identity the caller as "El Apredido."

■ ■ ■

Mompox, Colombia

Chico ran out the side door of the hospital. The second policeman was there waiting for him. He put his arms out to grab Chico, but Chico ducked and swung the burlap bag with the two remaining pineapples at him. The bag glanced off the officer's head, knocking him off balance. As he fought to regain his balance, Chico kicked the officer in the groin with the force of an NFL placekicker attempting a 62 yard field goal, and he dashed past him.

Chico heard the moans and cries of the cop as he ran around the corner and darted into an alley. Chico knew the streets and alleys of Mompox better than a city engineer. Since his parents' murder he had survived on these streets. He ran down one street after another, turning right, then left, darting into alleys, scaling fences. Holding his sombrero in one hand and his burlap bag in the other, he zigzagged through the streets and around pedestrians, bicycles, and horse drawn rickshaws. He thought briefly about seeking refuge at the largest and second oldest church in Mompox, Iglesia de la Inmaculada Concepcion, but he hadn't seen the inside of a church since his parents were murdered. And he knew Padre Brian Laline, a missionary priest from Dublin, Ireland, locked the doors after Mass every morning. Instead, he dashed across the cobblestone path of Parque de

Bolivar and around the tall statue of Simon Bolivar. He crouched for a moment in the lengthening shadows of the Bolivar monument and recalled his father and Uncle Felipe arguing over coffee one night about Bolivar's reputation. His uncle called Bolivar, the Liberator of Spanish South America and told how with the help of almost all the able men in Mompox, Bolivar formed an army which won victory in Caracas. His father, however, held a different opinion. He claimed Bolivar was a "false liberator," a deserter, a conspirator, a liar, a coward, a womanizer, and a looter. Looking up at the statue, Chico wondered which one was right. Or, possibly, could they both be right?

More and more people were starting to come out for the evening festivities. He could hear music played in nearby cabarets and saw small groups of people talking and wandering the streets. He left the park and walked up Calle 18. He didn't think he was being followed, but he wasn't sure. Approaching the Mompox cemetery, he threw his burlap bag with the two pineapples over a fence and then scaled it holding desperately onto his sombrero. A group of cats scattered in all directions as he ran behind the tomb of Alfred Serrano, known by locals as "El Gato," the Cat. After his death, Alfredo's family found a cat at his grave one day. They gave the cat some food and now visitors to the cemetery often see dozens of cats around his gravesite. Cats weren't Chico's favorite animal. He never understood the stories about Alfred Serrano, his love of the feline animals, and the tradition of people leaving food for the cats that resulted in their proliferation around his gravesite. Chico's conclusion was people were sometimes crazy.

At the far end of the cemetery, Chico stopped and listened. Only the sounds of distant music and laughter in the growing darkness could be heard. Chico felt safe here – at least for the time being – or until the police brought out the dogs. He crawled in the shadows of a stone angel and began to worry about the Padre and Sergio. He had given Padre a cellphone, but he didn't know the number. He pulled his large sombrero down over his eyes and curled into a fetal position behind the gravestone of his parents. The ghosts of the past danced in the shadows of the night. This was a place he had visited often, but never at night. He thought about Sergio, the Padre, the unidentified woman in the hospital, Alejandro López, his parents, and the jaguar. For the first time in a long time, Chico was scared and he began to cry.

■ ■ ■

Darkness fell on Mompox like a thief in the night. Somewhere in the distance, people were laughing, dancing, and playing music while El Apredido sat at his large desk planning the final phase of his plan. El Capitán and his own men had taken care of the Mexicans and soon they would catch the boy who stole Alejandro's motorcycle.

When the phone rang, he eagerly picked it up. "Have you got the kid yet? Where is the priest?" he asked. When the only sound he heard was silence, he looked at the caller ID. The call was coming from Alejandro's cellphone. But how could this be? Alejandro was dead. Then a voice calmly said, "I came in peace, yet you tried to kill me."

"Who is this?" El Apredido demanded.

"I came in peace, but you have awakened the devil in me and I am now your worst enemy."

"Who is this?" he demanded.

"What's in a name? Remember? Just beware. I am coming to get you."

"You don't know who you are talking to. I control this town. You are a dead man!"

"Say your prayers tonight, El Apredido, because I am coming for you. You won't know where or when, but I will be there. Your days are limited."

"You don't scare me. Five of your men were killed this afternoon and fed to the caimans. You can't get me!"

"There are none so blind as those who cannot see. The graveyards are filled with indispensable men. Do not delude yourself. You are far from indispensable. Three of your men are already dead. Do you recall Macbeth's saying how he was steeped in blood so deep that returning were as tedious as going forward. Know this and mark it well. Vengeance is in my heart, death in my hand, blood and revenge are hammering in my head. Your days, El Apredido, are numbered."

"You don't scare me!" El Apredido shouted into the phone. "I will get you and feed you piece by piece to the caimans!" But the line was dead. Beads of perspiration formed on his forehead. He loosened his red bowtie. The room was suddenly hot, stiflingly hot. He opened the window to get more air and then jumped back. This was foolish. He paced up and down the room avoiding the open window. He was so close to completing his revenge, to making his statement to the world. He had eliminated the five Mexicans sent by S.R. There might be more later, but it would be too late then.

He stopped before the painting of Abraxas. What if the priest wasn't sent by S.R.? Then who had sent him? He already killed three of his men. One was cut in two by his own AK-47; another's head had been blown off, and now Alejandro had been shot between the eyes. Whoever he was, he was good.

He went to the credenza and made himself a drink. The priest was a fool to think he could fight El Apredido and the forces he had. He would have the last word, not this mysterious, meddlesome priest whoever he was. El Apredido smiled to himself. He would indeed have the last word. He poured an ounce of Tanqueray London Dry Gin, an ounce of freshly squeezed lime juice, an ounce of Green Chartreuse, and an ounce of Luxardo Maraschino liqueur. He poured the improbable mixture into a tall stemmed glass. The pale green, innocently-looking drink was said to have originated in a private athletic club in Detroit during America's Prohibition-era. Theoretically, the mixture of such strong flavors shouldn't work together, but they did. The end result was a surprisingly potent, complex, delicious drink called "The Last Word."

El Apredido smiled, sipping his drink, and avoiding the open window. "The foolish priest will soon be a dead man," he said looking up at the painting of Abraxas. "He does not realize that I, like The Last Word, am greater than the sum of its parts."

And Abraxas seemed to smile back at him and nod.

■ ■ ■

12

Mompox, Colombia

While Cavanaugh and Fran waited in Bogotá for the long bus and ferry ride to Mompox, a Russian made Mi-17 helicopter with twin turbine engines, 57 mm rocket pods, Kevlon armor plating, and a loading ramp lifted off a secluded airstrip in the Andes Mountains near Bogotá. It flew low following the Magdalena River. At times its rotor blades skimmed the tops of trees lining the river banks. It was a big helicopter capable of carrying up to thirty armed soldiers and an armored vehicle. It bypassed domestic airports in Monteria, Cartagena, and Corozal and the small local airports in Magangue and Mompox. Instead it circled the town of Mompox, its lights searching for a suitable landing place. A mile outside the town, it landed in a clearing. Twelve armed men in camouflage uniforms exited the copter and took up defensive positions around it. Each man carried a PP-2000 submachine gun with Zenit-4TK laser sights complete with a 44-round magazine of armor-piercing ammunition in the stock of the weapon, a MP-443 Grach pistol, and three RGN fragmentation grenades.

The loading ramp in the rear of the helicopter opened and a specially equipped black Cadillac Escalade / ESV with tinted, thick bulletproof glass, run-flat tires, and rocket-propelled grenades rolled onto the soft ground. A thin man dressed in a multi-colored flowered shirt, blue designer denim jeans, and a Yankee baseball cap emerged from the copter, looked around at the lights in Mompox, and took a deep breath. The air was damp and he could smell the Magdalena River. He tugged his jeans up and motioned back to the helicopter. Two more people walked down the ramp.

One was a balding man in his sixties with a large stomach, a full moustache, and a nervous tick. He held a large satchel in his left hand and a smaller black leather bag in his right. The other was a beautiful, tall, statuesque woman in a long flowing blue gown. Her skin seemed to glow in the moonlight. Her long, straight jet-back hair fell over her shoulders. Two of the soldiers fell off the perimeter defense line and opened the doors of the vehicle for the man and the woman. After they were secure in the car, the men climbed in themselves. The thin man in the colorful shirt waved to the helicopter pilot and, as it slowly ascended, he and another armed guard joined the others in the Cadillac.

In the car he spoke into a walkie-talkie in Spanish. "Maintain your positions. We are proceeding to San Juan de Dios Hospital to see my sister. Will inform you when we arrive."

Amid some ambient static, the response came. "Copy that, Chago."

■ ■ ■

Father Bennis stretched. Where was Chico? It was dark now. The only light came from a full moon. There was an ominous quiet surrounding him. Judging from the stars, he estimated he was somewhere to the west of Mompox. What lay between him and Mompox, however, he did not know. Were there wetlands, swamps, rivers, farms, homes? He didn't know. He did know, however, that somewhere in the darkness there were snakes and at least one dangerous jaguar.

It was at times like this that prayer usually helped. Peering into the darkness, the first words that came to his mind were, "My God, my God, why have you forsaken me?" But had his God really forsaken him, or had he forsaken his God? How could he pray after what had happened, what had almost happened, and what he was planning to make happen?

He felt the cold metal of the gun in his hand. He had been trained carefully to use it, and he had learned well.

His thoughts switched to María Isabelle. He recalled first meeting her in Havana, Cuba. She was a nurse and sister-in-law of Diego Velasquez, a professor at the University of Havana with whom he was staying. When Bennis was shot by a hired sniper back then, she had cleaned his wound and nursed him back to health. They became close. He sensed her growing attraction to him, but dismissed it. He resisted her advances. She was kind, caring, and beautiful, but he was a priest. When events developed and her life became endangered, he called in a favor from a former Washington, D.C. contact engaged in subversive activities he knew from when he was a Black Ops officer, and both María and he were extracted from Cuba.

Fr. Bennis called in another favor and secured an assignment at St. John Berchmans in Staten Island where he convinced the pastor to hire María as "chief cook and bottle washer." But there were problems. The pastor saw María's presence in the rectory as "inappropriate." He also noticed the growing attraction they had for each other. The pastor did not want another scandal. For his part, Bennis also realized his affection for María was deepening and becoming a distraction. Maybe, he felt, he was falling in love with her. Maybe, he wondered if the priesthood was no longer his calling. He requested a "leave of absence" from his vows to "find his mind" and make a decision. There was a time when he thought it could work out. He thought he could serve two masters. Could he love his God and María at the same time? Or would he come to hate one and love the other, or be devoted to one and despise the other? He decided to give it a try.

Jack Bennis accepted a teaching assignment at a private high school and María got a job in a healthcare and rehabilitation center as a nurse's aide. Things did not work out, however, and he told María it wouldn't work out for them and that he was committed to being a priest. He thought the situation between them was totally resolved when she announced her engagement to Francisco Thomás, a maintenance worker at the nursing home.

But again things didn't work out as he expected. María broke her engagement to Francisco and continued her advances to the priest. She was in love with him and nothing he could do seemed to dissuade her. When he thought she had been kidnapped by a sadistic killer with a personal grudge against him, Jack Bennis prayed to his God to save her. He bargained with God that if He saved her, he would leave the country and vowed never to see her again.

Once again, however, things didn't work out as he had planned. She wrote to him asking for his help, and here he was. Thomas à Kempis wrote about this when he said, "Man proposes but God disposes." Sometimes Bennis felt like God had a sense of humor. But María's shooting was far from funny. The man responsible, he vowed, must pay. The Lord may have said that vengeance was His, but Jack Bennis believe his God was a forgiving God. As the Bible stated, there is a time for everything, a time to be born and a time to die, a time to love and a time to hate.

He walked slowly down to the water bank. A flash of lightning lit up the night sky. A storm was coming. If he followed the water's edge toward the glow in the distance he would reach Mompox.

He hesitated. Where was Chico? The boy would not abandon him and Sergio. He said he would bring back food for them. Had something happened to him? His eyes drifted to the shadowy building on stilts in the middle of the water. The distant sound of a chainsaw floated over the waters. And then the sounds of screams.

The priest clutched María's .45 in his hand. He took a deep breath. There was a time to make war and a time to kill.

■ ■ ■

Bogotá, Colombia

Aunt Jo's chauffeur dropped Cavanaugh and Fran at the bus terminal in Bogotá and then rapidly drove away. As they watched the limo disappear, Fran asked, "Now what? How do we get to Mompox from here?"

"I haven't got a clue," Cavanaugh admitted. "Maybe you could ask someone."

"Oh, is this another of those male things where guys don't ask for directions?"

"No. You speak Spanish. I don't."

Fran huffed and went into the terminal. Fifteen minutes later she returned. "Well, Mr. Columbus, according to everyone I asked, it will probably take from eighteen to twenty hours to go from here to Cartagena and then, barring rain and hoping the roads aren't washed out, another four to five hours to Mompox."

"You have got to be kidding me!"

"I wish I were. And that's the good news. The bad news is we missed the last bus. The next bus, or Copetran as they call it, doesn't leave until tomorrow morning."

"Shit! Now what do we do!"

"Well, let's think about it. We have no luggage. We have no reservations." She looked around and spotted a bench across the street. "I guess we could camp out there for a day or two."

Cavanaugh grunted and thought of the dead blackbird in the back of his car. Then he reached into his pocket and pulled out Lt. Marion Fraumeni's business card. Fran was right. He hated asking for directions. But this was different. He dialed Fraumeni's cellphone. She picked it up on the third ring. "What can I do for you, señor Cavanaugh?"

He explained their situation and their desire to get to Mompox as soon as possible. Fraumeni listened and then said, "I know someone who has a private plane. They could fly you to Cartagena and you could hire a 4X4 from there."

"What will he charge?"

"Who said it was a 'he'?"

"Sorry about that."

"What's in your wallet?"

"What?"

Fraumeni chuckled, "*She* takes credit cards."

Cavanaugh nodded. "How do we get to this friend of yours?"

"I'll pick you up in an hour."

Two hours later, Fraumeni pulled up in a blue 2004 Chevrolet Grand Vitara. Cavanaugh looked at his watch and then asked, "What happened to the Ferrari convertible?"

"That's the company car. If you want a ride, get in."

It was dark when they arrived at a private airport outside of Bogotá. Fraumeni parked the car and told them where to wait. Another hour later, a Cessna 182 Skylane pulled up the runway and the pilot motioned for Cavanaugh and Fran to climb aboard. Cavanaugh noted it was a single-engine, four seated plane. He didn't like flying to begin with, but looking at this small plane he was more apprehensive than usual. As he climbed aboard, the pilot turned to him and said, "Welcome aboard, señor and señora Cavanaugh."

Fran smiled. Cavanaugh's jaw dropped. The pilot was Lt. Fraumeni.

■ ■ ■

Lightning flashed across the sky in the distance as they took off. "It's liable to be a bumpy ride," Fraumeni warned.

"Why are you doing this?" Cavanaugh asked. "You are going out of your way for us."

"Maybe I'm a sucker for a sob story. The truth is, however, your former partner, Morty Goldberg, did me a favor or, as I believe you say back in the States, a 'solid.' He asked me to look out for you, and I'm trying."

"What did he do?" Fran asked.

Fraumeni ignored the question as she switched on dials and the plane banked to the left. "I would fly you to Mompox, but a storm is approaching. Your best bet is to hire a 4x4 to take you from Cartagena to Mompox. Don't try to drive it yourself. The roads are for the most part unpaved and treacherous. Once you get to Mompox, you won't need a car. Mompox is small and isolated. That's part of its beauty. Its remoteness has preserved its character and charm. It is in the middle of a *ciénaga*, a wetland created by the Magdalena River and its tributaries. You could get there by boat or by bus, but the time schedules are frankly unreliable. The ride from Cartagena to Mompox, I must warn you, will be hot, dusty, and rough. If it rains, as predicted, the roads may get washed out. If that happens you might be better off taking a motorized canoe or *chalupa*, as we call it, or even the ferry. There are a lot of options. I wish I could fly you directly there, but I have work tomorrow and the weather doesn't look good."

The flight was as she predicted rough and bumpy. Cavanaugh wondered what Goldberg had done that merited Fraumeni going out of her way for them. She avoided all questions on the matter and concentrated on flying. For his part, he started to worry about his brother and María. Why hadn't he heard from him again? How did María get shot and why? What kind of problem had his brother gotten himself into this time?

Suddenly, his cellphone rang. He fumbled for it and flicked it open. Fraumeni looked at the flip-phone in wonder. "Where did you get that relic?" she asked.

"Fly the plane," he said and answered the phone. A small voice on the other end of the line whispered, "Señor Cavanaugh? This is Chico."

"Chico, how are you? I was wondering about you. How is my brother and his lady friend?"

"Señor, the lady is in the hospital. She is hurt bad, very bad."

"We are on our way. Where is she?"

"Señor, she is in San Juan de Dios Hospital."

"Is my brother with her?"

"No, señor."

Cavanaugh looked out at another flash of lightning lighting up the night sky in the distance. It was followed by rolling thunder. "Sorry, Chico. I can't hear you very well. Can you speak up a little louder?"

"No, señor," he whispered again. "He is not with her. I am in the cemetery."

"Oh, my God! What happened?"

"Señor, I am hiding."

"Who are you hiding from?"

"The Policía."

"Where is my brother?"

"Señor, I left the Padre with Sergio in the forest by the swamp."

The plane bounced in the turbulence of the approaching storm. Cavanaugh looked at the gauges and then at Lt. Fraumeni. She was fighting with the controls. He knew less about a plane's gauges than he did about a computer which was practically nothing. He did know that when the gauges gyrated up and down and red and yellow lights started flashing, things weren't going well. Fran reached over from the rear seat and clutched his shoulder. "We're having a bit of a problem here, Chico. You are cutting in and out. We are on our way. Can you hold on for a couple of hours more?"

"Sí, señor. I will try. It is raining very hard. But I am with my parents."

"Chico, can you put your father on the phone? I need to ask him some questions."

"No, señor. He is dead."

Cavanaugh heard a loud crack of thunder on the other end of the line and then he lost the connection.

■ ■ ■

Mompox, Colombia

"Something is happening, El Apredido!" The police chief's voice was panicky. He spoke rapidly and sounded out of breath.

El Apredido checked the clock on his wall. It was 2:37 in the morning. "What is so important that you wake me at this ungodly hour? Go, prick thy face, and over-red thy fear, thou lily-livered boy!"

"My men report a helicopter landing in a clearing outside of the city."

El Apredido sat up and looked out his bedroom window. Rain poured down like a cow pissing on a flat rock. Lightning flashed across the sky and thunder rumbled in the distance. "Where exactly is this helicopter?"

"They say it took off."

"Why did it land?"

"I don't know."

"Did anyone get off?"

"They could not see."

"You scullion! You fustilarian! You rump-fed runyon! How do I function with fools like you? Check with your men. Someone must have seen something." Then he added, "What about the boy?"

"We have not found him yet."

"And the priest?"

"He seems to have disappeared."

"No one disappears unless I make them disappear. Find them!" He rubbed his eyes and remembered the unidentified woman in the hospital. "Do you still have people at the hospital?"

"Sí, El Apredido. One man is still there."

"Check with him and get back to me." He looked again at the clock. *Who would land a helicopter in a storm like this and then take off?* He stood slowly and wrapped a black smooth stretch-cotton robe with soft fleece lining around himself and walked into his den.

On top of his 17th century credenza, underneath the abstract painting of Abraxas, he found the crumpled message he had previously discarded. He unfolded the letter and read it again. "You may think you are secure in Mompox, but, trust me, you are not. My people are on their way…."

Was the helicopter sent by S.R.? Had S.R. arrived in Mompox? A chill ran through his body. Was he about to experience the "serious repercussions" S.R. had promised?

El Apredido looked up at the painting of Abraxas. He rolled up his right sleeve and touched his own tattoo of Abraxas, the demon from Hell who had dominion over the cycles of birth, death, and resurrection. Was he about to witness the "bloodshed" S.R. promised? He stared at the figure in the painting and it seemed to raise its shield and nod.

He opened the top drawer of the credenza and withdrew a Glock Model 18 with two full magazines of 33 rounds each. He liked this weapon because he could switch it from semi-automatic to fully automatic. It was like having a handgun that could become a machine gun at the flip of a switch. He would be ready for S.R. He smiled and nodded at the painting. "Cry Havoc," he shouted, "and let slip the dogs of war! Let the priest or S.R. come. I will be ready for them."

■ ■ ■

13

Mompox, Colombia

It was almost 4:00 a.m. when Cavanaugh and Fran arrived in Mompox. The last leg of their journey had been excruciating. The roads were bumpy and partially washed out and they had to get out frequently to push or pull the 4x4 they hired through mud and knee-deep water. It was not the kind of "honeymoon" either of them anticipated.

The driver's name was Pablo. He was tall and thin with a full head of stark white hair. Fran thought he was handsome. Cavanaugh thought he wore a wig. He spoke no English, but that did not stop him from constantly talking. Fran carried on a conversation with him and translated for Cavanaugh.

For his part, Cavanaugh concentrated on the road and couldn't believe Pablo could drive and talk so much in the driving rain. He never shut up even when you could not see the road because of the wind and rain.

Pablo did give Fran a basic idea, however, of what to expect in Mompox. He knew where the hospital was, but he wasn't impressed with it. He said it was built back in the 1500s and was one of the oldest hospitals, if not the oldest in Colombia, and that it was badly in need of repairs. In fact, he told them the staff had not been paid in over six months. Both Cavanaugh and Fran worried about María receiving adequate treatment there. But Pablo commented it wasn't that bad and from what he heard about medical treatments under "Obama Care" it might even be better than some places in the United States.

Cavanaugh remembered Chico and asked Fran to have him take them first to the cemetery. Pablo's enthusiasm over the cemetery almost resulted in their tumbling down a ravine. He told them the cemetery was one of the feature items in Mompox. He said they should come back during Holy Week for the traditional celebration of the Serenade to the Dead. He gestured with his hands about the size of some of the white stone tombs and warned them not to be upset with the number of cats in the cemetery. Fran knew Cavanaugh's love of animals did not extend to cats so she did not translate that part of Pablo's never-ending narratives.

When they entered Mompox, Cavanaugh spotted a number of police cars lining the sides of the road. Pablo waved at one police officer sitting in his patrol car smoking a cigar and explained that was Adrian, his second cousin once or twice removed. He wasn't sure anymore. Adrian smiled and waved at them through the rain. He told Fran how Adrian had been a waiter, but the money was better being a police officer. He heard the drug dealers paid him well for looking the other way. It wasn't the kind of life Pablo liked, but Adrian was family. He was telling them about Adrian's prostate problems when they arrived at the historic Mompox cemetery. It was dark, but the rain had subsided. Pablo did not understand why they wanted to get out at the cemetery and offered to wait, but they paid him and walked down the dark brick path into the cemetery.

They both were wet and muddy, but it felt good to finally get out of the car and away from Pablo's constant babblings. Cavanaugh nicknamed him "Jabber-jaws" and marveled that anyone could talk that fast for such a long time without seeming to take a breath.

"What do we do now?" Fran asked. "Maybe we should go to a hotel first and dry off."

"No. We need to find this Chico kid. He knows where my brother and María are. There'll be time to dry off later."

"We're in a cemetery, Tom." She motioned to the white graves all about them. "Later never came for these people."

"Why do you have to be so negative, Fran? Why don't you take the right and I'll take the left and we walk around and see if we can find Chico?"

"Are you out of your mind? I'm not walking through this cemetery alone!"

Just then two cats ran across their path and disappeared behind some gravestones. Cavanaugh jumped back. "What was that?"

"Cats! Pablo warned me there are a lot of cats in this cemetery."

Cavanaugh shuddered. "Okay. You're right. We should go together. Just stay close. The sun will be coming up soon."

Fran smiled and poked Cavanaugh in his arm. "Maybe we should wait until the sun comes up and Dracula goes back to this coffin." Cavanaugh flinched, but realized the pain in his arm was less which was a good thing.

They followed the perimeter of the cemetery. The sky began to clear and the rain stopped. They were so wet already they didn't seem to notice. They spoke little and when they did it was in whispers as if they feared waking the dead. Occasionally, a cat would scamper across the white tombs decorated with artificial flowers.

As the darkness dissipated, they could see more clearly. Then, they saw a body. They almost missed it. It was behind a statue of an angel and between two white sepulchers stacked on top of each other. There, huddled in a fetal position was a small boy wearing a large sombrero pulled over his head. He was motionless. Fran saw him first. "Tom, there's a body over there," she said pointing and gripping his arm tighter.

Cavanaugh stepped in front of Fran and motioned for her to stay back. Moving closer, he whispered, "Chico, is that you?"

A head peeked suddenly out of the sombrero and the boy sprang to his feet and prepared to run. "Hold on, kid! It's me – Cavanaugh, the Padre's brother. You spoke to me on the phone. We came here to help!"

The boy stopped. He crossed his arms. He was shivering.

"This is my wife, Fran. Can you tell us what happened? Where are my brother and María? And what are you doing here?"

The boy studied them for a moment and then looked at the sky. The sun was rising. "Señor, we must go. The Policía are looking for me. The

Padre is with Sergio. The woman is in the hospital." He grabbed his burlap bag and said, "Sergio will be hungry. We must hurry."

"Where are we going? Who is Sergio?"

But the boy had turned and was zigzagging through the graves toward a forest of trees in the distance. Cavanaugh and Fran looked at each other, shrugged, and followed after Chico.

■ ■ ■

When the police chief pulled up in front of San Juan de Dios Hospital, he knew something was wrong. The rain had stopped, but a large black Cadillac Escalade / ESV with tinted windows blocked the main entrance.

A tall man stood in the shadows. He wore a camouflage uniform and carried what looked like a submachine gun. Was he a member of FARC, the revolutionary army forces of Colombia? Was this some kind of terrorism on their part? But everything was quiet. It didn't feel right for FARC.

El Capitán spotted the patrol car assigned to the hospital at the far end of the parking lot. He drove there, but the car was empty. The police officer assigned to watch the hospital was nowhere in sight. What was going on? He wouldn't abandon his post.

El Capitán exited his vehicle to survey the area. Then he saw it. The small red dot moved slowly and deliberately across his car, up his arm and centered on his chest. He knew instantly a laser-mounted weapon was aimed precisely at his heart. He raised his hands and moved cautiously back to this vehicle. He expected to feel the bullet before he heard the shot.

Was this what life was all about? What would El Apredido's money do for him and his family if he were dead? He realized this was about the woman – the woman whom El Apredido's man shot at the ferry. This was not about him. This was not about FARC. El Apredido had killed and intimidated far too many people. He had been a coward to go along with El Apredido's demands. He knew about the chop-house on the marsh where El Apredido tortured and killed anyone who stood up to him. He recalled the boy Chico whose parents were killed by El Apredido's chief assassin,

Alejandro López. He knew, but had done nothing. He had looked the other way and allowed him to go on. He had taken the abuse, the curses, the threats. And for what? For money, for greed? As he looked down at his chest at the small red laser dot, he realized what a fool and a coward he was. He slowly raised his right hand and made the sign of the cross. Then he gripped the steering wheel, closed his eyes, and waited for the bullet that would end it all.

But it didn't come.

He opened his eyes. The red laser dot was gone.

He took a deep breath, made another sign of the cross in thanksgiving, and then drove away. He had been given a message. If he had not been killed, then most probably, Stephano, the police officer assigned to the hospital would be okay. Whatever this was about, it wasn't about him. This was about El Apredido. Driving away, he knew there was one more thing he needed to do.

■ ■ ■

The sun was up when Chico, Fran, and Cavanaugh finally reached the spot where Chico had left Father Bennis. As they worked their way cautiously through the dense forest, birds and invisible animals scattered ahead of them. Fran narrowly avoided stepping on a brightly colored, highly venomous coral snake. Cavanaugh pulled her away just in time. Chico stopped them twice to point out pit viper snakes which were also poisonous and thrived in the forests and scrublands of Colombia. Fran and Cavanaugh stepped carefully and were extremely vigilant as they followed the boy with the big sombrero.

It seemed they walked for hours through the tangled jungle. Through the trees they could see the outskirts of the Mompox wetlands. At a large evergreen tree, Chico stopped and waited for them to catch up. The tree had many dark, pointed spines and a smooth brown bark. Chico pointed to the spines of the tree and explained, "Señor and señora, I call this tree a 'Monkey no-climb tree' because of the sharp spines. Sergio hates this tree. It is not far from here."

A short time later they saw an A-frame shelter built between two trees. It was covered with foliage, boughs, pine needles, and branches from near-by trees and shrubs. A horizontal branch was lashed with vines to two more branches on each end. Chico froze in his tracks. Cavanaugh noticed fear in the boy. "What's the matter, Chico?" he asked.

"Señor, I do not know where this came from? It was not here when I left."

Cavanaugh moved closer, and Sergio, Chico's tailless pet spider mon-key jumped out of the shelter and hopped into Chico's arms. In his hand he held a half-eaten mango.

A voice from the shelter called out, "It's about time you got here, Chico. We were beginning to worry about you." Cavanaugh peered into the shel-ter. There on a bed of leaves, pine needles, and grass lay his brother, Father Jack Bennis. The priest rose, crawled out, and gave his brother a bear hug. "Well, well, look what the wind blew in! What are you doing there?"

"We heard you and María got yourself into some kind of trouble. We thought you might need some help."

"We?"

Cavanaugh turned and Fran stepped forward. "Hi, Jack. It's good to see you."

Bennis whirled toward his brother. "Why did you bring Fran with you? Have you completely lost your mind? It's dangerous here! She could get hurt."

Fran moved forward and slapped the priest across his face. She reared back and swung again. Bennis ducked and the punch glanced off his arm. Cavanaugh grabbed Fran by both arms and pulled her back.

"Just who do you think you are talking to? You misogynous bastard!" she screamed. "It was *my* idea to come here! María's hurt. Tom and I want to help. We don't need your condescending bullshit!" She looked at his shelter and added, "You may know how to survive in the jungle, Jack, but you don't now shit about women!"

Chico stepped behind a tree with Sergio in his arms and said nothing.

Bennis rubbed his face. He felt the stubble of his fledgling beard. "I apologize, Fran. I just don't want you hurt. There have been a number of attempts at killing us since we got to Mompox. I didn't want you involved. I wanted to protect you."

Fran's face was red. A tear rolled down her cheek. "You don't get it, do you? You and Tom. Are all men like you? You say you want to protect us, but you really want to control us!"

"I'm sorry if I offended you, Fran, but it is dangerous here and I feel I have enough blood on my hands already. I don't need any more."

Cavanaugh put his arm around Fran and looked at his brother. Jack Bennis' shirt and pants were ripped and filthy. He looked more like a homeless drug addict than a priest. The drug reference reminded him of his quest to find Salvatore Anthony Russo, but he dismissed the thought and asked, "Tell us what happened."

For the next hour, Father Bennis told them about the letter he received from María, his trip to Mompox, his conversation with El Apredido, the man who followed him, his meeting with María, the murder attempt by the man on the motorcycle, their rescue of Margarita, her death in the hotel bomb, and María's shooting at the ferry. They sat in the shelter and listened. Whenever Bennis mentioned the man on the motorcycle, Chico would interject, "His name was Alejandro López. He killed my parents."

When he finished, Chico filled in some gaps. He told how he followed the Padre and the woman from Alejandro's shooting at them at the café. He gave more details about the shooting at the ferry, and he told them how he hid Alejandro's body, stole his motorcycle and weapon, and led the Padre to safety in the jungle.

Cavanaugh and Fran asked a number of questions.

Fran was concerned about María's condition and the need for the best medical treatment.

Cavanaugh wanted to know more about this El Apredido person and the drug he was said to be producing.

Chico eyed the collection of fruits the Padre had assembled in the shelter including zapote, grandadilla, camu-camu, and bananas. He held out the burlap bag with the two pineapples he had bargained for and said, "Padre, I thought you and Sergio would be hungry so I brought you some pineapples, but I see you do not need them."

"Thank you for your thoughtfulness, Chico. You didn't need to do this. They say there are between 2,000 and 3,000 fruits that can be found in the rainforests. I was once trained to learn how to survive here. Sergio and I would not grow hungry."

"But what about María?" Fran asked. "How is she doing?"

Chico answered. "I checked at the hospital with my friend Nancy. She knows everything that happens in the hospital. She told me the woman you speak of is still in a coma. The doctors removed three bullets from her back, but one of them was very close to her spine. They do not know if she will walk again."

"What can you tell us about this El Apredido? Who is he and what kind of drug is he supposedly making here?"

"He is a bad man," Chico said.

"I don't know his real name. Everyone calls him El Apredido which means 'The Learned One.' From what I have been able to put together from María and others, he is making a unique genetically-altered drug some call the Devil's Breath. The drug is combined with other drugs and causes its victims to lose their memory and their free will. I came to Mompox to ask him to stop."

"Oh, Jack, how naïve can you be? Don't you remember Mom telling us that fools rush in where wise men fear to go? How could you expect this character to stop just because you asked him?"

Fran reached over and touched Jack Bennis' hand. They exchanged glances and she said softly, "But wise men never fall in love so how are they to know?"

Bennis lowered his head and nodded. "I tried to get him to stop the peaceful way. Maybe it was naïve and foolish. In any case, it didn't work. Now Margarita is dead and María has been shot. Now I have to do it another way. I owe it to them and to the others who would be affected by the Devil's Breath."

■ ■ ■

14

San Juan de Dios Hospital, Mompox

Stephano Sanchez sat on a folding chair outside María Isabelle's hospital room. Why was he guarding an unidentified woman? It made no sense to him. He was bored. He had read the sports pages of the local paper three times. His eyes were tired. The lines on the paper began to double and blur. He had trouble concentrating. Maybe he needed glasses. He closed his eyes to rest them and thought of how much he had enjoyed being a barber before joining the Mompox Police Department. He made more money now, but he was bored. When he cut hair for a living, he knew all the gossip in the town. He knew who was sleeping with whom. He knew who was selling and who was buying drugs. He knew who the best jeweler was and how much he made for a living. When he was a barber, he could give his opinions to his customers on everything from cooking and politics to sex and medicine. He enjoyed joking with his regulars. He felt the pulse of the community and reveled in it. As a police officer in Mompox, however, no one trusted him. The people who shared intimate stories and politically incorrect jokes with him in his barber shop now regarded him with suspicion, deceitfulness, and hostility. His uniform conveyed power, authority, and status, and the people resented him.

Stephano drifted off imagining how monotonous and dull his job as a police officer in Mompox was. But here he didn't have to combat the danger in Cali or Medellin. He didn't worry about a traffic stop leading to an armed attack or a sniper firing from a rooftop or a young burglar fleeing with an automatic gun tucked into his belt. While danger was always a possibility in a domestic dispute or the arrest of drunken revelers, the money he received from bribes, payoffs, and kickbacks were lucrative compensations he looked forward to. He had a good house, his wife had fine jewelry, and he had money in the bank. He was dreaming about the wisdom of his choice to pursue material gains over happiness when he felt the cold muzzle of a Grach pistol pressing against his forehead.

He dropped the newspaper and froze. His hands shook. His eyes widened and he saw a tall, muscular man in a camouflage uniform staring down at him. The man's face was scared and pock-marked, but there was death in his dark eyes. "Move and you are dead," the man whispered.

Stephano shifted his eyes and saw another man leveling a submachine gun at him. He raised his hands slowly and wished he were still a barber.

■ ■ ■

A tall, thin man dressed in a multi-colored flowered shirt, blue designer denim jeans, and a Yankee baseball cap entered María Isabelle's hospital room. Angela Vicario, a heavyset nurse in her early fifties, and Dr. Dionisio Iguarán, a young doctor who looked like he just got out of high school, hovered over her bed like a couple of honey bees buzzing over a fruit tree. "How is she doing, Doctor?" the tall man asked.

"Who are you?" Dr. Iguarán demanded. "Visiting hours are over! You don't belong here!"

Behind the tall man stood a tall, statuesque woman in a long flowing blue gown and behind her a nervous, short man with a black leather bag.

"What's the meaning of this?" Nurse Vicario shouted. "Get out of here before I call security!"

Then both the nurse and the doctor saw the stern faced man in a camouflage uniform blocking the doorway, holding a submachine gun.

"I am her brother," the man in the multi-colored shirt replied. "Work with us and nobody needs to get hurt."

The young doctor stepped away from María's bedside. The older nurse, however, folded her arms and blocked the man's passage. "I don't know what you want, but you have no right to be here!"

The tall, thin man suddenly slapped the nurse across the face sending her into a cart beside the bed. "Get out of the way," he said. "I warned you. I am not going to warn you again." As the nurse struggled to get up, the statuesque woman bent to help her.

The man addressed the young doctor. "Tell me what happened and what her condition is."

While the doctor explained, the man with the leather bag approached María's bed and read her chart. The nurse exclaimed, "You can't do that! It's confidential."

The tall, thin man motioned to the armed man in the doorway. "Shoot her if she opens her mouth again." The young doctor motioned to the nurse to be silent and told them the woman had been shot in the back three times at the ferry landing. A man who was with her was killed. Two of the bullets that hit her were non-lethal, but one was lodged close to her spine. They put her in an induced coma until they could determine the best method of treatment.

"Where are her X-rays?" the man reading her chart asked.

"In my office. I was waiting for the staff to come in today to discuss appropriate treatments. We do not usually treat critical cases like hers here."

"Carlos," the thin man said to the armed guard in the doorway, "take the nurse to the doctor's office and get the X-rays. If she causes any trouble, kill her."

■ ■ ■

When the police chief called El Apredido to inform him of the military presence at the hospital it was almost noon and El Apredido was fully dressed and clutching a Glock Model 18 in his hand. Ten of his armed associates guarded the perimeter of his house and another six patrolled the inside of the house awaiting orders.

It must be the woman, he thought. They came for her. But why? Perhaps the priest had sent a message. That damn priest was a thorn in his side. He must be removed. He told the police chief, "We need to end this situation. Have your man at the hospital kill the woman. Whoever she is, she is involved with that meddlesome priest. Her death will draw him out!"

El Apredido was not prepared for El Capitán's answer. "I have had enough of your orders! If you want her killed, you will have to do so yourself. I am through answering to you!"

"You insolent rogue, you have lived too long! I pay you well to do what I say. You know what I will do to your family. I will chop your wife and children up piece by piece and feed them to the caimans!"

El Capitán laughed, "You will have to find them, El Apredido. They left Mompox hours ago with a police guard!"

"I will torture and kill you slowly. I'll spurn your eyes like balls before me. I'll unhair thy head. Thou shalt be whipped with wire and stewed in brine, you lily-livered coward! You owe me!"

"I owe you shit! I have had it with your killings, your intimidations, your drug dealings. I will have no more of it! You are on your own now!"

El Apredido felt his blood pressure rising. He shook his Glock in the air. "You are a dead man, El Capitán!" He went on talking and shouting insults and threats into his phone, but the line had already gone dead.

■ ■ ■

Cavanaugh sat cross-legged in his brother's shelter and asked about the drug called the "Devil's Breath." Bennis explained, as far as he could learn, it was a derivative of scopolamine, but it had long lasting effects. Supposedly, it acted like a hallucinogenic and an amnesiac. It was said to have a hypnotic effect on its victims.

"Unlike normal drugs," he said, "this one robs its victims of their free will and they have no memory of what they do while under its influence."

Cavanaugh thought of his encounter with Big Louie and how he was able to get him to hand over two hundred dollars. When he tried to give it back, Big Louie didn't believe he gave it to him.

"Why are you so interested in this drug, Thomas?"

"We came here to help you and María, but before I left, Fran's aunt and cousin asked me to find a guy called Salvatore Russo. He seems to have been developing a drug with similar, long-lasting effects."

"It's a strange world, Thomas. But I don't think there is a connection. María's brother's name is Santiago Rodriguez."

"But, Padre," Chico said while sharing a banana with Sergio, "they have the same initials – S. R."

Cavanaugh never believed in coincidences, but then again he never believed in omens either. He wanted to question what El Apredido's real name was, but, for the time being, decided to let this one slide. "So how are we going to get this El Apredido character and get María the medical treatments she needs? Fran tells me this hospital she is in dates back to the 1500s and the doctors are working there without pay. We need to get her to another place."

"First, we have to get rid of El Apredido. He ordered the hit on María and me. I don't think he knows who she is – or at least not yet – which could give us some time. If he knew she was with me, he would probably have her killed to draw me out. And it would work."

Father Bennis turned to Chico. "Do you know where this El Apredido lives? I doubt he lives in the chop-house shack in the middle of the wetlands."

"Sí, Padre, you are correct. He lives in a big house with carved doorways, flowers from the balconies, and a beautiful courtyard. The house overlooks the Magdalena River. It is one of the most beautiful old buildings in Mompox."

"Good. Now we are going to need to prepare." Fr. Bennis turned to his brother and Fran. "Are either of you claustrophobic or afraid of the dark?"

"What are you talking about, Jack?"

"Well, Chico here has discovered a series of tunnels made by the Muisca Indians a long, long time ago…."

Chico stood up. "No, Padre! They will tell!"

"No, they won't, Chico. They're family. We need to go back and get the AK-47 and the motorcycle before it gets dark and your jaguar friend becomes hungry."

Chico adjusted his sombrero, rubbed his hands together, and frowned.

"I know you don't like the idea, Chico, but if we are going to stop this El Apredido, we are going to need the gun and the motorcycle." Bennis hesitated and then added, "We don't want him hurting any more people like he did to your family."

Chico lowered his head and nodded, and then he and Sergio led the way back to the Muisca tunnels. As they trekked through the jungle, Bennis turned to Cavanaugh and Fran and said, "Brace yourselves for something you have never seen before and something you must promise to keep secret. We're family here and we need to stick together."

■ ■ ■

The way El Apredido looked at it, he had lost three of his loyalist "drones," but there were always more "drones" to take their place. They answered to him and him alone. The police chief was a fool. After this situation was resolved, he would hunt him and his family down and butcher them all like pigs in a slaughterhouse. No one crossed El Apredido and got away with it.

But the Jesuit priest was proving to be an extreme nuisance. S. R. was smart to send him. But the reinforcements he sent were not as good. His men had killed them all, dismembered their bodies and fed them to the caimans in the wetlands. Was S. R. behind the helicopter landing and the armed vehicle at the hospital? Had S. R. himself come with even more force this time? But what was at the hospital that he would risk coming to Mompox for in the midst of a violent storm? It seemed logical it had something to do with the woman shot at the ferry. What was her relationship to S. R.? And what happened to the priest? Where was he?

El Apredido paced up and down his room, consciously avoiding the window. He glanced at the complete works of Shakespeare in his bookcase. He thought of Shakespeare's Julius Caesar and how he said it was most strange that men should fear death seeing that death was a necessary end that would come when it would come. And yet, he was afraid. His hands were cold and shaking. He didn't like this feeling. It wasn't like him to be afraid. He looked back at the painting of Abraxas and shouted, "Who is this damn priest?"

On his large desk lay the detailed plans for his destruction of the world's economy. It would all be coordinated. It would start small and escalate rapidly like a wildfire in parched woods. The timing was essential. A series of power grid outages along the Eastern seacoast of the United States; a nuclear crisis at Indian Point and Nine Mile Point 1 and Nine Mile Point 2 in upstate New York, and the synchronized blockage and disruption of traffic on all bridges and tunnels into and out of New York City. A communication would be sent to all major media outlets across the world in anticipation of the "main event." He grinned, "And It would all be done without firing a shot from a remote 'frozen in time' town in Colombia, South America."

The Devil's Breath was the key ingredient. The key people had already been "infected" with the drug and were under its hypnotic effect. They would have no recollection of what they did and no control to stop themselves. The new formula they had developed would enable the drug to be dispensed as a gas. The damage would be done before anyone realized it. Markets would collapse. There would be panic in the streets. Riots would ensue. Looting was a guarantee. Chaos would spread across the globe. It would be the start of a new world order.

The unsuspecting "drones" were in place. The seeds had been planted. He knew how to manipulate people. He studied human nature enough to anticipate behavior. Enough would react to influence the rest, and they would react like lemmings going over a cliff.

But El Apredido realized it would be a pyrrhic victory if he were dead and did not live to see the fruits of his destruction. He concluded, the priest must die, the woman must die, and, if he got in his way, S. R. must also die.

He looked back at the portrait of Abraxas and its chicken-like head seemed to smile and nod in agreement.

■ ■ ■

Father Bennis prepared some torches from dead leaves and twigs to carry into the caves. He told them it would save batteries and better light the way, but he also wanted to see the flow of air through the tunnels. Perhaps, he thought, there were other exits from the unexplored tunnels.

Their first mishap occurred quickly. Climbing down the narrow entrance to the subterranean tunnel, Fran fell and twisted her ankle. "I'm all right," she insisted, but her limp told everyone – including Sergio – it was a lie.

As they proceeded slowly through the tunnel, they could see more clearly. Bennis noted the ground was wet and water dripped from the ceilings and rolled down the walls. Cavanaugh helped Fran, but he too noticed the water.

Chico led the way. He cautioned, "Be careful, señor and señora. The ground is wet and muddy. I think it is because of the heavy rains last night." Bennis and Cavanaugh looked at the water but said nothing.

When they reached the large open area, the walls seem to dance in gold from the light of their torches. Cavanaugh and Fran stood speechless. Fran asked, "What is this place?"

"As near as I can explain," Bennis began, "this is part of an ancient series of subterranean tunnels built by the Aztecs, the Incas, the Muisca, the Mayans and probably a number of other groups to hide their possessions from marauding Conquistadors in the sixteenth and seventeenth centuries. Erich von Daniken wrote a book called *The Gold of the Gods* about a secret network of underground tunnels such as this throughout parts of South America. Supposedly, these civilizations hid their treasures of gold and precious metals in a labyrinth of secret tunnels."

"That sounds ridiculous," Cavanaugh said.

"Maybe, but when I was studying to become a priest, I came across references of various Catholic priests who, in their quest to convert the natives, came across what they called a subterranean 'Village of the Underworld.' One group of priests wrote about exploring a series of tunnels and discovering a huge room, similar to this one, supported by a sophisticated arch-roof buttressed by large stone pillars. As they advanced, however, they were overcome with a horrible, putrid, dark smell and numerous snakes that lurked in the shadows of their torches."

"What did they discover?" Fran asked.

"Well, nothing like this," Bennis admitted. "They were petrified and declared the place an entrance to Hell and placed large stones in the entrance so that no one could enter it again."

"That sounds like a horror story you would tell Girl Scouts around a campfire."

"I agree, Fran," Cavanaugh said, "but I seem to remember vaguely reading somewhere once about some Spanish explorer who claimed there was a 'garden of the sun' buried in some underground passage." He looked around the room and asked, "Do you think this could be it? How the hell did you find this place?"

"Chico accidently found it when digging after his parents were murdered."

Cavanaugh moved through the statues. "Do you think this could be real gold?"

"It's possible, maybe even probable."

"This must be worth millions!"

Fran limped over to the altar. Behind it she could see and hear the waterfall. She lifted a gold chalice. "This is heavy," she said. "If this is solid gold, this alone would be worth well over a million dollars!"

Chico clutched Sergio with his left arm and held his torch up high. "It is not for sale!" he shouted. "This is a sacred place!"

Fr. Bennis explained. "Chico is convinced greedy people will exploit these sacred items of the Muisca for profit, that some would melt the gold destroying the remnants of an ancient civilization, and that modern-day Conquistadores would desecrate the work of a lost culture."

Cavanaugh felt the intricate details on the head of the gold shepherd guarding his flock of sheep. He nodded, "He's probably right. Everything seems to be about profit nowadays. I think some people would sell their own mother for a few extra dollars, let alone a million or two."

"So where does that leave us?"

Bennis smiled. "You always were the practical one, Fran. My brother needs you." He walked to the AK-47 resting on the side of the nine foot statue of Goranchacha. He lifted it up and handed it to Cavanaugh. "Thomas and I are going to take the late Alejandro's weapon and motorcycle and go to the hospital to see how María is doing. Along the way we may meet some of El Apredido's men. You, Fran, stay here with Chico and Sergio. We will call you when we need you."

"But I want to go with you!" Fran insisted.

"Your ankle injury will hold us back. I will call you when things have been taken care of."

"How are you going to call us?"

"I will take Alejandro's phone. You keep yours."

"But, Padre," Chico said, "You don't know where I left the motorcycle."

"I will follow the trail we left."

"He's good at that," Cavanaugh said checking the AK-47. "He makes MacGyver look like a Webelo."

"I don't know what 'MacGyver' and 'Webelo' are."

"Chico, my brother means that years ago I was trained to survive in the jungle and to follow trails. It was part of my life a long time ago when I served in the Special Forces. Say a prayer for us. That jaguar of yours is not the only dangerous animal out there and we can't tell where our path will lead until we reach the end of the road."

■ ■ ■

The tall, thin man in the multi-colored shirt stepped closer to María Isabelle's bedside. He removed his Yankee cap. The tall, stately woman stood behind him. Dr. Peters, the short man with the black leather bag, went to work immediately. "Why is she intubated?" he asked the young doctor.

"She was unconscious when she arrived and had lost a lot of blood. Her lung was collapsed and she had trouble breathing. We induced the coma to alleviate her pain, ventilate her lungs, and prevent the possibility of asphyxiation."

"What is her current condition?"

"She is stable. Her vital signs appear to be normal, but she was shot three times. One bullet passed completely through her causing only superficial muscle damage. One bullet is lodged in her liver. The third bullet is close to her spinal cord. She may never walk again."

The nurse returned with the armed guard. Her lip was swollen and a thin line of blood flowed from her nose. She gave the X-rays to Dr. Peters. He looked at her and said, "Wipe the blood and the sullen look off your face and you will be fine." He studied the pictures for a few minutes, nodded, and then extracted a needle from his black leather bag. He pulled back the blanket covering her feet and stuck the needle in her foot testing her reflexes. "Excellent knee and ankle jerk, no upturning of her toes," he muttered to himself.

Then he turned to the tall, thin man in the multi-colored shirt and said, "She has sensation and good reflexes, Chago. With physical rehabilitation she should walk again, but we need to get her out of this hell-hole."

Chago nodded and the tall woman behind him touched his shoulder. "I told you Dr. Peters would know, didn't I? He is the best."

"You did, Aunt Joe."

Dr. Peters examined María Isabelle with his stethoscope and rechecked her chart. "Her vital signs are good. Her blood gases are good. Her lung was probably aspirated but has re-expanded." He turned to the young doctor and said, "Take her off the respirator, remove the intubation, and bring her out of the induced coma. Your tests indicate no evidence of brain injury. We are going to move the patient to a medical facility better equipped to treat cases like this."

"But you can't!" the young doctor objected. "She needs treatment. The roads in and out of Mompox are too treacherous. The ferry would take too long."

Chago stepped forward and placed both hands on the young doctor's shoulders. "We have our ways, Doctor. Now step aside and do as Dr.

Peters tells you. This is my sister you are dealing with. If anything happens to her, I am holding you responsible. And you do not want to anger me. Understand?"

The guard from the hall approached Chago and whispered in his ear. "The cop's radio went off. His chief advised him to get out of here. He warned him that El Apredido was sending men here to kill the woman. He said he had had enough of El Apredido's abuse, threats, and violence and, after he did one more thing, he himself was getting out of Mompox. He advised the cop to do the same."

■ ■ ■

Jack Bennis found Alejandro's Harley-Davidson without any trouble. He drove and his brother clung to him for as if his life depended on it. Cavanaugh had the AK-47 slung over his back. "Go easy, will you, Jack? I don't want to fall off this thing. I don't have a helmet, you know."

Bennis accelerated and narrowly avoided a huge tree. "Hang on, Thomas. Have I ever let you down?"

"Are you kidding? What about the time you lit my pajamas on fire?"

They hit the root of a mangrove tree and flew into the air. Bennis felt his brother's arms tightening around his waist.

"Come on, Thomas, I was just checking if your pajamas really were flame-retardant." A low hanging branch narrowly missed their heads. "I just was looking out for my baby brother."

"You were a freaking pyromaniac!"

They skidded through a muddy patch and a rafter of wild turkeys scattered ahead of them.

"And what about the time you scared the hell out of me when you started crying, 'Help! The Crawlspace Monster's got me' and then you climbed out of your bed and grabbed me!"

Bennis shouted over the noise of the Harley-Davidson, "You always were a ninny! I was trying to make a man out of you!"

"What about the time you glued my sneakers to the floor?"

"You may have a point there, but Mom grounded me for a week for that one. You were lucky though. I was planning to put the glue inside your shoes."

They skinned trees and flew over rocks and boulders until they left the woods and entered the quiet streets of Mompox. Bennis slowed down. He checked carefully for police and El Apredido's men. The only things in the road were chickens running loose. "If you were honest, Thomas," he said, "you would recall how you used to rip up my homework and once you hid a term paper I had worked on for a month."

"You never proved it was me!"

"I suppose my guardian angel stole it or the dog we never had ate it!"

"I'm not admitting anything, but you deserved it!" Then Cavanaugh started to chuckle. "Do you remember those peanut butter and jelly sandwiches Mom used to make for us to take to school?"

"Yes. I seem to remember that some of them had a lot more jelly than others."

"Yeah, well that was to cover up the poops I mixed in with the peanut butter."

Bennis slammed on the brakes and started to retch. "You didn't!"

A cock crowed in the distance. Cavanaugh smiled, "No, but I almost did. You're lucky I have a conscience."

"Some of those sandwiches did taste a bit funny. You did it, didn't you? Admit it!"

"You'll never know," Cavanaugh said and pointed to an old three story orange brick irregular shaped building that looked more like a prison than the San Juan de Dios Hospital the sign in front said it was. In the parking lot was an unoccupied police car and blocking the main entrance to the hospital was a large Cadillac Escalade and a fully armed man in a camouflage uniform.

"We'll take this up later, Thomas. I promise. But now's not the time. I don't like the look of that armored car and the empty patrol car. Chico showed me a back entrance. We can go through the kitchen and up the stairs. Things could get messy fast. Stay close. I don't want to lose you."

As they started to go in the back entrance, they both heard the screeching of tires and turned to see three late-model Ford Fusions pull into the parking lot and then a series of shots rang out.

■ ■ ■

15

Chago heard the shots, too. "Contact base, Manuel, and have the helicopter pick us up here. Tell them we are being assaulted." He withdrew a Smith & Wesson Model 629 .44 Mag, capable of killing a cape buffalo, from his waistband. "You and Bayardo cover the stairwells."

"We need more time, Chago," Dr. Peters said. "María is starting to come out of the coma."

Chago bent over his sister. "María, you will be fine. We are taking you to a better facility. Who did this to you?"

María's mouth was dry. Her voice harsh. "Chago? Is that you? Where is Jack?"

"Jack? Who is Jack? Did he do this to you?"

"No," a voice came from the doorway. Chago turned to see his two soldiers backing up with their hands in the air. Two white men, one with an AK-47 and the other holding a .45 pistol stood in the doorway.

"Jack," María said trying to get up. He ran to her and clutched her outstretched hand. "I am here, María."

The woman in the blue dress spoke. "The one with the AK-47 is the man I told you about. His name is Cavanaugh. This must be his brother, the priest who was with María."

The sounds of gunfire and explosives echoed through the hospital halls. Cavanaugh spoke first, "Listen, folks, we don't have much time. We are here to help. There are three carloads of guys with guns coming here. We need to work together."

"Chago," María's voice was weak. "Jack is a priest. I asked him to help me stop that drug you told me about. He came here to talk to El Apredido."

"That was foolish. Who shot you?"

Bennis answered. "A man named Alejandro. I killed him, but not before he was able to shoot María. He was sent by El Apredido."

"Listen, guys," Cavanaugh said, "we don't have time to chit-chat here. I don't hear anymore firing outside. Pretty soon they will be coming up the stairs looking for María. I think it's time to shit or get off the pot. What do you say we work together? We can talk later."

"He is right, Chago," Aunt Jo said. She slowly lifted up her long flowing blue gown in the most provocatively sexy move Cavanaugh had ever seen and withdrew two Desert Eagle .50 caliber handguns from ankle holsters on both legs. Cavanaugh nodded appreciatively. He liked her style. Aunt Jo definitely wasn't your typical 92-year-old woman.

Fr. Bennis stood and looked around the room. He spoke to the young doctor. "How many patients are on this floor?"

"She is the only one."

"Good. Chago, have your men wrap those two oxygen tanks in the corner with blankets. Pour those bottles of isopropyl alcohol over the blankets and then roll them and the anesthesia machine down the hall blocking the stairwell they will be coming up. Then you and your people take María down the stairway at the other end of the corridor. My brother and I will create a diversion for you. One shot in the oxygen tank should work, but we could use a couple of your RGN fragmentation grenades as a backup."

"My men will stay with you."

"No. You will need them when you leave the hospital. There may be more of El Apredido's men out there."

"He is right, Chago," Aunt Jo said. "Give them the grenades. We need to go!" She took the large valise Dr. Peters had carried with him and turned to Dr. Dionisio Iguarán. "When we are gone, there will be some damage. Take this, repair the damage and upgrade this hospital. What is left divide among the staff."

The two camouflaged men returned and started wheeling María down the hall. Aunt Jo, Chago, and Dr. Peters followed them. They could all hear the sound of people on the stairway by the oxygen tanks. "Go quickly. Take care of María," Bennis said. "I will take care of El Apredido."

■ ■ ■

Fran limped around the huge cavern in the flickering lights from the torches. The images painted on the walls seemed to dance in the shimmering lights. Fran noticed the flames flowed in the same direction. She looked around the room at the different tunnels. She felt a slight breeze coming from one of the tunnels. "Chico," she asked, "where do those tunnels go?"

"I do not know, señora. I only know where two of the tunnels go – the one the Padre and your husband went out and the one we came in. I have been afraid to go into the other tunnels. There is a bad smell in that one on the left. It smells like something is dead in there."

"What about the one on the right? There seems to be a breeze flowing from that one." She started to walk toward the tunnel.

Chico ran after her. "No, señora, please do not go there. It is bad luck."

"There is a stream of fresh air coming from that tunnel, Chico. You can see it in the flames from the torches. Let's see where it goes."

"I do not like this, señora. Let us wait until the Padre and your husband return."

Suddenly, they both felt the ground beneath them shutter and the muffled sounds of gunfire and explosions echoed down the tunnel. Sergio clung to Chico's neck. Fran picked up a gold and silver spear from one of the statues and started down the dark tunnel on the right. "Bring a flashlight and follow me, Chico," she said. "There must be an entrance to these tunnels somewhere. These statues didn't walk here by themselves. I think it may be down this tunnel. This is where the air is coming from and the noise of explosions."

Chico, Sergio, and Fran walked slowly into the tunnel on the right. The walls were wet and smelled of mold. As they continued down the winding tunnel, their feet splashed in water. "We should go back, señora. Sergio is afraid."

"Listen, Chico. I hear running water ahead."

Their lights flashed upon a collection of rocks ahead blocking their way. Through the rocks, a slight stream of daylight could be seen. "Help me, Chico. The passage is blocked. Help me move some of these rocks. I think this is an entrance to the tunnels."

"It is not good to fool with the gods, señora. We must go back."

Fran stood in ankle deep water and began to remove the stones by herself. She used the spear to pry some of the stones loose. The rocks cut her hands but she worked feverously. As the rocks fell, her hands were bloody, but they saw a trickle of water and sunshine on the other side. Chico placed his flashlight down, pulled his sombrero down, and bent to help her. Sergio joined in as if it were a game throwing rocks in all directions. The sounds of gunfire decreased as they heard an approaching whoop-whoop-whoop passing over them. Gradually, they managed to open a gap in the rocks big enough to squeeze through.

Chico and Fran looked down at a narrow path behind a waterfall. Inching their way carefully along the slippery, moss covered rocks, they saw through the thick foliage beyond the cascading waters glimpses of smoke rising from the town of Mompox below them.

■ ■ ■

The only sound in the parking lot of San Juan de Dios Hospital's parking lot when the helicopter landed was the whoop-whoop-whoop of the helicopter blades. Bodies of El Apredido's men lay strewn across the asphalt like Lego blocks discarded by distracted children. Three Ford Fusions smoldered from direct hits from the 57 mm rocket pods on the helicopter.

As Cavanaugh and Bennis emerged from the hospital, they saw María being carried into the Mi-17 helicopter and Chago's men policing the area for weapons and bodies. Walking toward María's brother, Bennis pocketed his gun and raised his hands. "Chago!" he called out. Four armed men pointed their submachine guns at him and his brother.

Chago waved his men away and approached Bennis. He spoke in Spanish. "Thank you for telling me about my sister. What do you want?"

"I have a question. Why did you tell María Isabelle that you were working for a drug cartel in Medellin and wanted to get out? As far as I can see, you are the leader of the cartel."

Chago rubbed his thin, drawn face and scratched his nose. He closed his eyes for a few seconds, pursed his lips and then stared with tired, unblinking eyes at Bennis. He didn't look well. "When I saw my sister, I did not know what to say. I left home so long ago and have done so many things she would not approve of. I told her a story to hide the person I have become."

Aunt Jo glided quietly up to him and placed her hand on his shoulder.

"No one is compelled to continue along the same paths in life. It's not easy, but with the help of God we can all change," Bennis said. "You told your sister about this drug called the Devil's Breath. Why? She came here planning to kill this El Apredido, and because of her I came to try to talk him out of what he was doing."

"I will be honest with you, Padre. I had heard stories about this drug and its ability to put people in a hypnotic state and rob them of their will and their memories, but I knew nothing about it. I was curious about learning more. I never thought she would come to this godforsaken place to kill El Apredido."

"She did it for you, Chago. And I did it for her. She almost got herself killed because of you. It's never too late to change."

Aunt Jo tugged at Chago's arm. "We must go," she said.

Santiago "Chago" Rodriguez extended his hand and smiled. "Thank you, Padre." His grip was hard and strong. He shook his head back and forth, "Trust me, Padre. I have no interest in this El Apredido person. I will think about what you have said and I will take care of my sister. I promise."

Father Jack Bennis observed a number of dark, decaying teeth in Chago's smile. He shook his hand saying, "And I will take care of El Apredido. I promise."

■ ■ ■

As the helicopter rose into the sky and a fire engine siren approached, Cavanaugh turned to his brother. "You don't believe him, do you?" he asked.

"About taking care of his sister? Yes. She is family. He'll do right by her."

"No, I mean about that other crap about not being interested in El Apredido and the Devil's Breath."

Bennis smiled, "Thomas, he's a pathological liar and a drug user. He has a typical meth mouth caused of excessive drug use. Lying is as natural as breathing to him. It's part of his trade."

"I was hoping you would notice. The way he stared at you was typical of liars. It was freaking scary the way he stared at you. I took a course at the Police Academy given by the famed criminalist John Dearie. He said people who lie often maintain uncomfortable eye contact. Most of us look away occasionally, but Chago locked eyes on you like a laser. 50% is normal, but that guy looked like he had a crush on you."

"I took a similar course with Professor Dearie in Quantico, Thomas. He also indicated people touch their face often when lying. Did you see how he kept scratching his face and nose?"

"Yeah. I read somewhere where Bill Clinton touched his nose dozens of times when lying to the Grand Jury about his relationship with Monica Lewinsky. But he never touched it when he was telling the truth."

"I don't know about that, but Chago's smile was as phony as a three dollar bill. A real smile involves the whole face including the eyes. His mouth was the only part that smiled. He was lying through his teeth as corroded as they were."

"So what do we do now?"

Bennis looked around at the parking lot. It looked like a war zone. "We get out of here and find this El Apredido character before Chago does. We still have miles to go, Thomas, before we sleep and I have a promise to keep."

■ ■ ■

El Apredido heard the gunfire and the explosions and the whoop-whoop-whoop of the helicopter. He clutched his gun in his hand and peered out behind the burgundy drapes in his den. As the helicopter slowly disappeared in the distance following the Magdalena River eastward, a momentary silence seemed to fall on Mompox like a woolen blanket had suddenly been thrown over the town. He smelled the dissipating odor of gunpowder and moisture in the air. A cock crowed somewhere in the distance and Mompox seemed to awaken from its slumber.

He tried calling the men sent to the hospital. But there was no answer. He tried calling the police chief, but the call went to voicemail. He tried calling the hospital, but no one answered. He was alone.

But there was still time. The pieces were all in place. He was smart, some would even say brilliant. He had earned an M.A. degree at Yale and a PhD in English Literature at NYU. He knew what he was doing and they were completely in the dark. They would be blindsided by his sudden, elaborate plans.

There was still time. Saturday and Sunday the Stock Markets in New York would be closed. Monday the world would hear from El Apredido and the world economic system would begin to crumble. Disruption, panic, riots, pandemonium would follow. The richest people in the world control the mainstream media, industry, trade, banks, schools, unions, energy supplies, healthcare, pharmaceuticals, research and government. When their system begins to crumble, El Apredido believed, they would also crumble. He who controls the world's money controls everyone. The rich know this and prosper from the debt of others, whether they are the poor, the middle class or state governments. Once their system is destroyed, they will lose their power and influence. The world will no longer be manipulated and controlled by the few. When the corrupt, powerful, wealthy conspirators lose their power, the people will rise up and assume a new world order. The present system only supports people with power and money. Once the system of wealth and power are transferred away from the conspirators and given to the hands of the masses who desire a better, fairer world, El Apredido will have reached his goal.

He gathered the plans on his desk and then looked up at the painting of Abraxas on the wall. He smiled and the painting seemed to smile back at him. Abraxas was the perfect symbol for this quest. He rolled up his sleeve and stroked the meticulous tattoo of the creature with the head of a rooster, the body of a man, and the legs of serpents, and it filled him with pride. Abraxas' hands clutched a whip and a shield, symbolic of wisdom and power. It was the perfect symbol. Carl Jung once called Abraxas the driving force of individualism, the supreme power which combined both the power of God and the devil and stood above both of them. Abraxas combined both good and evil, light and darkness.

El Apredido knew the Knights Templar used Abraxas in some of their seals during the Crusades. The Knights were a force to be feared. They were loyal and devoted totally to their cause just as El Apredido was to his. They went into battle without making a noise. They were committed to destroy the enemy or to die trying. And so was he.

People had died in his private crusade and more people would die. There would be much pain and suffering before the new world order would be established. He knew this and accepted it. It was a necessary part of his plan. The end would justify his means. He echoed Macbeth's words aloud, "Things bad begun make strong themselves by ill!"

He folded his plans quickly and carefully and placed them in a traveling bag. Outside bells were ringing and sirens screamed. He did not hear the door behind him slowly open. But he did hear the cocking of the gun. He turned and stared at the door.

"You!"

That was his last word as his precious plans dropped to the floor and a hollow-point bullet ripped through his heart, exactly seven inches below his red bowtie.

■ ■ ■

16

Tom Cavanaugh stood outside El Apredido's large colonial manor over-looking the Magdalena River. The house was enclosed by a high stone-walled fence and a wrought-iron gate. The whitewashed house with its red-tile roof and multi-colored flowers draped from its balconies would have made a picture-perfect postcard image against the clear blue sky.

As the sun beat down on him, he looked in the distance at the Moorish-style tower of the beautiful white San Barbara Church with its gold-paint-ed columns. He turned and stared at the open heavily carved large oak door of the mansion. He moved the AK-47 from one sweating hand to the other. He didn't like being out here alone. He wanted to be with his brother, to lend support if he needed it. But his brother insisted that he stay outside and guard the perimeter.

It reminded him of stakeouts he had been on when with the New York City Police Department. Then he would read stories about strange events and arcane facts to pass the time away. Now he had nothing to do but think.

A motorized boat called a *chalupa* went by on the Magdalena River. Somehow it seemed out of place in this isolated island-city that seemed frozen in time. He heard the sounds of chickens and birds and the clip-clop of a donkey-driven rickshaw on the cobblestone roadway close by. An eagle soared high above, and he remembered the blackbird in the back of his car. And then his first job as an unlicensed private investigator – to locate Salvatore Anthony Russo – came back to him. There were a number of things about this El Apredido that reminded him of Sal Russo. "El Apredido" means "The Learned One," and Sal Russo certainly was a smart guy. Russo had earned multiple degrees at big name schools. Cavanaugh recalled almost not graduating from high school because of trigonometry. Maybe that was the reason he never tried to balance his checkbook.

He felt the bump on his head. Russo's friends told him about his involvement in drugs. The letters he decoded from Russo's girlfriend indicated he was working on developing some long-lasting drug which made people do things they ordinarily wouldn't do. Cavanaugh saw that it worked when he got Big Louie to give him two hundred dollars. According to his brother, María, and Chago, El Apredido was working on a drug that would put its victims in some kind of a hypnotic state and rob them of their free will and memory.

It reminded him of the brainwashing of Sergeant Raymond Shaw in the movie *The Manchurian Candidate*.

Cavanaugh noticed two fishermen casually tying their long canoe to a mangrove tree by the bank of the river. What better place for Sal Russo to develop his Devil's Breath than in a quiet, isolated place like Mompox? It would make sense that gold-toothed, obnoxious Aunt Vincenza wouldn't want the police arresting her darling grandchild. Should he call her now and tell her he located her grandson and tell her he is a major drug dealer, a murderer, and a really "bad guy"?

He turned and looked back at El Apredido's house. "I shouldn't have let Jack go in there alone," he said. He knew Jack had a score to settle with El Apredido. He had had María shot and killed Chico's parents. No, Jack should not have gone into the house alone. There was something special between María and his brother. He didn't want to think about it, but he knew it was there. He had to stop him.

Cavanaugh started running toward the house. Then he saw Jack Bennis standing in the doorway. He looked pale.

"What happened, Jack? What did you do?"

The priest shook his head. "He's dead, Thomas."

"What did you do?"

"Nothing. I found him dead on the floor of his den. He had been shot once in the chest and then twice in the back of the head. I didn't do it! He was dead when I got there!"

"Holy shit!" Cavanaugh said. "Who was he, Jack? Was he the guy I was supposed to find? Was he Sal Russo?"

Bennis looked beyond his brother. "I have no idea, Thomas. Someone got to him before I did."

"I need to find out." Cavanaugh pushed his way passed Bennis. "Where's his body?"

"On the second floor, but what are you going to do?"

"I'm going to get his fingerprints. I need to find out if he is or was Sal Russo. Did you touch anything up there?"

"Only the door."

"Good. Now it's your turn to stay here. I'm also going to wipe your goddamn fingerprints off anything I think you may have touched."

Bennis grabbed Cavanaugh's arm. "I didn't kill him, Thomas. I swear I didn't."

"Save it for the confessional, Jack. I really don't give a shit. I'm just covering your ass."

■ ■ ■

Cavanaugh found El Apredido lying face down on an oriental carpet in his den. Blood seeped from the wounds in the former drug dealer into the carpet forming a new pattern of scarlet. The huge exit wound in his back contrasted with the relatively small entry wounds in his head. The first shot had killed him. The second and third shots in the back of his head would have blown his face apart. There was no way he would recognize El Apredido as the Sal Russo he had seen in the photo in Carolyn Hendershot's apartment.

Were the shots in the back of the head to insure his face would be unrecognizable? Were they the *coup de grâce*? Or were they meant as an added act of contempt and revenge?

He knelt down and felt El Apredido's neck. It was still warm. Whoever killed El Apredido had done it recently. His old detective skills kicked in. It didn't look good for his brother.

Cavanaugh stood and looked around the room. There were some papers scattered on the floor. A painting of Abraxas similar to the one he had seen in Carolyn Hendershot's apartment had been slashed. Why would his brother do that? He looked back at the body on the floor. He crouched down again. The skin on El Apredido's right arm had been scraped after he had been shot. It looked like a tattoo had been removed after he had been shot. But why?

It didn't make sense. Why would someone kill El Apredido, then shoot him the back of the head and then slash his painting and slice something from his arm? Or had El Apredido slashed the painting and his arm before he was shot? The lack of blood from the peeled away skin on his arm indicated that it had been done after he was dead.

"What do you think?" a voice behind him asked.

"I told you to wait outside."

"I thought I could help," Fr. Bennis said as he stepped gingerly into the room avoiding touching anything. "That's just the way I found him. What do we do now?"

Cavanaugh avoided stepping into the puddle of blood on the carpet. He shook his head. "It looks like he was shot with a high velocity round in the chest. When he fell forward, someone shot him twice in the back of the head. Whoever did it, slashed the painting over there and cut something off his arm. It doesn't add up. He would have had some bodyguards around him. Where are they?"

"I didn't see any on my way up here."

"Neither did I. Let's take a look around. Don't touch anything! When we get outside, I'm going to call Lt. Fraumeni. I met her in Bogotá. She helped us get here. Maybe she can help us get out of here."

In the kitchen on the first floor, they found two of El Apredido's bodyguards stuffed in a storage cabinet. The blood from their slashed throats had seeped out onto the white tile floor. Their bodies were cold and their blood was beginning to coagulate. Cavanaugh breathed a sigh of relief. The bodyguards had been killed quietly before he and Bennis arrived. Maybe his brother had not killed El Apredido. Maybe. But then, who did?

■ ■ ■

Cavanaugh called Lt. Fraumeni from the courtyard in front of El Apredido's house and told her what had happened. She told them to stay where they were and she would contact the local police. Both Cavanaugh and Bennis had an uneasy feeling about this, but they complied. An hour later, Lt. Fraumeni called back. "I've been unable to reach anyone but a clerk at the Mompox Police Station," she said. "Apparently, the Chief of Police there has left town and so has most of his department. I've received permission to come to you to handle the investigation since Chago was involved."

"Chago left with his sister in a helicopter. He's not involved," Cavanaugh said.

"Did you see him get into the helicopter?"

"Well, no, not exactly."

"He had a lot to gain with El Apredido's death."

"Can you tell us who this El Apredido really is? I've been working a case back in New York to find a missing guy named Salvatore Anthony Russo who seems to have been developing a drug like the Devil's Breath. I have a feeling he might be El Apredido."

"I can't say for sure. We will have to check fingerprints and dental records when we get there."

"I don't think dental records will help much as his face appears to have been blown apart by two shots to the back of his head."

"Then fingerprints will hopefully do it. Stay where you are. We'll be flying out to you in a few hours."

When they finished their call, Cavanaugh turned to his brother. "Are you hungry?"

Jack Bennis smiled. "Famished. Let's get Fran and Chico and get something to eat."

"And leave this place unguarded?"

"You're not a cop anymore, Thomas. We have food back in the tunnels or we could stop and get some arroz con coco or maybe some Soledeña sausage. I haven't had a hot meal in days."

"You can really eat after seeing that bloody scene back in the house?"

"Of course I can, and so can you. Maybe you would like to try a yucca fritta instead? It's a meat and cheese stuffed yucca. They say it's a Colombian favorite."

"Are you nuts, big brother? Do you know who you are talking to? How about a double-meat cheeseburger instead?"

"We have a few hours before your police lieutenant gets here. Let's go now. From what I have heard the people in Mompox pretty much mind their own business. I have one more thing I need to do before the police arrive, however. I feel I owe it to Chico and others. I could use your help, but I have to warn you, it might get a bit dangerous. Let me know if you would rather not get involved. "

"You've got to be joking! We have come this far, we might as well finish whatever it is you've got in mind. I've just got another call to make that I'm not looking forward to, Jack. I've got to call Sal Russo's grandmother to tell her I may have found her grandson. She's not going to be a happy camper, although I doubt she ever was. The woman scares me."

"Hold off on that call, Thomas. You can call her after we check out El Apredido's chop-house in the middle of the lagoon."

■ ■ ■

The two brothers rode the Harley-Davidson through the quiet streets of Mompox and headed straight to the lagoon. They rode by restaurants, colonial buildings, artisans' shops, churches, placid plazas, and the cemetery. Mompox residents looked at them, but went on about their business. Chickens scattered in the road ahead of them. An occasional tourist would smile at the two men huddled on the motorcycle and wave. They avoided stopping to eat and meeting up with Fran and Chico in the tunnels. They skirted the wooded area and went straight to the lagoon.

A number of hollowed out wooden canoes lined the shore of the lagoon which looked like a combination swamp, marshland, and lake. Dilapidated, grey wood houses stood on stilts about five feet above the water. The houses were grouped close to one another and clothes hung on lines between the houses. In the woods behind them they heard the sounds of birds and monkeys chattering away. In the center of the water stood the building Chico had pointed out to Jack Bennis as El Apredido's house of torture, the chop-house. From the moment he first learned about this building, Bennis wondered about it. Why did El Apredido keep people away from it? Was it merely intimidation? Was it to instill fear in people, to demonstrate his power? Or could it be something else? What was he doing in this building? What was the purpose of torturing people and feeding their dismembered bodies to the crocodiles or caimans? There was something in that isolated building in the middle of the water that El Apredido did not want people to know about. But what?

Jack Bennis explained his theory about El Apredido's chop-house to his brother.

"I think there's a reason El Apredido wanted to keep people away from that building. I think it may have something to do with manufacturing the drug Devil's Breath. He would need a place where he could develop it in secret and away from the prying eyes of the police and local people. Why else would he have armed guards guarding the place?"

"It makes sense to me, Jack, but what are you planning to do?"

"I'm going to visit it and see what's going on in there."

"Have you completely lost your mind? You said there are armed guards there! Chico told you they kill anyone who comes close to it. How do you plan to get there?"

"We borrow one of these canoes and row out to the building. We tell them we just came from El Apredido which we really did. They won't be expecting any trouble. We will use the element of surprise. Do you remember watching *Charlie Chan at the Wax Museum* when we were kids?"

Cavanaugh shook his head. "And what does Charlie Chan have to do with anything?

"His advice was good. 'Always prefer to utilize element of surprise, never to be victim.' Plus, if anything should go wrong, you have the AK-47 and I have a .45."

"And just what do you expect to find from this hair-brain scheme of yours?"

"We won't know until we get there, but I do have my suspicions."

"Jack, I seem to remember your friend Charlie saying something about an anxious man who hurries too fast sometimes stubs his big toe. Maybe we should wait for Lt. Fraumeni from Bogotá."

"Fair enough, Thomas. But timing is important here. If we want to find out who killed El Apredido we have to act now. You can stay here if you want and I will do this myself. I realize you have a wife and child to worry about. I have no one."

Cavanaugh grabbed his brother by the arm. "Hold on! Don't try to give me a guilt trip again. You did this when we were kids. We're in this together. I may think you're crazy, but I'm not about to let you go out there by yourself."

Bennis stared at Cavanaugh. "Are you sure you want to do this?"

"Is the Pope Catholic?"

"Okay. Then let's take that canoe tied to the mangrove tree and get started."

Cavanaugh slung the AK-47 over his shoulder and took a deep breath. Together the two brothers untied the canoe and started rowing out to the chop-house in the middle of the lagoon.

■ ■ ■

Fran and Chico sat on the narrow overgrown pathway carved into the side of the hill. They had inched their way under the waterfall by holding on to rocks and vines. Fran was tired and sat down with her back against the moist rocks. Chico and Sergio did the same. They looked out through a clearing in the trees at the serene scene below them. Fran inhaled deeply. The odor of clean, fresh air and the aroma of wild flowers and dense foliage were in sharp contrast to the musty, dank smell of the tunnel they had dug their way through.

Fran held the spear she had borrowed from one of the statues in the cave and dug it into the ground beside her. "The dirt is loose, Chico. The rain must have loosened some of the dirt and gravel under the rocks on this footpath. Over the years, fallen trees, undergrowth and erosion have made this path almost impassable and extremely dangerous. I can see why no one would find this pathway."

"Sí, you are right, señora. We should go back now."

"No, Chico, let's take a break and enjoy the moment for a while. Listen to the sounds of the birds and look at that beautiful sky. I think I can see a heron in the water below."

"Sí, señora, but I think we should go back. Sergio is getting nervous."

Fran extended her hand to the spider-monkey and it jumped into her lap. She tickled its white belly and it wrapped its long, slender arms around her neck. "I never thought spider-monkeys could be so tame."

"Sí, señora. Sergio lost his tail to the jaguar in these hills. I helped him. Monkeys like him use their tail to climb trees, get food, and get around. Now that he has no tail. I take care of him, and he is my friend."

Fran smiled and pointed the spear out to the lone house in the middle of the lagoon. "Do you know who lives in that house, Chico? It's so far from the other houses on the shoreline."

"That is a bad house, señora. El Apredido uses it to torture people. Anyone who goes near it is killed. He cuts their bodies up and feeds them to the caimans."

"Now why would he do that, Chico? That sounds like an old wives' tale."

"I do not know what an old wives' tale is, señora, but it is true. I have heard the chainsaw at night and the screams of people coming from that house. And I have seen body parts floating in the water. It is a bad house, señora. On my parents' graves, I promise you, it is a bad house. It is a death house."

■ ■ ■

Both brothers rowed in silence toward the chop-house. Each was caught up in his own thoughts.

Jack Bennis thought of Chico and how much the boy missed his parents. El Apredido had robbed him of something most of us never appreciate until it is gone. He thought how many things he would have liked to talk to his own parents about, how many thoughts he would have liked to share with them, how many questions he would have liked to ask them. He reflected on his father. His father was a bad man. He raped his mother, murdered Bennis' stepfather, and tried to rape his baby sister. As he rowed toward the chop-house and his oar hit the water, he recalled how he strangled his father to death with a lamp cord. Part of him would have done it again, but another part of him wished he could have talked to his father. Why was he the way he was? What motivated him? Did his father really love or even like his wife and family? Did he wish he could control himself better? Did he drink to forget or for regret? Or was it a disease he had no control over? What was life like for him growing up? Bennis looked ahead at the foreboding shack in the middle of the lagoon and thought how we can sin not only by what we do, but by what we fail to do.

For his part, Tom Cavanaugh's thoughts as he dug his oar into the water were about his brother's references to Charlie Chan. He remembered sitting in front of a 10" TV screen with his mother, his Aunt Mary Jane, his little sister and his brother watching black and white movies on Channel 5. He remembered watching wrestling and old Charlie Chan movies under a "fort" built from the couch cushions. Thinking back now, many of those movies would be considered racist. The actors who played Charlie weren't Asian and the comic relief came mostly from one of Charlie's many sons or from his black chauffeur, Birmingham. He recalled watching *Charlie Chan in Egypt* and remembered being upset even as a small boy by the stereotypical performance of the black actor Stephin Fechit. It was demeaning and insensitive, and yet Lincoln Theodore Monroe Andrew Perry whose stage name was Stephin Fechit made millions playing such stereotypical roles. It was a sign of the times back then, but the times had definitely changed. Sometimes, he felt, "political correctness" went overboard. In the case of racial bias and stereotyping, however, he thought, things had changed for the better. As they grew closer to the looming chop-house ahead, he realized this was not unfortunately the case in everything.

The closer they came to the chop-house, the more Cavanaugh thought back about his childhood. He liked it best when his father was not at home, which was most nights. Then they could all gather around the small TV and escape reality for a little while or until his father returned drunk and looking for a fight. Maybe that was why they liked watching wrestling; it was an escape from the real world. Everyone had his or her favorite wrestler. Cavanaugh's favorite was the barefooted Argentina Rocca. His Aunt Mary Jane somehow always seemed to cheer for the bad guy. Killer Kowalski and the Iron Sheik were her favorites. His mother's favorite was the former ballet dancer Ricky Starr. His little sister hooted for the huge 600 lb. overall clad Haystacks Calhoun. He couldn't remember who his brother's favorite was, but he thought it was probably Bruno "The Living Legend" Sammartino.

Jack Bennis' words came like a slap in the face. "We're almost there, Thomas. I don't see any guards. Be ready. I'm going to tie the canoe to one of the pilings."

■ ■ ■

17

It felt good to rest for a while on the narrow path. Fran looked at her hands. They were cut and filthy. Digging through the rocks had been more exhausting than she realized. Her fingernails were broken. She smiled thinking about whether she could make an appointment in Mompox for a manicure and pedicure. She examined her arms and legs and concluded she could use a warm bubble bath and a sleep in a comfortable bed.

"Señora, look!" Chico said. "Out on the lagoon! There is a canoe going toward the chop-house. This will be bad for the two fishermen in the canoe. We should go now."

Fran followed Chico's gaze. It was hard to see from where they were, but one of the fishermen wore a black shirt. The other wore what looked somewhat like a green and white shirt. It took a moment before she realized Cavanaugh was wearing a Jets' green and white jersey and Bennis was wearing a black clerical shirt. "No!" she screamed. "It can't be! We must warn them! Stop! Go back!"

Sergio heard it first. He jumped from Fran's arms into Chico's arms and started screeching loudly. Then Chico heard it. It was a low sound like a hacksaw cutting through wood. It was difficult to hear it with the waterfall behind him and Sergio's panicked shrieking, but he recognized it immediately. It was the ominous sound of the jaguar, and it was close.

Chico pulled Fran's arm and searched the trees around them. "Señora, we must leave! The jaguar is close!"

"But Tom and Jack are in that canoe!"

Then Fran heard it, too. It sounded like a deep, chesty cough. She looked up and saw the yellow and tan black-spotted head of a jaguar preparing to pounce from the tree above them.

■ ■ ■

So much can happen in a second or two; a text message when driving, the reflexive action of closing your eyes when sneezing, a careless word said never to be recalled. The unexpected happens with sometimes tragic results. Looking at the jaguar ready to pounce, Fran saw her father's face. Emotions overwhelmed her. He was angry. She pulled away to defend herself as the jaguar leapt from the branch above them.

As she shielded herself and pulled the spear closer to her, she didn't hear Sergio's screeching, Chico's warnings, or the cascading waterfall. She saw the jaguar's dark eyes honing in on her like a deadly laser. Its wide open mouth revealed huge powerful pointed canine teeth capable of puncturing a bowling ball. She felt its warm, strong fetid breath just before it hit. Then the impact of the jaguar's almost 200 lbs. hit her.

Its claws ripped through her blouse. She pulled back away from the jaguar's hungry jaw. Its body felt like it was crushing her. Suddenly, she lost her balance and slipped from the narrow path. Fran and the jaguar tumbled into the dense foliage beneath them.

She didn't know the jaguar has the strongest bite force of any cat. She didn't know it kills by biting the head of its victim. She didn't know the jaguar can kill anacondas and crocodiles. Fr. Bennis could have told her about an ancient Indian legend that the jaguar was the god of darkness, that its coat represented the stars and heavens, and that some ancient peoples believed eclipses were brought about when the jaguar swallowed the sun. Cavanaugh, her trivia-loving husband, might have told her the Aztec warrior god Tezcatlipoca is depicted as a jaguar and the jaguar played a chief role in Mayan rites with human sacrifices made to the Jaguar god.

But Bennis and Cavanaugh weren't there, and, as she fell through branches and trees with the violent slicing claws of the jaguar slashing at her arms and legs, her only thought was to survive. She closed her eyes and held on tight. Limbs and branches broke as she and the jaguar tumbled. Images of her infant son, her husband, and her family flashed before her. She didn't want to die.

When they hit the sandy ground of the beach below them, she thought this was the end. She had no fight left in her. Her arms were bleeding. Her body ached. But suddenly she realized the jaguar's deep, hoarse-like coughing roar had stopped. Its flailing limbs went lack. She opened her eyes and looked into the still eyes of the jaguar. Blood leaked out of its mouth as its tongue rolled out and its jaws slowly closed like a descending drawbridge.

She tried to push its heavy body off her and saw the gold and silver spear from one of the statues in the tunnel protruding through the jaguar's breast plate and exiting from its back.

■ ■ ■

As they approached the chop-house, they both heard the chilling sound of a chainsaw followed by a series of terrifying screams. Jack Bennis turned to his brother and put his index finger to his lips. He tied the canoe up to a piling next to a yellow motorized canoe similar to the larger *chalupas* seen on the Magdalena River carrying passengers to the mainland. Slowly and cautiously the brothers climbed the ladder to the dilapidated deck of the house. The screams and sounds of the chainsaw seemed louder now and even more frightening.

They stood momentarily before the door, took a deep breath, and then kicked the door open. They entered the dark room prepared for the worst. Both had their guns at the ready. But as they moved into the darkness amid the sounds of screams and sawing, cutting sounds, they didn't believe their eyes.

What looked like an elaborate sound system with speakers set up at each window broadcasted the deafening screams and chainsaw sounds. Bennis moved quickly to the generator in the corner and cut off the power. Suddenly the terrorizing sounds ceased. They looked around the dark room. There were no tortured bodies, no chainsaws. The room was empty except for the sound system and the generator.

"So much for the chop-house," Cavanaugh said.

Bennis nodded. "They set up a solid state digital beam which when crossed sets off the sound system. Brilliant idea. It keeps intruders away and instills fear."

"But Chico said he had seen body parts in the water."

"I don't doubt they killed people here and dumped their bodies in the water. But this system insured people would fear El Apredido."

They both heard the sound of a glass breaking in another room. A light was coming from the bottom of a door in the corner. "Looks like we're not alone, Jack."

Suddenly, bullets ripped through the door. They dove for the floor. There was more crashing of glass and then they smelled smoke. "Stay behind me, Thomas," Bennis said as he barged into the door and rolled on the floor. Cavanaugh followed.

The shooting stopped and they looked around. They were in a laboratory of some sort. Overturned tables, broken glass beakers, test tubes, measuring equipment, and various drug paraphernalia were tossed about the room. On a long table in the corner a stack of papers were ablaze by an open window. Cavanaugh rose to put out the fire. That was when he saw them. Five bodies lay motionless behind an overturned table. Each had been shot in the chest and then in the head. "Jack," he said, "there are bodies over here. Looks like they were shot just like El Apredido was."

Bennis moved cautiously to the window where he saw the yellow motorized canoe they had tied their canoe next to rapidly speeding away. "Looks like we have a problem," he said. He pointed to the diminishing canoe in the distance. There was one driver wearing what Cavanaugh thought was a colorful shirt of some sort.

"Shit!" Cavanaugh said. "We just missed him again!"

"That's not our only problem," Bennis said as he pointed to the canoe they had borrowed slowly floating away.

■ ■ ■

Behind them the fire intensified. They felt it on their backs. "What do we do now, Jack? We have no boat. The water is rampant with crocodiles. And the wood is so dry this place is going to light up like a tinderbox in a few minutes."

Bennis looked around the room. "The fire is going too fast. I don't see anything to put out the fire, but I have an idea. Let's go back to the other room and use that audio system to ask for help. And while we're doing that, you might try saying a few prayers."

Cavanaugh called Lt. Marion Fraumeni and told her what was happening. "She's still an hour away," he told his brother. "We'll be toast or fish food by then."

The priest went to the sound system and started asking in Spanish for help. Cavanaugh stood at the door, listened to his brother's message. He watched fishing boats in the lagoon stop, listen to the message, and then row away from the chop-house. "It's not working, Jack. They're still afraid of this place. The boats are moving away from us."

They heard burning wood crackling in the other room. The roof started to collapse. One of the pilings gave way. The building listed to one side. Smoke flowed under the door and breathing became difficult. Bennis kept broadcasting messages asking for help, but no help came. The fire now was coming through the wall. They could see the fire coming through the ceiling.

"Hold on, Jack. I've got an idea. It may not work, but it's worth a try. Give me the microphone and go to the door. Keep waving for help."

"What are you going to do?"

"Somehow I think this Devil's Breath drug is mixed up with the guy I was hired to find. It sounds like the drug he was working on. If I'm right, he might have experimented with it around here."

"So what are you going to do?"

"It's a long shot, but we don't have much time. I'll keep hoping and let you do the praying. Maybe between us something will work."

Fr. Bennis stood at the door desperately waving his shirt while over the loud speaker he heard his brother's voice asking a question over and over again, "Have you ever been to Cozumel?"

■ ■ ■

Fran lay exhausted in the sand. She struggled to get up, but the jaguar's heavy body and an assortment of tangled bushes and broken branches held her pinned to the ground. In the distance she heard a voice coming from the chop-house. It was Tom's voice repeating over and over again, "Have you ever been to Cozumel? Come to the chop-house. We need help!"

It didn't make any sense. Then she remembered the fishermen in the canoe – the black shirted one and the one with the green and white shirt. They were Tom and his brother.

She looked through the trees. She could see the water and a yellow *chalupa* speeding away from the notorious chop-house in the middle of the lagoon. Smoke billowed from the house. She had to get up. She had to help them. But the more she moved, the more thorns and briers dug into her. She screamed as loud as she could, "Help! Someone please help!"

Suddenly, she felt a branch being lifted from her leg. It was Sergio. He was trying to help. He screeched incessantly, but there was little he could do.

She looked back to the chop-house in the distance. There were flames shooting from its roof. Tom's voice continued, "Have you ever been to Cozumel? Have you ever been to Cozumel?"

She shouted, "Please, someone please help!"

A dark figure appeared between the trees. Behind it came another. And then another. They moved slowly, cutting back the thick underbrush cautiously. Fran continued to cry for help. Her voice cracked. She was crying. When they were a few feet away, they froze. They looked in fear and disbelief at the jaguar on top of her. One of the men pointed his fishing rod at the yellow and tan black-spotted coat of the massive cat, and they all stepped back. Fran sobbed, "It's dead! It's dead! Please help! My husband is on that building in the lagoon. He is in trouble. Please send someone to help him. Please!"

■ ■ ■

18

That night Dr. Dionisio Iguarán and Nurse Angela Vicario treated Fran's cuts and bruises. She had no broken bones, but numerous lacerations, scratches, and abrasions. Her most serious injuries were deep incisions on her arms and legs from the jaguar's claws. Some of them required stitches.

Lt. Marion Fraumeni and Sergeant Diego Coyle, a tall, muscular red-headed police officer she brought with her from Bogotá, sat with Fr. Jack Bennis, Tom Cavanaugh, and Chico around Fran as the doctor and nurse worked. "You are all lucky to be alive," Fraumeni said. "I told you to wait for me. You all could have been killed."

"It was close," Bennis said. "I'd say it was more than luck, however. I'd have to call it blessed. I am grateful someone heard the plea message I transmitted."

"I don't think it was your message, Jack. I think they responded to my message."

"Your message? Are you crazy? Your message made no sense. Why would anyone come to our aid if they had been to Cozumel?"

"Did you see the glazed look in the fisherman who arrived?"

"Of course, I did. I also smelled his breath. He smelled like he had swallowed a bottle of rum!"

"Can we get back to the situation at hand, gentlemen? You can argue about this later. Did you see anyone at El Apredido's house before you entered it?" Coyle asked.

"No," Bennis said. "It was quiet when I entered the house. I was surprised there were no bodyguards. We found them later in the kitchen. Their throats were slashed. El Apredido's body was still warm, so I think we just missed the killer."

"The only thing I heard after Jack went into the house was what sounded like the clip-clop of a donkey-driven rickshaw going by. I didn't see anyone, however."

Nurse Angela Vicario spoke up. "If you ask me, I think the Police Chief killed him."

"No one asked you, Angela," Dr. Iguarán said as he stitched up a deep cut on Fran's leg.

"Why do you say that?" Fraumeni asked.

"Because everyone knew that El Apredido was abusive to El Capitán. They hated each other. Ask anyone. He cursed him out and threatened him constantly. And, according to one of the men with that devil in the ugly colorful shirt who hit me, El Capitán told his men El Apredido was coming to the hospital to kill that woman."

"What does that have to do with anything?"

"I heard him say that El Capitán was leaving town, but he had one more thing to do. That was to kill El Apredido!"

"He never said that, Angela! He warned his men and said he was leaving, but he never said he was going to kill El Apredido!"

"But he had reason!"

Dr. Iguarán stopped suturing. "Angela, you are doing it again. You never got along with and the Police Chief. You still blame him for sending your brother to prison for killing your cheating husband. What about the man in the colorful shirt who slapped you and threatened to kill you if you said anything else."

"He must mean Chago," Cavanaugh explained. "Like you said, Lieutenant, he would have a lot to gain from El Apredido's death. They both were drug dealers and this new drug El Apredido was developing could be a valuable asset to the leader of a drug cartel."

"But he left in the helicopter, Tom. We saw him."

"Actually, Jack, we didn't see him leave. We saw him go to the helicopter, but I never saw him get in. Did you?"

"No, but there was no reason he wouldn't. He was taking his sister to a better equipped medical facility."

Sergeant Coyle spoke up. "I checked with the local hotels. A man in a colorful shirt checked into Portal de la Marquesta. He could be the same man."

Lt. Fraumeni raised her hands. "Hold up, everyone. We are making a lot of assumptions here. Let's stick to the facts. Fr. Bennis and Mr. Cavanaugh, why did you go to El Apredido's chop-house? And what did you find there?"

Bennis spoke first. "When Chico told me about the chop-house and the sounds that came from it, I was suspicious. I thought there must be some reason why they were keeping people away from the house. The thought occurred to me that they might be using the house as a drug lab. I thought we might be able to find something that would show who killed El Apredido."

"He does that at times," Cavanaugh said. "Sometimes he thinks he's the entire police force and knows more than anyone else."

"That's not true, Thomas. I knew with the death of El Apredido that chop-house was the place we could find information he did not want anyone else to know. I figured whoever killed him would want that information and we needed to act fast before it was gone. It looks like I was right. But we missed the killer again and almost got killed in the process."

Lt. Fraumeni brushed a strand of blond hair from her eye. She looked over at Fran. "And what were you doing fighting a jaguar in the mountain?"

Fran grimaced and glanced at Chico. "We were just doing a bit of hiking. The jaguar caught us by surprise."

"The lance you killed the jaguar with, where did you get it?"

Fran looked at Cavanaugh. Cavanaugh looked at Bennis. Bennis looked at Chico. Chico looked back to Fran. His eyes widened and he adjusted his large sombrero.

"I ... I don't remember now. I'm really pretty tired. My head is pounding and I hurt all over."

"Can we hold off with the questions, Lieutenant?" Cavanaugh asked. "Fran was almost killed by that jaguar. She's been through a lot."

"I agree," Dr. Iguarán said. "The patient needs rest right now."

"Okay, but I am curious about that lance. It looks like it is made of precious metals."

"Were you able to identify El Apredido from his fingerprints?" Cavanaugh asked quickly trying to change the conversation.

Fraumeni checked with Coyle. Coyle shook his head. "I faxed his prints to headquarters. They have no record of him here in Colombia. I took the liberty of sending them to your friend, Detective Iceberg, in New York."

"That's Detective Goldberg, not Iceberg," Cavanaugh said.

"Whatever," Coyle shrugged. "So far no record of his prints. I'll try Interpol next."

"So we still don't know who he was," Cavanaugh said. And then, as if on signal, his cell phone rang. He looked at it and groaned. The call was from Salvatore Russo's grandmother, Vincenza Russo.

■ ■ ■

Vincenza Russo got right to the point. "Mr. Cavanaugh, did you locate my grandson yet?"

Cavanaugh glanced at the bloody spear in the lieutenant's hands. "We have encountered a few difficulties, Mrs. Russo. There has been a murder, and we are with the police down here right now."

"Where are you? You sound far away. You are breaking up."

"I am in a small town in Colombia called Mompox."

"What the hell are you doing there? I am paying you to locate my grandson, not traipse around the world! You told me you were going to Mexico!"

Cavanaugh walked toward the door. "There have been some developments …."

"I explicitly told you the police were not to be involved!"

Cavanaugh's face reddened. He felt the bump on his head. He turned and looked at the doctor bandaging his wife. Part of him wanted to tell her that her grandson was a coldblooded killer and a drug dealer. Part of him wanted to tell her that her grandson was dead. But another part of him told him he still did not have all the facts. "I don't have all the facts yet, Mrs. Russo, but, as I said, a man has been murdered down here. It's far from definite, but there are some indications the man might be your grandson. They are checking his fingerprints now."

There was a pause on the line and then the woman stated flatly, "He's not my Salvatore!"

"I hope it is not the case, Mrs. Russo. I will call you when I know for sure."

"You are wasting your time and my money, Mr. Cavanaugh. Whoever you are talking about is not my grandson!"

Cavanaugh looked back at the police officers. Coyle had some papers in his hands and was showing them to Fraumeni. "I really have to go now, Mrs. Russo. I will call you when I hear anything new." He disconnected the call before she could say anything else and walked over to the police. "What do you guys have there?" he asked.

"I really don't know," Fraumeni said. "These papers were found in El Apredido's room. They seem to be some schedule or plan of some sort together with a long, rambling essay, but I don't understand what they mean."

Cavanaugh looked at the papers and his brother moved closer to see. They studied the papers for a few minutes and then exchanged looks. "This reads like Ted Kaczynski's manifesto, *Industrial Society and its Future*," Cavanaugh said.

"I don't understand," Fraumeni said. "Who is this Kaczynski person?"

"Kaczynski was probably before your time. He was known back in the late 1970s and early 1990s as the 'Unabomber.' He mailed a number of homemade bombs in his personal nationwide campaign against modern technology."

Fr. Bennis read through the essay. "This is more about dissolving our worldwide economy system. There are quotes in here from Thomas Jefferson about the right of the people to alter or abolish any form of government that becomes destructive of its original purpose and establish a new government. There is a quote in here from John Locke that when a government ceases to function for the people, it may be dissolved and the people are free to establish a new government that works in their best interest."

Cavanaugh took some of El Apredido's essay from his brother. "Somehow he seemed to think we human beings have an obligation to care for each other and support the whole human race."

Bennis stared at him. "And we do, Thomas. It's called the Golden Rule: Do unto others as you would have done unto you."

"Yeah, but El Apredido seems to have taken it to another level. He seemed to think the end justified the means. His plan would wreck the world economy and force a new world order. Apparently, he felt out of chaos and anarchy, a new and better system would be born."

"That is ridiculous," Officer Coyle said. "How would he go about doing this?"

"That's what the elaborate schedule is about. Somehow he planned to create a panic in New York City by creating a power crisis and then closing all the entrances and exits to the city. The resulting panic would close the stock markets and throw everything up in the air. It might grow into a worldwide pandemic. Banks, corporations, industries would collapse. Riots would ensue. People would revolt against the establishment and the world order would be reversed."

"Sergeant Coyle is right, Thomas. This is delusional at best. He could never accomplish this. There are too many checks and balances to prevent something like this from happening."

"You're probably right, Jack, but it would cause a lot of problems. People around the world are pretty upset about the way politicians and leaders have been running things. The rich get richer while the poor get poorer. I can only imagine what a nuclear threat would mean to a city of over eight and a half million people who are literally trapped with all roads, bridges, and tunnels blocked – if even temporarily."

"How could he do that?" Lt. Fraumeni asked.

"That's what this schedule is all about," Bennis said. "Every entrance into and out of New York City has been marked including the airports."

"That would still be impossible!"

Cavanaugh shook his head. "El Apredido was convinced of the need to rebuild our economic system. To rebuild it, he felt, it must first be destroyed. That, I believe, is where the drug called the Devil's Breath comes in. Using it, he could control the minds of enough people to cause a panic. I have personally seen how this drug works. It can make a person do something he or she never wanted to do. It robs them of their free will. He's been planning this for a long time."

There was silence in the room for a few moments and then Chico said, "El Apredido was a bad man."

Lt. Marion Fraumeni smiled. "Apparently a lot of people thought so, too. The question now is, who killed him?"

"Whoever killed him, I think, went to the chop-house to destroy the lab there and take information about the Devil's Breath," Bennis said.

"He was probably the man in the colorful shirt who set the fire in the lab, set our canoe adrift, and sped away."

"I saw the boat through the trees as it was speeding away. I couldn't get a good look at the driver, but I did see someone wearing a colorful shirt in it," Fran said.

Diego Coyle turned to Lt. Fraumeni. "That brings us back to the man who checked into Portal de la Marquesta. A colorful shirt is not much to go on, but I think we should check him out."

"You are right, Diego. We should ask this man a few questions. Meanwhile, I ask you all to stay close by. I will need to speak to you again." She studied the spear in her hands and added, "When you feel better, Mrs. Cavanaugh, I would like to ask you some more questions about this weapon you used to kill the jaguar. It looks very old and very valuable."

■ ■ ■

"I need to get out of this hospital," Fran said. She looked at Dr. Iguarán. "No offense, Doctor, but I never really liked hospitals."

"I understand, señora. Sometimes I don't like them very much either."

"Do you have any suggestions where we might spend the night?"

Nurse Vicario spoke up. "My friend works at La Casa Amarilla. I have never stayed there, but she tells me it is clean and comfortable and they give you free breakfast."

"Food sounds good," Cavanaugh said. "I almost forgot I was hungry. Where is this place?"

"It is close to the river and the forest, not far from the Church of Santa Bárbara. My friend Rosario can get you rooms. She is a good person. She has had many problems in her life. Her brother was killed in a gunfight in Medellín. He was part of Pablo Escobar's security force. Pablo was killed trying to escape on the rooftop of the house he was hiding in. Rosario was very close to her brother. Then her son drowned in the Magdalena River the week before Easter. He was so anxious to take part in our procession in the Serenade to the Deceased. Poor Rosario ended up spending the night in the cemetery grieving for her brother and her son. She still believes …."

"That's enough, Angela," Dr. Iguarán said holding up his arms. "I think it might actually be TMI – too much information. I think our visitors should know La Casa Amarilla, while beautiful and clean, is a hostel and has few private rooms which can be expensive."

Fr. Bennis stepped forward. "I think I may have been there before. María Isabelle stayed in a hostel by the church. It will be a treat to get something to eat, take a bath, and get some sleep. I have no problem staying in the dorm rooms with Chico, and Thomas and Fran can take a private room."

Fran smiled and reached for Cavanaugh's hand. "This can be our honeymoon!"

"Some honeymoon! You almost get killed by a jaguar, and I almost die in a fire!"

"The key word is *almost*, Thomas. We can all thank God the tough part is over."

Cavanaugh helped Fran up and said, "Something tells me, Jack, it's not over yet. God seems to have a sense of humor at times. The killer of El Apredido and the men at the chop-house are still out there somewhere. You know what they used to say, 'The opera's not over until the fat lady sings.' "

■ ■ ■

19

That night Lt. Marion Fraumeni, Diego Coyle, Tom Cavanaugh, Francesca Cavanaugh, Fr. Jack Bennis and Chico ate a family style dinner at the hostel. They were served bean tostada with guacamole, chipotle salsa and Spanish rice. Cavanaugh complained throughout the meal about not having the juicy cheeseburger he was craving. He didn't touch the guacamole despite Fran's insistence it was rich in fiber, potassium and other essential nutrients. "It's a great source of vitamin E and C," she told him. "It helps fight cancer and improves the absorption of nutrients from other foods. It's good for you!"

"I don't care what you say about it," Cavanaugh said. "I don't like the way it looks, the way it feels, and the way it smells. And besides, I don't like the name 'guacamole.' It reminds me of a giant, green mole of mucous."

Four young backpackers chuckled as they checked their I-Phones and eavesdropped on the conversation at the table next to them.

"Any news from Interpol about the mysterious El Apredido?" Fr. Bennis asked.

"Nada," Coyle said. "There is no record of his fingerprints on file anywhere."

"How can that be?" Fran asked.

"He doesn't have a criminal record and never worked in a civil or federal service job. The question is, who was he?"

Fraumeni said, "We are checking other sources but they will take time. Bank records, passport files, airport security tapes and other places. But without a name to go on, we may honestly never know for sure who he was."

"Thomas, do you still think this guy might be the Sal Russo you are looking for?" Bennis asked.

"From the picture I saw of him in his girlfriend's place, he's about the same size and build, but I can't be sure. I never saw him in person like you did."

"What are you going to tell his grandmother and mother?"

"I have no idea. The grandmother assured me El Apredido definitely isn't her precious Salvatore Anthony Russo."

"How can she be so sure?"

"I don't know. I feel the old woman is holding out on me. I would think the battleax might have known El Apredido, but I never told her who was murdered. When I told her we were checking fingerprints, she just said she was sure it wasn't Russo."

Diego Coyle poured himself another glass of red sangria. "We found a piece of crumbled paper in a wastebasket at the house. It was a message threatening El Apredido. It was signed S.R."

Chico spoke through a mouthful of tortilla. "Padre, you told me Chago's real name is Santiago Rodriguez. His initials would be S.R.!"

Fraumeni glared at the twelve-year-old. Fr. Bennis patted the young boy's arm. "It could be, Chico, but it doesn't mean he killed El Apredido. We think he left with his sister on the helicopter."

"Salvatore Russo's initials are also S.R."

"What did you find out about the man in the colorful shirt at the Portal de la Marquesta?"

Coyle answered. "He checked out a few hours ago. He paid in cash. Nobody's apparently seen him since."

A tall, slim backpacker at the table next to them leaned over. "We saw a man in a garish, mostly yellow, multi-colored shirt earlier today," he said.

Fraumeni and Coyle looked annoyed. "That could be him. Where did you see him?" Cavanaugh asked.

The backpacker put his I-Phone down and pulled his chair closer. He wore a black t-shirt with a wanted poster on the front of a forlorn looking black cat and the words "Wanted – Dead and Alive – Schrodinger's Cat." The other three backpackers stopped texting and looked up. "My name is Gerard," he said. "We saw a guy in a colorful shirt driving a rickshaw earlier today."

"Speak for yourself, Jerry," an anorexic looking brunette with multiple tattoos and pierced nose, eyebrows, and lips contradicted him. "I didn't see nothing! Don't try to involve me in your shit!"

"Gerard, where did you see this guy?" the priest asked.

"Back in the nice section of the town with the big mansions. He was driving a rickshaw pulled by a sick looking donkey. He caught my attention because he didn't look like your typical rickshaw driver, if you know what I mean."

"I heard a rickshaw going by the side of El Apredido's house," Cavanaugh said. "But I didn't see who was driving it."

"Can you give us a description of the man you saw?" Bennis asked.

"Not really. The sun was in my eyes and the guy turned away when he saw us. His shirt was what caught my eye. He seemed to be too dressed up to be a local."

"Could you identify him if you saw him again?" Coyle asked.

"No, he couldn't!" the thin brunette asserted. "What's the matter with your hearing? You heard him say he couldn't give you a description. What part of that don't you understand?"

"Easy, Felicia," Gerard said. "Let's not start another fight here."

"It's your own fault, asshole. You go sprouting off stuff you don't know diddly about. When are you ever going to learn to mind your own freaking business?"

"Thanks for your help," Bennis said. "You seem to have confirmed our suspicions."

"And what are your suspicions?" Felicia asked.

Cavanaugh dipped his fork in his guacamole and said, "That, young lady, is none of your freaking business!"

■ ■ ■

"I may have a picture of the guy," a heavyset young man at the backpackers' table offered. All heads turned toward him. "I can't be sure, but I took a lot of pictures today and I think I got one of that skinny donkey pulling the rickshaw."

"Maurice, when are you going to learn to keep your mouth shut?" Felicia said.

"They are looking for a murderer, Felicia. Give me a break. I don't know who this guy is, but nobody should get away with murder."

"Can you lend us your camera, Maurice?" Coyle asked.

"Sure. I left it in my backpack. I'll go get it."

Felicia grabbed Maurice's arm, "Hold on! You guys aren't going to keep his camera as some kind of evidence, are you?"

"We just want to check the pictures. He can keep the camera," Coyle said.

Maurice pulled his arm away. "I'll go get it for you. I should be right back."

"Let me go with you, Maurice," the fourth person at the table said. "I need to take a piss anyway." He seemed to grow as he stood up. He was a lot taller than the others and wore a red t-shirt that said, "When life gives you lemons, make lemonade."

Cavanaugh looked up at the man as they left. "Who is the tall guy?" he asked. "He looks like he a basketball player."

"That's Scott Shushansky. He's studying archeology at Boston University. Actually, we are all studying archeology in some way."

"Oh, great! Why don't you tell them about your last bowel movement, Gerard? How many times do I have to tell you to keep your mouth shut?" Felicia said.

"What is this archeology?" asked Chico.

"What are you writing – a freaking book, kid? If you are, leave that chapter out!"

"Ease up, Felicia. The boy asked a question. He deserves an answer."

"I give up!" she said turning around and folding her arms. "You are incorrigible. You would talk to the wall if you thought it was listening."

Gerard looked at Chico and explained, "Archeology is a complex science that analyzes the activities of human beings who lived in the past by studying the artifacts or things they left behind which tell us about their culture and civilization."

Chico tapped his fingers nervously on the table. "Why… why are you here in Mompox?" he asked.

"Centuries ago there was a group of people in this area known as the Muisca. They were a powerful people partly because of the precious resources in this area such as emeralds, copper, coal and gold. They were known to offer gold to the Goddess Guatavita which is part of where the legend of the Golden City of El Dorado started."

Lt. Fraumeni glanced at Fran, but said nothing.

Suddenly, they heard screams from the dormitory area. Coyle jumped up first and headed toward the screams. Everyone else followed. When they got to the dorm area, they found a young woman crying hysterically. Coyle held the woman in his arms and asked, "What's wrong? What happened?"

The woman didn't answer. She pointed toward the restroom. Fraumeni moved toward the restroom. Bennis and Cavanaugh followed. Chico held Fran's hand. Gerard and Felicia stood frozen. "Where are Maurice and Scott?" Felicia whispered.

"Coyle," Fraumeni called, "come here."

Fran moved to the young woman who was sobbing uncontrollably. Bennis and Cavanaugh followed Coyle. On the floor of the restroom, the lanky body of Scott lay in a growing puddle of blood. His throat had been cut.

"Where's the other guy?" Coyle asked.

Cavanaugh saw him first. Maurice was lying next to his cot. His knapsack was open and the contents thrown over the cot. His throat had also been cut. Cavanaugh and Bennis exchanged looks. "My bet is his camera is gone," Cavanaugh said.

Bennis didn't answer. He bent over the body of Maurice and gave him his last blessing.

■ ■ ■

Only two of the Mompox police force drifted back to work; Stephano, who had been a barber and was sent to guard María Isabelle at the hospital, and Adrian, who had been a waiter and the second cousin once or twice removed from Pablo, the taxi driver who drove Fran and Cavanaugh to Mompox. But the Police Chief was nowhere to be found. Fraumeni had to call for reinforcements. Since her arrival, El Apredido and two body guards, five men in the lab at the chop-house, and now two anthropology students had been murdered. Ten people had been killed, not including an unknown number of El Apredido's men who had been killed and then carted off by Chago and Aunt Jo in the helicopter. Multiple homicides in multiple locations and not enough personnel to investigate thoroughly, it was an unworkable situation. Sergeant Diego Coyle put it succinctly. "It's a cluster-fuck!"

The two Colombian police officers took Gerard and Felicia to the Mompox police station to put them under protective custody. Stephano was sent to secure El Apredido's house and Adrian to secure the sight of the hostel murders. The five bodies in the scorched chop-house sank into the lagoon and became food for hungry caimans.

Chico slept in a bed for the first time in months. Before he fell asleep with his sombrero clutched in his hands, he prayed for his friend Sergio whom he left in the jungle. He asked that God take good care of him.

Jack Bennis smiled looking at Chico cuddling his sombrero. He turned to his brother and said, "He's a good kid, Thomas. He's been through a lot."

Cavanaugh nodded. "So have we, big brother. Fran fell asleep as soon as her head hit the pillow."

Bennis covered Chico with a light blanket and then walked outside with Cavanaugh. "It's not over, Thomas. I was hoping it was, but whoever killed El Apredido is trying to cover his tracks by eliminating anyone who might have seen him. The question is, why?"

"Aside from not wanting to get caught, I have the feeling it all goes back to that drug, the Devil's Breath. Someone doesn't want us to discover its formula. Why else would they destroy the lab in the chop-house?"

"That means anyone who came in contact with him is a target."

"I still have this nagging feeling that Salvatore Anthony Russo is involved in this in some way."

"Do you still think Russo might have been El Apredido?"

"I'm not sure. The grandmother was pretty adamant when I said they were checking fingerprints that it wasn't her precious Salvatore."

"Maybe she knew he didn't have a criminal record."

"Maybe. El Apredido's manifesto indicated he intended to wreck the world's economy using this Devil's Breath. It's hard to believe a traffic jam in New York would cause the riots and mayhem he was looking for, but if you throw in a nuclear malfunction and a blackout, you never know. Stranger things have happened in our political systems."

"But who do you think killed El Apredido?"

"Fraumeni seems to think it may be Chago or the Police Chief."

"Chago would benefit from the Devil's Breath. He has the facilities, but we saw him leave. I can't believe he would come all the way here to help his sister and then stop and go back to kill this El Apredido. I think he would eventually hunt him down and probably torture him slowly for hurting his sister, but I think his priority now would be taking care of María."

"And the Police Chief?"

"I am sure he hated El Apredido, but he would not have the facilities or the contacts to make use of the Devil's Breath. True, he could sell it to someone who would, but then we would be able to find him. I can see him killing El Apredido, but not burning down the chop-house and killing those two innocent students."

Cavanaugh looked up into the dark sky. Millions of stars would normally light up the night sky in Mompox, but on this night dark, ominous clouds hid the constellations above. A rumble of thunder came from the distance.

"I just remembered something. Russo's friends told me about rumors of a Hispanic exchange student at Yale who was a possible source of the drugs he sold there."

"You're thinking that Russo and El Apredido knew each other?"

"Maybe. They told me Russo was against the huge profits made on Wall Street and by big businesses while there were so many people starving and homeless. A scheme like El Apredido planned would turn economies upside down, but would increase hardship and suffering across the board. It wouldn't help the poor. It would increase their discomfort."

"If we had a copy of this Sal Russo's fingerprints, Thomas, we could definitely rule him out as El Apredido."

"And what about that slashed drawing of Abraxas in El Apredido's house?"

"What about it?"

"I saw one just like it in Russo's friends' apartment. And another like it in his girlfriend's place. They told me Russo made it."

Another crack of thunder. Closer this time.

"Holy crap! I completely forgot. I borrowed a stack of letters from his girlfriend. They all contained coded messages. His fingerprints would be on those letters."

"Do you have them with you? We can give them to Lt. Fraumeni and she can check them out."

Cavanaugh shook his head. "Great idea, Jack, but they were in our luggage which we left in the cab that took us to Aunt Jo's brothel."

"I will admit I am curious, but I'm not going to ask you why you and Fran went to a brothel. I will pray for you both, but I am not here to judge you. That is your business. Fraumeni can have someone in Bogotá check out the cab, find your luggage, and have the letters checked."

"It's not like that, Jack! We were trying to find Chago! Aunt Jo was the only way we could reach him to tell him about María." Cavanaugh paused as rain started to fall on them. "What about Fraumeni and the spear Fran used to kill the jaguar with? What do we tell her? We can't tell her where she found it."

"Let's get inside before we drown. This rain is pretty heavy. We'll think of something. Right now Fraumeni's involved over her head with dead bodies."

As they re-entered the hostel, they smelled it immediately. Smoke. It was wafting from under the door of Cavanaugh and Fran's private room. Their room was on fire!

■ ■ ■

Cavanaugh crashed through the door. Flames and billowing smoke danced from the drapes by the window. He grabbed Fran who was still asleep and carried her out of the room and into the rain outside. Bennis ran directly toward the flames crying in English and Spanish, "Fire! Fire!" He pulled the sheets off the bed and used them to cover the drapes which he pulled off and threw through the window. Outside the rain was coming down in buckets. Lightning flashed across the sky and thunder seemed to explode all around them.

Adrian, the Mompox police officer who had been a waiter, ran into the smoky room as Bennis shoved the last of the burning drapes out the window into the torrential rain outside. "Wake everyone up," Bennis ordered.

"It looks like you got the fire out already," Adrian said.

Bennis pointed to the broken glass on the rug. "Someone deliberately set this fire trying to kill my brother and his wife. Whoever did it might still be around. Wake up everyone and check out all the rooms."

"But it's pouring outside. Where is everyone supposed to go?"

"Until we check out this hostel, it's a simple choice – burn to death or get a little wet!"

Outside, Cavanaugh put Fran in a wooden rocking chair and asked, "Are you okay?"

Fran coughed as rain pelted her in the face. "What's going on?"

"Your room was on fire. I just got you out. You were sound asleep." He reached down and prepared to give her CPR.

Fran pushed his hands away. "What the hell are you doing? I'm all right."

"Are you dizzy or confused?"

"No more than normal."

"Are you short of breath? Were you burned anywhere? Open your mouth. I want to see if you have any burns inside your mouth and throat!"

"Knock it off, Tom. I'm okay!" She struggled to stand. "What happened? How did the fire start?"

Jack Bennis appeared in the doorway behind them. "Somebody broke your window and set the drapes on fire. The fire was deliberate. Looks like our mysterious 'friend' in the colorful shirt wants all of us dead!"

■ ■ ■

Fran coughed and grimaced. "This is ridiculous. Every bone in my body hurts. I want to go home, Tom."

"There will probably be all sorts of police and military here in the morning if his rain lets up," Cavanaugh said. "I don't think they'll want us to leave."

"Screw them!" Fran said. "We have a son back home to worry about. If we hang around here much longer he'll be an orphan!"

"There's an early morning ferry that leaves in less than two hours," Bennis said. "You could walk to the ferry if you wanted to, but it's pouring out."

"Fran's right, Jack. There's no need for us to stick around unless you need us. We're wet already and we don't have any luggage. We could be on that ferry in less than an hour."

Bennis rubbed his hands together. "I can manage things here. You guys get going. I'll tell the lieutenant about the letters in your luggage. Chances are the cab driver may have turned them in already. I'll ask her to have them check for fingerprints."

"My ex-partner, Morty Goldberg, should be able to help, too. He and the lieutenant are friends."

"Sounds like a plan. We'll text you with any information we find."

"Text?"

Fran smiled. "Tom doesn't know how to text, Jack. Have them text me and I will give him the message."

Bennis reached over and hugged each of them. "Go with God," he said and gave them a blessing. He watched them walk slowly into a wall of rain toward the ferry. Lightning flashed around them and thunder reverberated through the night like a roaring, hungry tiger.

■ ■ ■

20

Adrian, the distant cousin of the cab driver who had taken Fran and Cavanaugh to Mompox, returned to tell Bennis the hostel had been cleared and no other fires were found. Bennis looked around at the stunned travelers and found Chico clutching his sombrero in one hand and the lance that killed the jaguar in the other.

"Keep an eye on things here," Bennis told the police officer. "I'm taking Chico and going to the police station."

"It's pouring out," Adrian stated. "It hasn't rained like this in ages. We are liable to have floods if it continues like this. It would be safer to stay here."

"There's something I have to tell the Colombian police officers."

"How are you going to get there?"

"The old fashion way – we'll walk."

Adrian scratched his head. "You are crazy to go out in this storm. Do you even know where the station is?"

"No," Bennis smiled and then looked at Chico, "but Chico does."

Chico's eyes lit up. He pulled his sombrero over his head. He looked at the water pouring down from the heavens. He smiled again and said, "This way, Padre." And the priest and the twelve-year-old started jogging through the cascading rain and flashes of lightning.

■ ■ ■

Jack Bennis tried to stay up with Chico as he followed him through the rain. The boy ran fast jumping over some puddles and splashing through others. Bennis was out of breath when they reached the Mompox Police Department. More defecting members of the Mompox police had returned, but no Police Chief. El Capitán was still missing.

A bolt of lightning hit a mango tree close by. Bennis stumbled and fell head first into a large puddle at the steps of the police station.

"Padre, are you okay?" Chico asked rushing back to help the priest.

"I'm fine, Chico. Thanks. Just a little winded and a little more wet," he laughed.

Inside the building, the two stood dripping wet as Bennis relayed his brother's information about Salvatore Russo's letters in his missing luggage. "Hopefully," he said, "the Bogotá police can locate the luggage he left in the taxi that took him to Aunt Jo's brothel. He thinks the letters should have Russo's fingerprints on them and you can compare them to El Apredido's."

While the necessary calls were made, Bennis and Chico asked permission to speak with the two backpackers, Gerard and Felicia. They found the anthropology students in a room at the back of the building drinking coffee. "I'd like to ask you a few questions about your work in this area," Bennis began.

Felicia spoke first. "What is this – a freaking inquisition? Two of our colleagues have been murdered and all you guys do is ask us stupid questions! Why don't you find Maurice and Scott's murderer for Christ's sake?"

"First, I'm not one of 'those guys.' I'm a priest, not a cop. I am curious about your studies."

Chico squatted at the priest's feet holding his dripping sombrero in one hand and the ancient spear in the other.

Gerard's eyes were red and puffy. It looked like he had been crying. "They were our friends, Father. We have been traveling through Mexico and Central America together. We have been following up on the work of Professor Guillermo de Anda. He has been studying the sacred rituals and geography of the Maya civilization. He is a special kind of anthropologist.

He's what you might call an underwater anthropologist and his work involves caves, cenotes, mountains, and woods."

"What is a cenote?" Chico asked.

"It's a natural pit, like a sinkhole. It happens when the ground gives way and collapses exposing underground water beneath it. Professor de Anda found a number of these cenotes in the Yucatán Peninsula of Mexico used by the ancient Mayans for sacrificial offerings. His discoveries in Chichen Itza are well-documented."

"This is ridiculous, Gerard. Why are you telling them all this? You never know when to shut your mouth."

"Why are you always so argumentative, Felicia? It's no secret what we're doing. We are simply following up on de Anda's work attempting to find possible subterranean caves of the Muisca in Mompox. The rumors of an ancient underground city of gold fascinated all of us and we decided to explore this region in hopes of finding the mythical El Dorado. If Professor de Anda found evidence of subterranean caves in the Yucatán Peninsula, maybe we could find similar caves in this area."

Chico moved his spear under his sombrero. Bennis asked, "But what makes you think there may be caves in this area?"

"That's a good question, Father. Scott was the researcher in our group. He studied journals and memoirs written by conquistadors and missionary priests. The Muisca occupied the highlands of Cundinamarca which bordered the Magdalena River. In a chronicle of the history and customs of the Muisca, Juan Rodriguez Freyle wrote in the early 1600s to the governor of Guatavita that the Muisca had a ritual at Lake Guatavita in which their new ruler was covered with gold dust, placed on a raft with gold, emeralds and all sorts of precious metals for him to offer to their god. The raft was burned in the center of the lagoon and the new ruler washed off the gold covering his body while his followers threw more gold, emeralds and precious gems into the lake. When he came out of the water he was lauded as their lord and king. "

"I read about this and how this ceremony gave birth to the legend of El Dorado. But the Spanish conquistadors knew about the El Dorado legend and actually dredged Lake Guatavita in search of El Dorado. They found some gold, but not much."

"We came to believe Lake Guatavita was only one of the Muisca's traditions. The Muisca Confederation, though little known, was as advanced as the Aztec, Maya and Inca civilizations. There is no reason to believe they too did not have underground tunnels and caves for religious services and safe havens to store their gold from the marauding conquistadors. If the waters of Guatavita represent the mother of the Muisca people, then we thought the mountains might represent the father of these people. And somewhere near the water and the mountains, the tangible world and the spiritual world would meet. That is what we are searching for. "

"But you have no tangible proof."

"True, Father, but dozens of golden artifacts have been found near the Magdalena River dating back to the Quimbaya civilization in Colombia from 300 to 1500. Many of the small gold figurines found resembled fish and insects, but some actually looked like airplanes."

Felicia suddenly looked at Chico. "What's that stick you have in your hand, kid?"

Chico pulled away. "It's mine," he said.

"Let me see it!" she demanded.

"No!" Chico said jumping up and moving toward the door.

"It looks old. Let me examine it!"

"No! It is mine." He pointed the spear at her. "Stay away from me. Make her stay away, Padre."

Father Bennis stood and stepped between Felicia and Chico. "I think you need to learn how to talk to people, Miss. Maybe you have been studying objects too long and have forgotten people have feelings."

"I want to see that spear. It looks like it could be a Muisca artifact. It looks like it is made of gold and silver. I need to examine it."

Bennis looked down at Felicia. "You need to back off, lady, and mind your own business. The spear is Chico's. You touch that boy or his spear and I will have you locked up in a Colombia jail for child abuse and attempted theft. That's not a threat. It's, as you might say, a freaking promise!"

■ ■ ■

It rained straight for four days and four nights. Cavanaugh was right about the Colombian troops and military arriving. But they didn't arrive to investigate the murder of El Apredido and the others. They arrived to assist in search and rescue, evacuations, door-to-door checks, and maintaining public safety during flood conditions as the Magdalena River overflowed, and roads were washed out, and homes flooded.

The Mompox Police Station became an evacuation center. 104 year-old Ana Sara Garcia claimed she hadn't seen such destruction since the earthquake in Popayan and the volcanic eruption of Nevado del Ruiz in Armero more than thirty years before. No one contradicted the old woman except Felicia who pointed out over 20,000 people were killed in Armero and somewhere less than 300 in Popayan while the only dead in Mompox were a few cats, a cow, and a number of corpses floating up from the graves of their historic cemetery.

There were numerous theories of why the sudden rains had occurred. Some blamed the La Niña or El Niño weather phenomenon. Some blamed deforestation and the destruction of the high-mountain wetlands and savanna wetlands which changed the water cycle in the country contributing to floods and favorable conditions for landslides. Some blamed the mining for gold and coal clogged the wetlands with sediment and contributed to the flooding. Still others claimed it was the beginning of the end. They believed the rains were a clarion call of the end of the world.

Through all the rain and turmoil, Fr. Bennis said mass every morning in the police station and heard confessions throughout the day. He administered to the sick, both in mind and in body. Chico was astonished at the work the priest was doing. But he worried about the fate of Sergio, his best friend. On the third night, as they were preparing to go to sleep, Bennis was praying his rosary when Chico asked, "Padre, why are so many people coming to you?"

Bennis replied simply by quoting something an old gunny sergeant had once told him. "There are no atheists in foxholes, Chico. When people are scared, they often turn to God. I wish they realized how much God can help each of us in our daily lives before disaster strikes, but sometimes that seems to be the way it is."

Chico sat on his cot with his legs pulled up to his chest. He stared at Fr. Bennis and then asked, "Padre, why did you become a priest?"

Bennis looked at the boy in silence and then answered slowly. "Sometimes, Chico, I think about that very question. There was an old Jack Bennis, a long time ago, who was a soldier. He killed people. That was his job. He took on a new role when he became a priest. Sometimes I wonder which role is the true Jack Bennis. Sometimes I think I am still struggling to find the true me. I know when I accepted God, I never felt better in my life. It was like a burden had been lifted from me. I really felt the Holy Spirit coming into my being. It is a blessing to be able to help other people. Still, I sometimes think I am pretending – that the true me is the soldier, the killer. I struggle, Chico, like all of us to be the best person I can be."

"Padre, how will you know which is the real you?"

Bennis nodded his head. "That is a great question, Chico. When I have doubts and problems, I sometimes turn to one of the Psalms – Psalm 23. It says, 'The Lord is my Shepherd: I shall not want…. He restores my soul. He leads me in right paths for His Name's sake. Even though I walk through the darkest valley, I fear no evil, for You are with me; Your rod and Your staff – they comfort me.'"

"And is that all, Padre? Does that work?"

Bennis rubbed the back of his neck. "To be honest, Chico, not always. I forget sometimes. I know God is my friend, but sometimes I don't act like I am His friend. I'm not perfect, Chico. None of us are. Sometimes I fall. When I do, God is always there to help me get up again."

Diego Coyle walked into the room Chico and Bennis were staying in. He folded his muscular arms and said, "The Lieutenant told me to tell you they found your brother's luggage. It was turned into a police station in Bogotá. We checked the letters from that Salvatore Russo to his girlfriend Carolyn Hendershot. There were only two sets of fingerprints on the letters. One was Hendershot's and the other was your brother's."

Bennis put his rosary beads in his pocket and stood. "Are you sure?"

"We checked and re-checked. Your brother's ex-partner, Iceberg…."

"Detective Goldberg."

"Whatever. He confirmed your brother's fingerprints and Hendershot's. Apparently, she has a record of being picked up for soliciting and drug possession. The soliciting charges were dropped for lack of corroboration and the drug possession charge dismissed on the basis of insufficient quantity and her claims she didn't know what the substance actually was."

"How is that possible?"

"I have no idea. What I do know is that once this rain stops the Lieutenant and me are out of here."

"What about the person who killed El Apredido?"

"To be brutally honest, he was a drug dealer. One dealer kills another. That's one less for us to worry about."

"But what about the two anthropology students who were killed?"

Coyle shrugged his shoulders. "Collateral damage. It happens every day. You get used to it after a while. We have to get back to Bogotá. We are turning everything over to the Mompox police. It's their problem now."

"This doesn't seem right."

"It is what it is, Padre. Life is not always fair, as you should know. The weather forecast is that the rains will stop sometime tomorrow. There will be a lot of cleanup to do, but the military should help with that."

As Sergeant Police Officer Coyle started to leave, he stopped and turned to them. "Oh, I almost forgot, the Lieutenant wants to get another look at that spear that killed the jaguar before we leave. She thinks it might be an artifact of some Pre-Columbian culture and may be very valuable."

■ ■ ■

21

Staten Island, New York

Tom and Francesca Cavanaugh caught a Jet Blue flight from Rafael Núñez International Airport in Cartagena to Liberty International Airport in Newark, New Jersey. Cavanaugh booked the flight from Cartagena instead of Bogotá because he thought it would save time and money. The flight was less expensive, but he did not take into consideration the one stop in Ft. Lauderdale, Florida, entailed an almost eleven hour layover. They were exhausted, frustrated, and annoyed when they arrived in Newark and took a taxi home to Staten Island at 5:00 a.m. The plan was to drive into Brooklyn and pick up their son and their dog from Fran's sister. Fran went to take a shower and change her clothes while Tom listened to a series of phone messages from Vincenza Russo inquiring about the progress of his search for her grandson.

After her shower, Fran fell asleep halfway through getting dressed. Tom never made it through the messages before he fell asleep in his favorite chair. At 10:30 a.m. the phone rang waking them both up.

Cavanaugh stumbled out of his chair to get the phone. It was a woman's voice on the other end of the phone. "Mr. Cavanaugh?" she said.

Cavanaugh shook his head and tried to find his awake voice. "Yeah. Who is this?"

"This is Deborah Russo, Sal's mother."

Cavanaugh checked his watch. What was Deborah Russo calling him at 10:30 in the morning? "Is there something wrong, Ms. Russo?"

"I want you to stop looking for my son, Salvatore."

Cavanaugh sat upright in his chair. "Your mother hired me to locate your son. Why do you want me to stop?"

"It's a long story, Mr. Cavanaugh. It is just that I feel it would be better for everyone if you stopped your investigation."

"Actually, I'm pretty deep into the investigation. I'm in the process of having the police check the fingerprints of a man who fits your son's description who was murdered down in Colombia."

"That is not Salvatore, Mr. Cavanaugh."

"How can you be so sure?"

"It's complicated, but, trust me, that man is not my son."

"I don't understand, Ms. Russo, but in any case I can't just stop looking for your son. Your mother paid me to find him."

"Tell her you can't find him. Tell her anything, but stop looking for Sal. It's not safe for anyone – including you and your family."

"What are you talking about?"

"I've said too much already. I warned you. Please don't tell my mother I called you. Goodbye."

"Ms. Russo, I don't understand. What are you talking about? Why are you warning me?"

But the line was dead and Cavanaugh was talking to no one.

"Who was that on the phone? " Francesca called from upstairs.

Cavanaugh stared into space trying to comprehend what had just happened. Then he looked upstairs and answered simply, "No one, Fran. It was just another telemarketing call."

■ ■ ■

Mompox, Colombia

It was still dark the morning the rain started to let up. Jack Bennis rolled out of his bunkbed. He stood, stretched, and reached up to higher bed. He whispered, "Wake up, little man. It's time we left."

Chico sprang up clutching his spear and his sombrero. "Where are we going, Padre?"

"I think it's best we leave before they start asking more questions about your spear."

As Chico climbed down, a head on the upper bunkbed at the other end of the room popped up and asked, "Where do you think you guys are going?" It was Felicia.

Chico froze. He pointed his spear at her. "Padre, make her stop!" he said.

Bennis raised his arms and walked toward Felicia. "We are leaving. Chico has a friend we have to check on."

Felicia swung her legs over the top of the bunkbed and dropped to the floor. "You're lying. I heard you talking about that spear. Where did you get it? It looks like it's made of some kind of steel and copper."

"It's made of silver and gold!" Chico stated.

Felicia's eyes widened. "That can't be! Where did you get it?"

Fr. Bennis spoke softly, "We are not quite sure what it is made of, but Chico's father brought it back to him from an expedition he was on years ago in Peru. The story is the spear was part of the ransom the Incas paid to Pizarro for the release of Atahualpa."

"You're lying. The treasures Pizarro received for Atahualpa were melted, refined, and made into bars which were shipped back to Spain."

"Not all the treasures were melted. Human nature being what it is, one of Pizarro's conquistadors stole this particular spear and kept it. He took it like many of our soldiers returned with German lugers and helmets from World War II. He wrote a detailed account in his journal of how he obtained it. Chico's father obtained the journal and the spear from a Peruvian dealer in antiquity. It has all been certified and documented."

"I don't believe you. Why were you trying to sneak out of here?"

"You don't believe a lot of people, Felicia. I think you need to trust more people. The Peruvian dealer can substantiate everything I've said. He told Chico's father about a vast subterranean series of tunnels in the northern highlands of Quito. If you must know, we didn't want unscrupulous treasure hunters destroying the few remaining relics of the Incas. I have told you too much already. I trust you will keep what I have told you to yourself. As a student of anthropology, you realize the importance of preserving the cultures of the past. We just need to get out of here before we have to answer a lot of questions that will create problems for a lot of innocent people and make a circus of the tunnels in Quito."

Felicia stared openmouthed at the priest and the boy as they quietly walked out of the hostel into the drizzling rain of the early morning.

■ ■ ■

Fr. Bennis and Chico sloshed through knee high water at times on their way to where Bennis and Cavanaugh left the motorcycle. After they were a few blocks from the police station, Chico stopped and looked up at the priest.

"What's the matter, Chico?"

Chico shook his head and tapped the weapon that killed the jaguar in the water. "Padre, you lied. You told Felicia a lie. My father did not get this spear from any Peruvian dealer. I found it in the tunnels by the lagoon."

"I know you did, Chico. But you have to admit, it was a pretty good story. I think Felicia may have actually believed it although I am not quite sure whether Quito is in Peru or Ecuador."

"But, Padre, you lied!"

Bennis rubbed his face. He needed a shave badly. He squatted next to Chico. "Felicia is a very pushy person. She is persistent, arrogant, and ambitious. I don't know the name for it, but she has a personality disorder of some kind. She's inflexible and has trouble connecting with people in socially acceptable ways. She wanted your spear. One way or another, she wasn't going to let you go without seeing it. She would organize a search for the Muisca treasures in this area. And she would have found the tunnels. I know how much you revere the ancient culture you discovered and that you do not want people destroying it. I respect your reasons for wanting to protect it. I told her a story to give her something else to think about and some other place to explore. But you are right, Chico, I did tell her a lie."

"But, Padre, you are a priest!"

"I told you, Chico, I'm not perfect. I am a human being with a lot of flaws. I try, but sometimes I come up short and make decisions that I feel are right. Sometimes my choices turn out not so right. This may have been one of them."

"Do you say that thing about your Lord being your herdsman leading you along dark mountain roads?"

"Something like that."

"Does it work?"

"I really believe God understands. I don't believe the end justifies the means all the time, but in this case I think He will understand and forgive me. I hope you will, too. Maybe someday in the future you will want other people to see and appreciate the discoveries you made of the Muisca treasures. If the right people were involved, a lot of good would come from it both for you and your sister and a lot of other people."

"What do you think I should do, Padre?"

Bennis looked up at the lightening sky and then down at the boy. "We all have to make our own decisions. I follow what I feel is right. I hope it's the way God wants me to go, but it may not be." He paused and then continued, "A group of four people in Chicago over a hundred years ago founded a club which is now found all around the world. It's called the Rotary Club. It encourages doing service to others. They have a Four Way Test they ask themselves when faced with important and difficult decisions."

"What is this test?"

"The test is simple. It's just four questions."

"What are the questions, Padre?"

"Is it true? Is it fair to all concerned? Will it build goodwill and better friendship? And will it be beneficial for all concerned?"

Chico looked up at the priest. "What you told that Felicia lady would not have passed that test."

"That is very true, Chico. I didn't want you to get into any trouble, and I wanted to respect your wishes. You have been my friend and I try to help my friends."

"What do you think I should do, Padre?"

"That's up to you, Chico. A lot of good could come from your discovery, but it is up to you."

The twelve-year-old's eyes widened. "I could get my sister and we could live together in our own house."

"That's possible, Chico. You're a smart young man, but you need to go to school and get an education. I could help you contact the right people who would do the right things for everyone. I know the curator of a well-known museum in Washington, D.C. His name is Professor Jereal Allbrook. We became good friends when I was in the Army's Special Forces Airborne Training and again when we took a special underwater demolition course with the Navy Seals. He has a PhD in anthropology from Harvard and PhD in Art History from the University of Chicago. He would make sure the Muisca artifacts are respected and their contributions appreciated. You would really like him."

Chico frowned. "Maybe I was wrong, Padre. Maybe I should not have kept these treasures to myself. It is selfish. Maybe more people should learn about the history and achievements of the Muisca."

"Maybe," the priest said. "But that is your decision."

Chico looked up at the sky. The sun was starting to come up. There were no clouds in the sky. A rooster crowed from somewhere near.

"Padre, can we go back to the tunnels? I want to look at them one more time."

Bennis smiled and patted the boy on his shoulder. "I was hoping you might say that," he said.

■ ■ ■

Staten Island, New York

Tom Cavanaugh sat for a long time staring into space. What was Deborah Russo's call about? Why did she want him to stop looking for her son? Why did she not want her mother to know about her call? Something was going on that he was unaware of. But what?

He got up and walked into the kitchen. He put on a pot of coffee and ran through a gamut of possibilities. None of them made any sense.

Vincenza Russo was the sister of Ralph Muscatelli, the mob boss his brother had killed. Did she know Jack Bennis shot her brother as he left a restaurant in Brooklyn? Did she have an ax to grind? She had been married to a successful Wall Street broker. Was she involved in some way with her grandson's drug dealing? He never checked if she had a criminal record. That was something he should have checked to start with. Was she responsible for his stolen car radio and E-Z pass? Could she have had something to do with his flat tires and broken headlight? But why? There was a lot more to this private investigation business than he had initially thought.

And what about Sal Russo's mother? What was Deborah Russo's story? He thought she dressed like a medium priced whore, but what did he know? Fran always told him the only taste he had was in his mouth.

He needed more information on Vincenza Russo and Deborah Russo. He checked his watch. It was almost 11:15 in the morning. He dialed a number he knew from memory. Morty Goldberg, Cavanaugh's old partner on the New York Police Force picked it up on the second ring. "What do you want now, meshuggener?" he asked.

"Morty, did I ever tell you how much I love it when you speak Jewish? It makes me feel warm and fuzzy all over."

"You are incorrigible! Sometimes I wonder how I worked with you for so long."

"Sometimes I wonder about that, too."

"I was planning on calling you anyway. I checked the fingerprints on those letters that Marion sent me from Sal Russo to his girlfriend. There were only two sets of prints on them. Hers and yours."

"That's impossible!"

"Improbable, not impossible. Who is this guy Sal Russo anyway?""

"It's a long story, Morty, I was hired to find him by his grandmother and his mother. But things haven't exactly worked out. Something is missing. I think he's involved in some new drug called the Devil's Breath. My sister-in-law Mary checked the Internet for information about him, but came up empty. It was like he didn't exist. I was hoping you could double-check him and two more names: Vincenza Russo, the guy's grandmother, and Deborah Russo, his mother. I need to know if any of them have any kind of criminal record."

"No promises. It's been pretty busy around here with political demon-strations and terror threats. But I'll see what I can do."

"Thanks, Morty. I owe you one."

"You owe me a lot more than one, meshuggener!" He paused a mo-ment and then added, "How is María Isabelle? Marion told me her brother supposedly took her off in a helicopter somewhere."

"Yeah, but I have no idea where she is. There has been some heavy rains and flooding down in Mompox and I haven't spoken to my broth-er. When I do, I'll give you an update. Thanks again for your girlfriend Marian. She really came through."

"Don't start, Cavanaugh! She's not my girlfriend! We met at a police conference and that is all!"

"You can tell me, Morty. I won't tell anyone else. She is very attractive and I wouldn't blame you...."

"Nothing happened, Cavanaugh! We are just friends! You have a sick, perverted mind!"

"Yeah, you're probably right about that." He looked up at the kitchen clock. "I hate to cut this call short, Morty, but unlike City employees I have a lot of things to do. Have a great day. And remember, your secret is safe with me!"

As Cavanaugh hung up he heard Goldberg shouting Yiddish curses into the phone. It was good talking to him again. He missed working with him. At times it was exciting, stimulating, and dangerous. At other times it was boring and uneventful. He rubbed the bump on his head and thought of the cuts and bruises on his wife, and he concluded retiring had not changed things that much for him. Langston Hughes was right. Life is definitely no crystal staircase.

■ ■ ■

22

Mompox, Colombia

Father Bennis retrieved the motorcycle of the man he killed who shot María Isabelle and they set out toward the jungle and the tunnels. The ground was very wet and muddy. Frequently they had to stop and push the motorcycle through or around muck and fallen branches and trees. But the mud and the trees weren't their only obstacles. The heavy rains of the previous few nights had driven snakes out into the open. The supersaturation of the ground might have accounted for the plethora of snakes they encountered on their ride. Chico, however, thought the clusters of snakes were an ominous omen.

"Padre, the snakes are all around us. This is a bad sign."

"It's a natural phenomenon, Chico. Snakes naturally seek higher ground and shelter from the rain. If we don't bother them, they shouldn't bother us."

"Padre, it means bad luck. They are all over the place. We should go back."

Bennis continued forward. "If we watch where we are going, we should be okay."

Chico held on tightly to the priest. Bennis could feel the boy's hands trembling. As the motorcycle made its distinctive noise, birds, monkeys, and other animals scattered away. The priest and the boy were forced to stop at one point. A large evergreen tree lay in a patch of mud across their path. Bennis and Chico got out to push the motorcycle around the tree.

Bennis noticed Chico's nervous energy. He had difficulty concentrating. "Do you think Sergio will be okay, Padre? He relies on me. I hope he was able to find food."

"Sergio will be fine, Chico. We left a lot of food at the shelter I built. He may have lost his tail, but he is able to take care of himself."

"I hope he wasn't hurt in the rains. What if a tree fell on him? I have a bad feeling, Padre."

Suddenly, Chico screamed, "Something bit me!" He looked down at a colorful snake at his heel. Chico knew that one of the most dangerous snakes was the coral snake. Its bite affects the nervous system and can quickly kill its victim. Its poison is neurotoxic and causes respiratory paralysis and suffocation within minutes.

"Padre, I am going to die! Please help me."

Bennis came to the boy and looked at the snake. "Relax, Chico. You are not going to die, at least not yet."

"But, Padre, that is a coral snake! Its bite is poisonous and kills quickly."

Bennis reached down and picked up the snake. Chico pulled away. "Be careful, Padre, it will kill you, too!"

Bennis held the snake by its neck. "Look, Chico. This looks like a coral snake, but it's actually a milk snake. Coral snakes are often red with black bands bordered by yellow. On this snake the red touches the black. In our Special Forces training, they taught us an easy way to tell the difference between the coral snake and the milk snake. Just remember the rhyme, 'Red touch yellow, kill a fellow. Red touch black, friend of Jack.' The bite might hurt for a little while, Chico, but it will not kill you."

Chico looked at the snake and then his ankle. His voice was shaky. "Are you sure, Padre?"

Bennis smiled. He wanted to say, "We'll find out in a few minutes," but instead he flung the snake into the bushes and said, "Yes, I am sure."

■ ■ ■

Staten Island, New York

Cavanaugh called up to Fran. "When do you want to go pick up Stephen?"

"I called Mary and said I will bring over lunch for everyone. It will be good to see my sisters again."

"I'll drive you over there. I want to see our son. But to be brutally honest, I really don't want to sit around and chit-chat with your sisters. I'm waiting for a call back from Morty and I have a few things I need to check out."

Fran came down the stairs. She wore a fuchsia terrycloth robe and was drying her hair with a white bath towel. Cavanaugh thought she looked beautiful. "I'll clean out the car and wait for you," he said.

"Don't be silly. It will take me a while to get dressed. You go ahead and do your thing. I'll take my car and we can meet at my sister's place."

Cavanaugh started walking toward her. She smelled good and clean. "Maybe we can find the time to do something else before we go?"

"Get out of here, Tom Cavanaugh. I just took a shower. There will be time for that later."

"There's no time like the present," he said putting his arms around her and kissing her tenderly. "It's been a long time."

She responded and seemed to melt into his arms. Then, suddenly, his cell phone rang. She pulled away. "It's your phone, big boy."

"I never liked cell phones!"

"Answer it. It may be important."

Cavanaugh fumbled for his phone. He checked the sender. It was Morty Goldberg. "I've got to get this, Fran. I'm sorry."

She smiled and resumed drying her hair. "I'll be here later. Maybe we can resume our little 'talk' later?"

■ ■ ■

Cavanaugh walked out to his car as he talked. "That was fast, Morty. I thought you were really busy. Did you find anything?"

"Not much initially. The grandmother is clean except for some parking violations. The mother was picked up for some minor drug charges when she was in high school."

"That's it?"

"Well, you know me. I like to do a little digging. I remembered you mentioned this Salvatore Russo was illegitimate and might have been the product of a high school Senior Prom visit to the Jersey Shore and your sister thought the father might have been the class valedictorian."

"Yeah, that might account for some of Russo's supposed brilliance."

"Well, I checked to see who the valedictorian was. Apparently, it was Jonathan Russell Carshook III."

"Sounds like one of those privileged rich kids. What's he doing now?"

"Not much. He's dead."

"What?"

"You heard me. He's dead. The interesting part is he died the day Salvatore was born."

"Was this some kind of sick coincidence?"

"Maybe, but Jonathan was murdered. His genitals were cut off and stuffed into his mouth."

"Who did it?"

"It's still an open case. The kid was on a vacation in Bermuda when it happened. It looks to me like it was a professional job. The investigation took place in Bermuda and the Russo family was never mentioned as there was no apparent connection at the time – until now."

"It sounds pretty circumstantial, Morty. Why would the situation change now?"

"Those letters sent from Sal Russo to his girlfriend."

"I don't get it. You told me the only fingerprints on the letters were Carolyn Hendershot's and mine."

"Exactly. Why weren't Russo's fingerprints on the letters?"

"Maybe he wore gloves?"

"Possible, but highly improbable. I think the answer lies in his father, Jonathan Russell Carshook III."

"I still don't get it. You said Russo's supposed father was murdered."

"There's not too much going on here at the present. The captain is out celebrating some Christian ceremony for one of his kids and the demonstrators have apparently gone home to take a much needed bath. So I called a friend in the Bermuda Police Service in Hamilton I met at a conference a while back."

"What's her name?"

"Her name happens to be Kathy Flynn, but it's not like that."

"Yeah, right. What did she tell you?"

"Kathy faxed me a copy of Jonathan's autopsy report. According to the report, Jonathan suffered from a genetic disorder called adermatoglyphia."

"I don't get it. What does this Jonathan what's-his-name's illness have to do with Sal Russo?"

"Adermatoglyphia isn't an illness. It's an inherited genetic condition. It is extremely rare but involves one copy of a mutated gene which results in the person's finger-pads being entirely flat. People who have this condition have none of the ridges that characterize normal fingerprints. Aside from the lack of fingerprints, these people are otherwise healthy."

Cavanaugh stopped when he reached his car. "Thanks, Morty. That is interesting. If Sal inherited this gene from his father, it could account for a lot of things. That might be the reason Grandma Russo was so sure the murdered victim in Mompox wasn't her grandson. When I told her we were checking fingerprints, she would have known Sal did not have fingerprints so he couldn't have been the victim."

"What do you plan on doing now?"

"I think I'm going to pay Carolyn Hendershot another visit."

"Be careful, meshuggener. These people may be dangerous."

"Thanks, Morty." He felt the bump on his head. "I'll keep you informed." Cavanaugh ended the call and opened his car door. The odor hit him immediately. He felt nauseous. "Oh, shit!" he moaned, "I forgot all about the dead blackbird!"

■ ■ ■

Mompox, Colombia

Jack Bennis thought he knew the way back to the tunnels. The heavy rains, however, changed the condition of the jungle. Broken branches, trees, and shrubs littered the jungle and made the trip slow and hazardous.

They inched their way through the woods checking overhanging limbs for snakes and other wildlife. Swarms of insects buzzed about them. Occasionally, they saw a dead capybara or a snake floating in a pond of water. When they finally arrived at their destination, it wasn't there. Instead of the small opening in the side of a hill that Bennis had tumbled into, a rapid flow of water poured out of the hole creating a small waterfall.

Chico looked around. Were they in the right place? He placed his hand in the water and the pressure pushed his hand back. "Padre, where has the entrance gone?"

"It looks like the rains have flooded the tunnel. I noticed water seeping down the walls when we were last in the tunnel. I think nature has reclaimed the tunnels."

"But how can that be, Padre?"

The priest remembered the anthropology backpackers speaking about the cenotes found in Mexico. If the tunnels were below an underground stream or a cenote, the heavy rains may have collapsed the tunnel walls flooding the tunnels. The water seeping down the walls of the tunnel may have been a harbinger of what was to come.

"I think the rain may have collapsed the tunnel walls. We can't get into the tunnel this way now."

"Maybe we can enter from one of the other entrances, Padre."

"We can try, Chico, but from the pressure of the water coming out my guess is the ground above the tunnel gave way from the weight of the water and flooded all the tunnels."

They drove around and checked the other ways they found to enter the tunnels. Bennis was correct. A landslide of mud and debris obliterated Chico's initial entrance. The narrow walkway under the waterfall had been washed away. The torrential rains of the previous nights had flooded the tunnels and made them inaccessible.

Chico looked up to the priest. There were tears in his eyes. "It's all lost, Padre. The Muisca treasures are buried and lost forever. What do we do now?"

Fr. Bennis reached down and adjusted Chico's large sombrero. "There are people who can use modern technology to get to the tunnels.

The man I spoke to you about could arrange an expedition to rescue the Muisca artifacts."

"But would he believe us? People have explored this area for many years. They found nothing. People believe it is a legend and nothing more. Who is going to believe a twelve-year-old boy like me could discover the tunnels when so many others tried and failed?"

Bennis pointed at the spear in Chico's hand. "Look at that spear you are holding. It's proof of the Muisca culture. The gold and silver in it are worth a lot of money. As a relic of another civilization lost and almost forgotten, it is priceless. I am sure my friend I told you about in Washington will be able to find the resources to excavate the tunnels without destroying or damaging anything."

Chico stared at the spear. There were scratches on it where he and Fran dug themselves out of the tunnels. The dried blood of the jaguar added another level of color and meaning to the ancient weapon.

"Do you really think so, Padre?"

Bennis pulled the boy to his feet. "I can't see why not. You and I saw what the tunnels looked like. So did Fran and my brother. We all have memories to hold and stories to tell. You are the one who discovered the tunnels, Chico. You are going to be a famous person. Your discovery will change our knowledge and appreciation of the Muisca civilization."

Chico rubbed the spear and smiled as Sergio jumped from a nearby tree into his lap and wrapped his arms around the boy's neck.

■ ■ ■

Staten Island, New York

The smell wasn't as bad as the bugs. Metallic-bodied blowflies, beetles, and maggots swarmed about the dead blackbird in the back seat of Cavanaugh's car. He had smelled dead bodies before, but the insects buzzing about him disturbed him more. He didn't think the insects needed an engraved invitation to their feast, but his broken side window had facilitated matters. He knew the smell would dissipate and the flies disperse. It was the blackbird, however, that had to go first.

Cavanaugh reached into the back seat and cradled the dead bird. He looked at its broken wings and lifeless eyes as the creeping maggots continued feeding. He had wanted to give it a more dignified burial, but he had things to do and a car to clean. The Beatles' song "Blackbird" came into his mind as he prepared to throw the bird into the adjacent cemetery. "Take your broken wings and learn to fly," he sang. "Take your sunken eyes and learn to see."

He tossed the bird, still wrapped in his handkerchief, high in the air and recalled the final refrain of the song, "All your life you were only waiting for this moment to arise." He returned to the car, opened all the windows, and turned on the air conditioner. The insects left first, but the smell of death lingered. He sat and thought about the song, the bird, and what had happened in the past few days. "Is that what it's all about?" he asked himself. "Are we just waiting for the end?" No. He believed there was more to it than that. "Do we ever achieve our true potential?" Probably not, but most of us do the best we can with what we have. "Do we ever really see things the way they are, not the way we want them to be or the way we fear they may be?"

Driving out of his driveway, he wasn't sure what the purpose of life was. But he cherished it and wanted to make the most of it. Right now, he had a case to solve and for the first time since he started looking for Salvatore Anthony Russo, he was beginning to see things a little clearer.

■ ■ ■

Mompox, Colombia

On their ride back to the police station, Chico held tightly to Fr. Bennis' waist while Sergio held tightly to Chico's neck. The ride was necessarily slow, but Chico had a million questions. "Will I be able to see my sister again?"

"I don't see why not. If you want I can arrange for the both of you to come to a school attached to St. Peter Claver Church in Cartagena where I am assigned."

"But, Padre, where would we stay?"

"I know a number of good people who would be privileged to have you both stay with them."

"Do you think this man in Washington will really be able to rescue the Muisca treasures?"

"I think he will jump at the opportunity."

"What will happen to Sergio? Can he come with me?"

"We will have him checked out by the doctor. Maybe they can repair his tail. Whatever happens, I will make sure he is taken care of properly. Maybe he would prefer to go back to the jungle instead of living in a city. The jungle is his home. Sometimes we have to let the things we love find their own way."

"What about that woman?"

Bennis stiffened. "What woman, Chico?"

"You know, Padre. The woman who was shot. I saw you two together. I think you love her."

The priest drove in silence for a few minutes. Chico asked again, "What about her, Padre? Do you love her?"

"I try to love everybody, Chico."

"But do you love her in a special way, Padre. I saw the way you looked at her in the hospital."

Bennis took a deep breath and said finally, "Yes, Chico. I think I do. She is a very special person to me. I have to admit I love her in a very special way. But I have no idea where she is now. Her brother took her somewhere to get her good medical care. I don't know where she is."

"Will you look for her?"

Bennis glanced back at the boy with the monkey around his neck and smiled. "You ask a lot of questions, young man."

"But will you, Padre?"

"I don't know, Chico. I told you once how I struggle to be the best I can be. I hope the way I go is the way God wants me to go, but I know sometimes it is not. I make mistakes like everyone else. I made a promise a while back that I would go away and not see her again. I am going to try to keep that promise. That promise was one of the reasons I came to Colombia. But somehow we met again. I didn't plan it and I don't think she did either. It happened. To answer your question, I will pray for her and her brother, but I won't try to find her."

"That doesn't seem right, Padre. If you love her and she loves you, you should go after her and find her."

"Life isn't always fair, Chico," the priest said as they pulled up to the Mompox police station. "You have seen that already in your own life. Let's go make a call to that friend of mine in Washington and see what he can do about rescuing those Muisca treasures."

■ ■ ■

23

Brooklyn, New York

Cavanaugh picked up a Box o' Jo and three glazed sticks from Dunkin' Donuts and parked across the street from Carolyn Hendershot's apartment building. He didn't know how long he would have to wait. He was tired. He tried to get some sleep on the plane and in the long layover in Florida, but the last few days had taken their toll on him. He hoped the coffee would keep him awake. The 410 calorie sticks were planned for breakfast, lunch, and possibly dinner. An empty quart sized bottle of orange juice under the front seat was for bladder issues. He was prepared for a possibly long stakeout.

If he were right, Salvatore Russo would be coming home to see his girlfriend as he promised. Whatever he had been planning was soon to happen. Was Sal Russo the S.R. who sent the threatening letter to El Apredido? Had Sal killed El Apredido and destroyed the drug lab? The Devil's Breath seemed to be behind it all.

El Apredido planned to disrupt the world's economy. His plan was elaborate and improbable. It would involve a lot of people from all different walks of life to pull it off. A drug like the Devil's Breath could rob people of their free will and get them to do things they would not ordinarily do. Cavanaugh had seen it work with Big Louie. But how would he be able to "infect" so many people with the Devil's Breath? There were a lot of unanswered questions.

Cavanaugh looked at students coming and going from Medgar Evans College across the street. He knew the area well. As a detective, he was involved in the arrest of a group of Rastafarians in one of the buildings. They had amassed a large number of weapons. He remembered when the college was formerly a Jesuit high school called Brooklyn Prep. Back in the 1800s, the land was originally the site of the Crow Hill Penitentiary. He smiled as he dunked a glazed stick into his coffee and observed the young students. How much things change over the years.

The students came in all different colors, sizes, shapes, and nationalities. Some wore tattered jeans; some wore hijabs that covered their heads and were fastened under their chins as a head-scarf; some wore football or soccer jerseys of their favorite team; a few wore burquas concealing all of the women's bodies including their eyes behind a mesh-like screen. They were animated, laughing, talking, gesturing, telling stories, texting. No two were alike, but all were similar.

He was on his third cup of coffee when he noticed a man with a navy hoodie walking behind five students from the college. The students had knapsacks slung over their shoulders or clutched books or laptops to their bosoms. The man in the hoodie walked head down trying to blend in behind the group. His hands were buried deep in his pockets. At Carolyn Hendershot's apartment building, the man peeled off the group and vanished into the building.

"That's him," Cavanaugh said to himself. Should he call Grandma Russo now and tell her where her grandson was and get this case over with? But he really didn't see his face. Russo's mother warned him to stop his investigation. But why? She sounded scared. He thought it was Salvatore Russo, but he had to make sure. If he were right, Sal Russo may have killed El Apredido, the men in the drug lab, and the two anthropology students and he may have tried to kill Fran and him. He checked his gun. It was loaded. Precaution, he knew, was much safer than daring. He got out of his car and slowly approached Carolyn's building.

As he entered the building, he failed to see another man in dark clothing watching him from the doorway of the college.

■ ■ ■

Mompox, Colombia

Father Bennis drove the motorcycle into the Mompox police parking lot and Chico hopped off cuddling Sergio in his arms. "What if the Lieutenant asks us about the spear?" Chico asked. "Will she arrest me? I don't want to go to jail, Padre."

"Relax, Chico. She may have left already. I promise you, no one is going to arrest you." He patted the boy on his shoulder and added, "You worry too much. Leave the talking to me."

When they entered the station, Mompox police officer Adrian Mesero stopped them. "Where were you?" he asked. "Lieutenant Fraumeni and Officer Coyle left. They were looking for you before they went back to Bogotá."

"We had something we had to do," Bennis said looking around. "Where is everyone?"

"If you mean those students, they left."

"They did? Where did they go?"

"I have no idea, Padre. The skinny obnoxious brunette with the big mouth made a phone call and then the two of them left. We had no reason to hold them here."

Bennis frowned. Why did they leave so quickly? Their friends had just been murdered. Chico tugged at the priest's elbow. "Padre, the call to your friend in Washington?"

Bennis nodded and asked permission to make a long distance call.

"Sure," Adrian said. "Use the one in El Capitán's office. He's not here. He'll never know."

After a number of voice messages, transferred calls, and long waiting periods, Father Bennis finally reached his former colleague Jereal Allbrook. "Dr. Allbrook, this is Jack Bennis. I'm calling you from Colombia about something we've found that I think will be of great interest to you."

"Jack Bennis? Is that you? How the hell are you? I haven't seen or heard from you in years. Where the hell did you disappear to?"

"It's a long story, Jereal. I called today with information about something I think you will be very interested in."

"I'll never forget how you saved my sorry ass in that demolition class we went through with the Seals. How have you been? It's been such a long time. Sorry I lost contact with you. You've got me at a bad time, but what are you up to now?"

"You may not believe it, but now I'm actually a Jesuit priest."

"You've got to be kidding! This isn't the Jack Bennis I once knew!"

"Yes, it is. Things happen. I changed. I've been following your rise to fame and success, however. Congratulations, Jereal."

"We've got to get together. I want to find out how you changed course and became a priest, but unfortunately I just signed off on a new project and there is a lot to do. I'm pretty pressed for time right now."

"I won't take up much of your time, Jereal. I wanted you to know about a subterranean tunnel a friend of mine discovered in Colombia. We had some bad weather down here and the rains flooded the tunnels, but they contain many magnificent artifacts of the Muisca civilization."

"Jack, where are you now?"

"I'm in Mompox. It's a small town declared by UNESCO as a World Heritage Site. It's located along the …."

"Along the Magdalen River. Yes, I know it well. My daughter was down there looking for the legendary City of Gold."

"Your daughter?"

"Yes. I've been married twice, Jack. I have three kids, two sons and one daughter. My daughter is from my first marriage. She's an anthropology student at Boston University. She just got off the phone with me a little over an hour ago. That's the project I just signed off on. She spied a gold and silver lance of some sort made by the Incas. I just arranged for an expedition to go down there to locate the dealer who sold this precious piece of antiquity."

"Is her name Felicia by any chance?"

"Yes. You must have met her. I have to admit, she's a bit rough around the edges, but she's good at what she does. I trust her instincts. She texted me a picture of this spear. It was in the hands of a sleeping young boy. It looks like a beautiful, unique artifact, not typical, I would say at first sight, of traditional Inca work. But I trust Felicia. She told me it came from Peru where one of Pizarro's conquistadors kept it from the ransom the Inca's paid for the release of king. She said a reliable source told her there was a Peruvian dealer who has documentation of the authenticity of the spear."

"I told her about the Peruvian dealer, Jereal."

"Well, there you go. I never knew you to lie and now that you're a priest I'm doubly glad I signed off on the project. It will strap us for the rest of year, but I believe it will be well worth it."

"But, Jereal, I have to tell you...."

"Sorry, Jack, but I really have to go now. I have a meeting with the President and I'm running late. It was great talking to you. We really have to get together. Give me a ring when you get into town."

Before Bennis could say another word, he heard the click as the line went dead.

■ ■ ■

Brooklyn, New York

Cavanaugh climbed slowly up the stairs to Carolyn Hendershot's third floor apartment. It was dark in the narrow hallway. A dog barked on the second floor as he went up the stairs. The scent of bacon and brewing coffee from one of the rooms mingled with the stale odor of dried urine and dust in the hall.

He stopped at apartment 3B and listened. A man and a woman inside were arguing. He recognized the woman's voice. It was Carolyn Hendershot's.

"I told you he was looking for you. What more did you want me to do?" Her Texas twang was gone; her voice, cold and hard.

"You didn't tell me he took the letters I sent you!"

"He didn't strike me as the kind of guy that could pour piss out of a boot without printed instructions let alone decipher your messages!"

"Well, you were wrong, Carolyn! He and his wife and brother showed up in Mompox and complicated an already complicated situation."

"What did El Apredido say about your plan?"

The man chuckled. "Let's just say he went along with it. He won't be a problem. I have the formula now and we will be able to carry out our plan without his interference."

The dog on the second floor barked again.

"Do you think it will work?"

"This was my plan from the beginning. Roberto got greedy. He wanted to destroy the world's economy. I just want to help the poor and the needy. If we use the Devil's Breath to take from the rich and distribute to the poor, it will help more people. The wealthy have more money than they know what to do with. The Devil's Breath will allow me to distribute this money to the needy without anyone knowing about it. It's a perfect, peaceful plan."

"You will be the modern day Robin Hood!"

"And you, my sweet Carolyn, will be my Maid Marian!"

Cavanaugh had heard enough. He withdrew his gun and kicked open the door.

"Freeze, Robin Hood. Your days of killing and stealing are over."

Sal Russo shielded himself behind Carolyn. "Who the hell are you?" he said.

"He's the man who stole your letters," Carolyn said.

Cavanaugh pointed his gun at them and nodded, "Greeting, Salvatore Anthony Russo, your days of killings are over."

"What's he talking about, Sal?"

"Nothing. He doesn't know what he is talking about!"

"Oh, you didn't tell Miss Lubbock Texas about your killing El Apredido and his men and then two innocent college students? How careless of you."

Carolyn turned to Russo. "You didn't do that, did you?"

"Your lover is no better than the real Robin Hood of old who murdered government officials and wealthy landowners. He is nothing more than a cold-blooded murderer."

"You don't understand. People like you never will. Sometimes to get things done one must do unpleasant things."

"The end never justifies the means, Russo. Those college kids didn't do anything wrong, and you tried to kill me, my wife, and my brother."

"Too bad I didn't succeed," Russo said as he pushed Carolyn forward into Cavanaugh and darted toward the window and the fire escape. Cavanaugh staggered back. He lost his balance and fell back. Carolyn crashed on top of him. As they struggled to get up, he saw Russo flying through the window. The next thing he felt was a sharp blow to the back of his head. Then all went black.

■ ■ ■

Mompox, Colombia

"What did your friend say, Padre?"

"Let's go for a walk. I'm hungry. How about you?"

The young boy ran after the priest. "But what did he say, Padre? When are they coming down here?"

They walked down to the river. It was another hot day. A slight breeze drifted off the Magdalena River. They passed the tree where Bennis and María Isabelle kissed. They passed the spot where El Apredido's man tried to kill him. They passed the hotel where Margarete died in the fire. In response to the boy's persistent questions, the priest's only answer was, "It's complicated, Chico."

Jack Bennis looked around at the river and the town of Mompox with its colonial mansions, red clay-tile roofs, and fragrant flower-draped balconies. Under other circumstance, it was a beautiful, restful town frozen in time. They stopped at Comedor Costeño, a rustic riverfront restaurant in the market area.

"Let's eat here. The restaurant has a great view of the river, table cloths, and ceiling fans."

"But Padre, you have not told me what the man said."

"I will, Chico. But it's complicated, and I'm hungry. Neither of us has eaten in some time."

Bennis ordered *pata guisado*, a marinated duck meat with a vegetable sauce and a touch of vinegar. Chico preferred the *sopa de pescado*, a soup made from various types of fish and vegetables and doused in homemade hot pepper sauce. From the speed with which Chico devoured his soup, it was clear he was hungry. He offered some to Sergio, but Sergio seemed distracted by Rickie, the restaurant owner's amusing dog who bounded from table to table doing tricks and begging for food.

Bennis ordered a second Club Colombia beer for desert while Chico had a large *salpicón de frutas*, a fruit cocktail made with bite size pieces of pineapple, papaya, watermelon, mango, apple, banana, and seedless red grapes. Sergio helped himself to pieces of the fruit. Chico followed up the fruit cocktail with a *merengon de frescas*, a meringue filled with whipped cream and guanabana. Somehow, he managed to finish up with a coconut flan.

Watching Chico consume the last pieces of his flan, Bennis began telling him about his brief conversation with his friend in Washington. "He's a very busy man, Chico. He had to go see the President of the United States in the White House."

"But what did he say about coming down here to rescue the treasures?"

"That's part of the problem, Chico. It seems the woman with the backpack at the hostel, the skinny one with the pierced nose, eyebrows, and lips and a lot of tattoos. It turns out she is the daughter of my friend in Washington."

"I do not understand, Padre. What does that mean?"

"Well, it means you were right about my lying to her about your spear. She spoke to her father and sent him a picture of the spear. She and Gerard left to go to Peru to find the antique dealer I lied to her about."

Bennis grimaced. Chico just stared at him.

"My friend is sending an expedition down to Peru to look for the tunnels I told her about."

"But they will not find them, Padre. I know where the tunnels are here in Mompox."

"I know, Chico. Right now we are going to have to wait a while and then contact him again."

Chico was about to say something when his cell phone beeped. He dug the phone out of his pocket. "It is for you, Padre. Maybe it is your friend?"

Bennis knew Jereal Allbrook did not have Chico's phone number. The only one who did was his brother. An icy feeling of dread swept over him. Something was wrong.

The message was brief. "If you ever want to see your brother alive again, call this number when you arrive in New York. Directions will be given to you then. You have 48 hours. No police or he dies." A photo was attached. It showed Thomas Cavanaugh tied to a chair in what looked like a stone cellar. He looked unconscious. There was blood on his face.

■ ■ ■

24

Abandoned Warehouse in New York Area

Pain pulsated through Cavanaugh's head. He tried to lift his arm, but it was tied to a chair. Where was he? How did he get here? Memories slipped in and out like a dense fog. He struggled to free himself. He felt nauseous. The room seemed to be spinning around. A voice close by spoke. He recognized the voice, but couldn't identify it.

"You're alive? I thought for a while you was deader than a peeled egg. I thought I heard the buzzards circlin'."

It was Carolyn Hendershot's voice. Where was she? He tried to open his eyes and the dizziness increased. He shook his head and his head felt like a knife was stabbing into his skull. He tried to speak, but even he couldn't understand what he said.

"Kickin' ain't goin' to get you nowhere unless you're a mule."

He turned toward the voice. Carolyn too was tied to a chair. "No use askin' me where we are cause I sure as shit don't have a clue."

He took a deep breath. "What happened?" he asked.

"Some big dude hit you over the head with a club. I thought he killed you. Then some other fat guy who probably hasn't seen his feet in forty years came in. They blindfolded me and carried the two of us to a van outside. That's pretty much it."

"What happened to Sal?"

"That seven-sided son-of-a-bitch left me high and dry and high-tailed it out of there down the fire escape quicker than hell could scorch a feather."

Cavanaugh tried to clear his head and stop the ringing in his ears. He had to focus. Think. Think. "How long were we in the van?" he asked.

"Hard to say. There were a lot of turns, some highway driving. Maybe an hour or two. I think we went up a hill or two. Hard to say. I couldn't see and I was scared. If it helps, when we finally stopped, the air seemed cleaner than New York's."

In his mind, Cavanaugh estimated where they might be. Upstate New York? Connecticut? New Jersey? Pennsylvania? He scanned the room. Peeling white painted brick walls, high barred windows, broken glass and accumulated dirt and grim on the floor, dangling incandescent lights and the lingering odor of oil. It could be an abandoned warehouse somewhere. But where?

His voice was slurred. "Did they say anything on the ride?"

"They was as chatty as a pair of oysters. I swear I heard more noise at a Quaker meeting. The only thing the fat one said was, 'Shut up!'"

Cavanaugh kept running the same thought over and over. Why had they been taken and held captive? Of what use were Carolyn and Cavanaugh to anyone? It didn't make sense. He shut his eyes and tried to think. Why Carolyn? The only reason he could come up with was her relationship with Salvatore Russo. Was she being held as ransom for Salvatore Russo? Was this all about the Devil's Breath?

If it was about the Devil's Breath, why had they bothered to kidnap him?

Perhaps, if he found out who they were, things would start to make more sense.

He heard the clang of a large metal door at the end of the room as it opened. A figure in black slowly approached. At least five more shadows moved forward in the shifting darkness. In the swaying overhead light he caught the glint of weapons. Who were they? What did they want from him?

The figure in black stopped in front of him. The light above him swung back and forth sending the person from darkness to light and back to darkness. He squinted, his eyes sensitive to the light.

"Well, Mr. Cavanaugh, I hope you are comfortable."

He recognized the voice immediately. He stared with unbelieving eyes at the person in front of him. It made sense now. He knew why he had been taken. He felt sick and vomited before passing out again.

■ ■ ■

Cartagena, Colombia

The early bird gets the worm, but the second mouse gets the cheese. It was something Jack Bennis learned a long time ago in basic training. His platoon sergeant called it the Seven Ps: Prior Proper Planning Prevents Piss Poor Performance. The advice had never let him down. But now he felt like a mouse in a deadly maze fighting against a time bomb. He had to secure a place for Chico to stay. He had to conceal in some way the ancient Muisca spear. He had to make arrangements to fly to New York to walk into a trap. And because his belongings had been destroyed in the hotel fire, he needed a passport.

The pastor of St. Peter Claver Church, Monsignor Antonio Passerio, was a kind, gentle eighty-year-old man who was well-known for a life of poverty, a love of nature and a belief in the power of spiritual prayer and meditation. He recognized God's presence in the world around him and gave freely to anyone in need. Monsignor Passerio said Mass humbly and heard confessions from daybreak to night. He was a priest of deep devotion to St. Louis Bertrand, the "Apostle to the Americas," who preached in Cartagena in the 16th century. St. Louis defended the natives' rights against the Spanish Conquistadors and spent much of his time as a missionary in the area from Cartagena and the Magdalena River. It was easy to get Monsignor Passerio to accept Chico and find a place for both Chico and Sergio to stay.

Carrying the ancient gold and silver spear from Mompox to Cartagena, however, was a bit more difficult. Chico and Bennis visited Ronaldo Vernon's Supermarket where they fastened a broom to the spear and wrapped paper bags around them. It was a clumsy, rushed effort, but it worked.

Airline tickets were simple. Unlike his brother, Jack Bennis knew how to work the Internet. He quickly made arrangements for the next available direct flight to New York City.

Once the reservation was secured, he reached for the phone. He knew he was walking into a trap of some sort. He didn't know why, but his brother's life was on the line. *Prior Proper Planning* was essential. There wasn't an option for *Piss Poor Performance*. He had to be prepared.

He still needed a passport, however, to get out of Colombia and into the United States. Security was tight. 9/11 changed everything. Time was of the essence. He took a deep breath and called the one person he thought could help.

■ ■ ■

Abandoned Warehouse in New York Area

Tom Cavanaugh stared at the figure in black in front of him. "It's you," he said. "But why?"

Vincenza Russo scratched the wart on the side of her nose. Her face alternated from dark to light as the dangling light bulb above swayed back and forth. "Salvatore has something I want," she said.

"The Devil's Breath?"

"You are smarter than you look, Mr. Cavanaugh."

"They tell me it's part of my charm."

Vincenza Russo smiled. The light sparkled off her gold tooth. "I am counting on your charm bringing your brother, the priest, to us."

Cavanaugh frowned. "What does he have to do with this? And, for that matter, what do I have to do with any of this?"

"You know too much. I wanted you to locate Salvatore for me. But you started digging into his life. I warned you not to involve the police, but you did."

"You've got to be kidding me! Sal's friends were about to rape his girlfriend. I called the cops to get her help and arrest those two perverts."

"I am not kidding, Mr. Cavanaugh. I never kid. For your information, Jacob Roberts and Dick Cranberry work for me. You should not have involved the police."

Cavanaugh struggled to get loose. "Redhead and Fu Manchu are nothing but educated fools. They tried to kill me and rape your grandson's girlfriend. You must have been following me, weren't you?"

"I needed to know where you were going and who you were talking to."

"You had someone steal my radio and flatten my tires, didn't you?"

"You were going too fast. I didn't want you to discover Salvatore's involvement in the Devil's Breath."

Cavanaugh glanced over at Carolyn Hendershot. She sat still and quiet. "I still don't get it," he said. "Your Sal has been experimenting with this Devil's Breath for some time. El Apredido, whoever he was, was manufacturing it and planning a crazy idea of wrecking the world economy with it."

Vincenza laughed. "El Apredido, as he called himself, was insane!"

"Yeah, but what about your grandson? He wanted to be the modern day Robin Hood!"

Vincenza shook her head. "Salvatore is a delusional, idealist. He always was and probably always will be. Look at this pathetic *puttana* he calls 'the love of his life.' He doesn't recognize the potential the variant of the Devil's Breath he created has."

Carolyn stared straight ahead like a frozen statue.

"And just how do you plan on using the Devil's Breath, Mrs. Russo?"

"Salvatore is a genius. I supplied him with the money and the backing to develop the Devil's Breath into an aerosol that could be used to infect many people at the same time. Imagine spraying the Devil's Breath into the aeration system of a bank. It would make bank robbery clean, effortless, and completely safe. Everyone affected would do as instructed, and no one would remember what happened. It would be the perfect weapon for the perfect crime!"

"If it's so effective, why kidnap Carolyn and me?"

Vincenza leaned forward. Her cold dark eyes bore into Cavanaugh. "Because Salvatore would not give me the formula! I funded his research. I supplied him with everything he needed, and he double-crossed me. He wanted to do good with the drug. He had visions of saving humanity!"

"Let's not get ahead of yourself, lady. Your grandson's a cold-blooded killer. He's not the Goodie Two-Shoes you make him out to be!"

Carolyn started to say something, but a quick gaze from Grandma Russo silenced her.

"We do what we have to in my family, Mr. Cavanaugh. It's a family trait."

A chill swept through Cavanaugh. Vincenza Russo was the sister of the Ralph Muscatelli, a notorious crime boss. "So you are using Carolyn here to get Sal to come and give you the formula."

"And he will."

"But what about me? Why bring me here, too?"

"You know the answer to that, Mr. Cavanaugh. I can see it in your eyes. You are the bait to bring your brother to me!"

"But why?"

"You and I know your brother, Jack Bennis, killed my brother. Another person was blamed for the assassination, but your brother was the real killer. My father figured this out and told me. He hired people to eliminate both you and your brother, but they were unsuccessful. I will not be. You see, Mr. Cavanaugh, another family trait of the Muscatelli family is we don't forgive and forget. We get revenge."

■ ■ ■

New York, New York

Father Jack Bennis caught Jet Blue Flight 1532 leaving Cartagena's Rafael Núñez International Airport at 2:30 the following afternoon. He tried unsuccessfully to get an extended leg room seat, but the plane was almost full, and he settled for a seat in the rear of the plane near the lavatory. It was noisy in the back of the plane with people coming and going to the restrooms and flight attendants moving about.

Sandwiched between an enormously overweight man whose after-shave lotion failed to cover up his body odor and penchant for cigars and a pregnant woman trying to breast feed a hungry infant, Bennis closed his eyes and pretended to fall asleep as he tried to say the rosary to himself. All sorts of thoughts, however, flew about his brain like a frightened flock of pigeons. His future was an uncharted, dangerous place. Images of the past reared their ugly scenes. He recalled how he had sinned through his own faults, in his thoughts and in his words, in what he had done and what he had failed to do. He saw the disappointed look in Chico's eyes looking up at him and heard the boy's voice saying, "Padre, you lied. You told Felicia a lie." Trapped between a malodorous fat man and a crying infant, he had only his thoughts, his conscience, his prayers, his fears, and his uncertain plans to keep him company.

The Airbus A320 arrived on time at 7:28 p.m. at JFK Airport. After the almost 180 passengers disembarked, Bennis called the number he had been given as instructed. He was given an address and warned to come alone and not to contact the police. Wearing civilian clothes, he blended in with passengers. In spite of everything, it felt good to have shaved, showered and to be out of clerical clothes.

Bennis called another number and waited for an Uber cab. The Uber driver made no objection to taking him to the address which proved to be over an hour away. The driver spoke little on the ride. Bennis didn't bother to check the route they were taking. It was dark and the driver was relying on his GPS mounted on the dashboard. Instead, Bennis spent his time praying, thinking about his brother and his brother's family, Chico, the killer of El Apredido, the Devil's Breath, and María Isabelle. Images seemed to skip through his brain like a kangaroo on steroids. The time sped by quickly. Then the car slowed down. He looked out the window at an abandoned industrial warehouse. This was it.

He exited the cab, tipped the driver, and watched him sped away. He felt totally alone. For a moment, he regretted not bringing a weapon. He checked his watch. It was almost 11:00 p.m. He took a deep breath. The air was clean and crisp unlike the building which appeared ominous and dirty in the darkness ahead.

Jack Bennis made the sign of the cross and started walking toward the door of the building. Like it or not, it was show time.

■ ■ ■

The door creaked as he opened it. Ahead a long dark, corridor led to another door. His steps echoed down the hall. There were muffled voices beyond the door. He paused. A woman and a man were arguing. Bennis didn't recognize the voices. Then he heard his brother's voice. "You're both crazy!" Cavanaugh shouted. "Give her the freaking formula, Russo, and take Carolyn and get out of here!"

Bennis opened the door. The shouting stopped. In the dim light, he saw all heads turn toward him. There was a stout, older woman in a black dress, a younger woman tied to a chair, five men with guns, and another man in a colorful shirt standing next to the woman in the black dress, and his brother tied to another chair.

"Get out of here, Jack! It's a trap! She's going to kill you!"

Bennis raised his hands and walked slowly forward. "And to whom do I have the pleasure of meeting?" he said.

Cavanaugh kept screaming, "Didn't you hear me? She's Ralph Muscatelli's sister! Get out of here, Jack! She's going to kill you!"

"I take it then, you must be Vincenza Russo," Bennis began, "and this must be your grandson, Salvatore Anthony Russo."

The older woman took one step toward Bennis. "And you, you must be Jack Bennis, the man who killed my brother."

Bennis felt a slight breeze on the back of his neck. He saw Sal Russo held some papers in his hand while Vincenza Russo held a Glock 26. He ignored the five men with guns who surrounded him and nodded to his brother and the other woman tied to chairs.

"I told you to get out, Jack! Don't you ever listen? She's going to kill us all!"

"I don't think so, Thomas." He turned to Vincenza Russo and asked, "What was all the yelling about when I came in? I hope I didn't interrupt something."

Grandma Russo gritted her teeth. "You are an impudent, arrogant son of a bitch. I should kill you right now, but I want you to suffer and see me kill your brother first.'

"So the way I see it, Sal here has a special formula of some sort dealing with the Devil's Breath. You know a lot of killing has gone on over this Devil's Breath. I can't see it's really worth all the effort."

"It's worth millions," the older woman said.

"She wants to use it to steal. I wanted to use it take money from the rich and redistribute it to the poor," Sal shouted. "She just a greedy, selfish crook like her brother!"

"If you meant it to help people, Sal, why did you kill your friend El Apredido?"

"He was a fool! He thought he could create a world economic crisis with it. I was the one who worked out the formula. I couldn't reason with him!"

"So you killed him and burned down the lab."

"Yes! And I would do it again. We had a deal to work together. He broke the deal."

"The deal involved Abraxas, didn't it. You drew that painting of Abraxas in his den."

"There was one in his friends' apartment and another in Carolyn's apartment," Cavanaugh observed.

"I imagine it was the symbol of your group. Abraxas represents crossing the borders between good and evil. Is that why you slashed his painting and cut off his tattoo?"

Sal waved the papers in his hand and shouted, "Abraxas was more than a symbol to us! He was our god! Carolyn and I shared his tattoo. He had no right to the tattoo or the picture. He was a traitor to our cause! I am glad I killed him! He deserved to die. He betrayed the deal we had!"

"And you, my own grandson, betrayed me! I funded your research. I gave you all you asked for to develop the Devil's Breath. I want that formula. Give it to me now."

"First, let Carolyn go!"

Bennis opened his arms wide. "Sal, do you really think this woman is going to let Carolyn go just because you hand her those papers? For all she knows, the formula might blow up in her face. No, she's going to kill Carolyn and you."

"Let Carolyn go, *Nonna.* This is the real formula. You have to believe me."

Vincenza Russo scratched the mole on her nose. "Sure, Salvatore, I believe you. Give me the formula and I will let Carolyn go. You have my word."

Bennis reached his hand out to Sal. "I wouldn't believe her, Sal. She's going to kill us all. We know too much. Give me the formula and I will hold it until you both are out of here."

"Don't listen to him. Give it to me. It's mine."

Salvatore Anthony Russo stood like a deer caught in the headlights. Bennis suddenly reached over and grabbed the Devil's Breath formula.

"You fool, you stupid bastard!" Grandma Russo screamed and fired one shot into Carolyn Hendershot's head. Carolyn fell back. Blood splattered on the white brick wall.

Sal stared incredulously at Carolyn's body. "Why? Why, *Nonna,* did you do this? I love Carolyn. I was going to give you the formula."

"I am through with bargaining. She was a *puttana* with a big mouth!" Vincenza Vincenza Russo turned her gun on Bennis. "Give me the formula, priest, or I will yank it out of your dead hands!"

Sal pulled out the gun he had killed El Apredido with. "You killed the only person I loved, *Nonna!*" he shouted. Before he could fire, however, his grandmother turned and fired three shots into his charging body.

Jack Bennis dived between grandmother and grandson and plowed into his brother tied to the chair. As he fell forward, he shouted, "Now! Now! Now!"

As he lay on top of Cavanaugh, he hear the puff, puff, puff, puff, puff, puff, of silencers going off in the darkness. Then they heard the clatter of guns hitting the concrete floor, followed by the thuds of bodies toppling to the ground.

A tall, dark figure in black stepped out of the darkness. "Will that be all, Padre?" he said in a deep, accented voice.

Bennis pulled himself up. "No. Thank you. Please convey my sincere thanks and deep gratitude."

The man nodded. "Do you want us to remove the bodies?"

"That won't be necessary. You have done more than enough already. "

The man nodded again. "No problem, Padre. A car is waiting outside to take you wherever you wish."

Bennis replied, "Thank you again," as the man faded quietly back into the darkness.

■ ■ ■

"What the hell just happened?" Cavanaugh asked as his brother untied him. "Who were those people?"

"I'm not quite sure, to be honest. The accent sounded Russian. Whoever they were, they did come through in the clutch, didn't they?"

"I don't understand. How did they get here and why?"

Bennis ran his hand through his hair. "When I read the text they sent me and saw they had you tied up and threatened to kill you if I didn't come to New York within 48 hours, I knew I was walking into a trap. I had a lot of preparation to do and little time to do it. My biggest problem was getting a passport. Mine had been destroyed in the explosion El Apredido planted in my hotel room. I also needed some backup so I called in a favor."

"A favor? Who did you call?"

"It would take too long to get a new passport through normal channels so I tried a long shot."

"A hail Mary?"

"You could definitely say that. I called Aunt Jo. I figured with her connections she could get me a passport whether legally or illegally. I didn't really care. All I knew was your life was on the line and I needed to get to you."

"But why Aunt Jo? What could she do?"

"She got me the passport and spoke to Chago about getting me some protection up here. He knew we helped his sister. I hoped he would help me help my brother."

"I'd sure say he did."

"I don't know where or how he got these people. I figured in his business he must have contacts all over the world. I called a number they gave me when I arrived at JFK. I deliberately left the outside door open hoping to make it easy for the help I was hopeful would come. I didn't expect the help would be so devastating and violent."

"You trusted the head of a drug cartel?"

"He knows his sister and I love each other. Yes, I trusted him. I didn't know what he planned, but I trusted he would come through in the end. Maybe if more people trusted and believed in him when he was a kid, things wouldn't have turned out like they did for him."

Cavanaugh stood and looked around. Carolyn lay slumped against the wall, still tied to her chair. Sal Russo lay on his back with three bullet holes through his colorful shirt. Grandma Russo lay sprawled at Cavanaugh's feet with her Glock 26 still in her hand. As the overhanging light swung back and forth, the bodies of Vincenza Russo's bodyguards lay like bags of woodchips in the shadows.

"She was going to kill her own grandchild for the stupid Devil's Breath formula."

"She was going to kill us all, Thomas. Some people will go to great lengths to get what they want."

Cavanaugh looked down at Sal Russo and then at Carolyn Hendershot. "They really loved each other, Jack. He was willing to give up the formula he developed to save her life. He really planned to use the Devil's Breath to help the poor and the needy. Somehow I feel sorry for both of them."

"You need to remember he killed a lot of people for that drug. He killed two innocent students and he tried to kill you and Fran."

"Still, I feel sorry for both of them." He paused and looked around. "Say, where's that formula? In the wrong hands it could cause a lot of problems. We have to find it."

"It's gone, Thomas."

"Gone? What do you mean? I saw it. Russo had it in his hand. Then you grabbed it."

"It's gone, Thomas. The only ones who knew the formula were El Apredido and Sal. They're dead. The Devil's Breath was a bad thing."

"What do you mean, 'It's gone'? Things don't just disappear. But where did it go?"

Jack Bennis opened his mouth, wiggled his tongue, and smiled. "It's gone. I ate it!"

■ ■ ■

25

Staten Island, New York

It was early morning when the car dropped Cavanaugh and Bennis at Cavanaugh's house. Fran was in the living room watching the news on CNN. "Where the hell have you been?" she began as they walked through the door. Bella, the cockapoo, Bennis had once rescued ran toward the men. When Fran got a good look at her husband's bruised face and the matted blood in his hair, she jumped up and cried, "What happened to you? Are you all right?"

Cavanaugh hugged his wife and whispered, "It's good to be home." Then he added, "Jack and I need something to drink."

"I'll put on a pot of coffee."

"No. I want something stronger. I feel like a beer. How about you, Jack?"

"I'll take a scotch if you have any. I need something stronger than beer."

The three sat for a long time discussing what had happened. At one point Fran pointed to the television. A three alarm fire was reported in an abandoned warehouse in upstate New York. Authorities were trying to contain the fire. Bodies had been recovered from the fire. Arson was suspected. No additional information was available at that time.

"What do you think, Jack?" Cavanaugh asked.

"I think whoever they are, they are thorough."

Flying over the raging fire in a helicopter, a CNN reporter indicated the factory had once been suspected as the site for manufacturing counterfeit handbags and sports paraphernalia. It was closed down and abandoned suddenly six years ago when a federal investigation began.

"Grandma Russo seems to have had her hands in a lot of things." Cavanaugh said.

Jack Bennis smiled and poured himself another shot of Glenfiddich. "It's good to be home again," he said. He took a long, savory sip, patted Bella's head, and added, "I wish I could stay."

"What do you mean?" Fran asked.

"I have to go back and check on Chico and his sister. Then we have to figure out what to do with the Muisca spear. And then there is Sergio. Spider monkeys can be quite noisy. Monsignor Passerio is a good man, but I don't know if he can put up with a monkey in the rectory for very long. There are a lot of loose ends I have to pull together."

"Did they ever locate the Police Chief?"

"No. From what I learned before I left, he cleared out his bank accounts and he and his family moved somewhere else. I doubt they are ever going to find him."

"What about María?" Fran and Cavanaugh asked together.

Bennis looked down at the dog in his lap. Bella looked up at him. Her eyes looked sad. He scratched her chin.

"Well?" Fran repeated. "What about María? Are you going to go after her?"

"I don't know where she is."

"Ask her brother, stupid!" Cavanaugh said. "He'll tell you."

"I don't know if that's a good idea."

"Oh, for Christ's sake, Jack, you love the woman and she loves you. You both know that. Go get her."

Bennis finished his drink and poured himself another. "You both have a lot of questions. Right now, I don't have the answers. To be honest, I have no idea where I am ultimately going. I am trying to follow the right path, but sometimes, I feel, I don't know what's right or wrong. The world is a crazy, mixed-up place."

"Come on, Jack, you're a priest. You're not stupid!"

"I'm human, Thomas, just like you and Fran. I can't claim to be better than anyone. I know I have feet of clay."

The three sat in silence for a minute. Then Fran asked a question that pierced the stillness. "What if María comes looking for you?"

Jack Bennis paused for a few seconds and then looked at his brother. "Can you remember back when we were little? You were a real worrywart. You would ask Mom a million questions. What would happen if you got sick like Davey down the block? What would happen if she lost her job? What would happen if we couldn't pay the rent? What would happen if it rained and we couldn't go to the beach? You had a million questions."

Cavanaugh lowered his eyes and nodded.

"Remember what Mom used to say in those situations? It was always the same response. Well, that's my answer here, too."

Cavanaugh looked up and smiled. The brothers clicked their glasses and repeated their mother's favorite saying together, "We'll cross that bridge when we come to it."

■ ■ ■

SOME CLOSING COMMENTS

I hope you enjoyed reading *Chasing the Devil's Breath*. If you could find the time, I would appreciate it if you could drop a brief review on Amazon. com.

A number of people helped make this endeavor a reality and were kind enough to read the initial drafts of *Chasing* the *Devil's Breath* and to provide needed information and feedback. In particular, I need to thank Robert Boyd, Jane Boyd, Jean Lucier Roland, Dr. Louis Gianvito, Mary von Doussa, and my wife, Diane. Thank you all.

I welcome the opportunity to answer questions and to speak at book clubs and other groups about writing and the writing process.

Please feel free to visit my website: http://www.george-hopkins.com/ and send any questions or comments you may have to me at Hopkins109@ aol.com. I will get back to you as soon as possible.

Sir Francis Bacon wrote, "Some books should be tasted, some devoured, but only a few should be chewed and digested thoroughly." My hope is simply that *Chasing the Devil's Breath* entertained you and gave you pause to think. All of the five other novels in this series surrounding the adventures of the priest and the detective can be ordered from your local bookstore and are available online at Amazon.com. and in Kindle editions. Thank you again for coming with me on this journey.

George R. Hopkins

CPSIA information can be obtained
at www.ICGtesting.com
Printed in the USA
BVHW03s2134210518
516974BV00010B/140/P